The Red Room

By

I0681150

P D Mitchellson

First Published in 2016

ISBN: 978-0-9956871-0-3

Disclaimer

This book addresses issues that include, but are not limited to:

Racism, self-harm, bullying and adult themes.

These issues/themes may be triggering to some readers, but are used in such a way as to educate the effects they have on others and in the hope that those reading this book will understand those effects.

These themes are in no way a representation of the author's thoughts, feelings or beliefs.

Readers discretion is advised adult content.

Any reference to names or character are in the public domain and do not have any association with the subject matter of this book

The Red Room

P D Mitchellson is the pen name for the two authors of The Mistress D trilogy starting with the first explosive erotic novel The Red Room.

The first book introduces Debra Fielding as Mistress D a wealthy and sophisticated woman living a glamorous life in Hampshire in England. She meets and becomes involved with Lucian Palmer Jones as handsome and struggling estate agent. On a luxury cruise they embark on an erotic and passionate journey into the world of BDSM and female domination. They plans are interrupted by Dominic Clayton a mentally unstable character who after meeting Debra becomes completely obsessed and will stop at nothing to get rid of Lucian and claim Debra as his Mistress.

Book dedicated to all those who appreciate

A real woman

Acknowledgments

We would like to thank friends and family who have supported us.

The girl's for their belief and being proud of their mum.

Our good friend Phil, a busy man who still found the time to help to shape and refine the story.

Book cover design by Emily

Bob our proofreader who saw things we couldn't see.

To the early sample readers who have gave us such wonderful feedback and encouragement.

Finally to you for purchasing the first in the Mistress D trilogy

Hopefully this book makes you laugh, cry and buy handcuffs & red shoes!

The Red Room

Prologue

Five years earlier

In the basement of one of Winchester's finest private residences, a naked and collared man knelt at the feet of a beautiful dark-haired woman. As he bent forward, a bead of sweat ran down his nose and splashed onto the hard Italian marble floor. His breath was laboured and came in short gasps. The woman stroked his head brushing away the wet strands of hair from his sweat-drenched forehead.

She lifted his chin slightly with her cane "There's a good boy." she said

At sixty-seven years old, being called a "good boy" was very comforting.

Reaching forward, she flicked the silver clamps attached to his nipples; he gasped, his eyes seeking hers.

"You know it's got to hurt don't you?"

"Yes Mistress," he said in desperation, knowing what was coming next.

She quickly removed each clamp, turning them ninety degrees and replacing them closer to the tips of his nipples to intensify the pain.

"Are you desperate my boy?" she said.

"Yes Mistress," he panted.

"Wank for me then!" she shouted into his face

Relaxing back on the elegant red velvet chaise longue, she drew on a slim Vogue cigarette and exhaled the smoke slowly through her lips.

She crossed her stockinged legs and hissed,

"Harder!"

He immediately gripped his stiff cock, jerking it more vigorously as she looked down into his pained eyes. His pale skin had turned blotchy pink around his neck and shoulders as he knelt there suffering for her.

She watched his face grow redder as he gritted his teeth at the renewed pain. Leaning towards him, she put her ruby red lips close to his ear and whispered: "I can make it much worse you know."

She reached down, tightly squeezing his heavy, swinging balls and digging her sharp red nails into his scrotum.

"Yes Mistress, please no Mistress!" he pleaded.

Placing her cigarette in a cut glass ashtray she reached down again, turning the clamps for the last time, knowing he couldn't control himself any longer. The man went into a spasm. His head flicked back, and his eyes rolled as he neared his climax.

She picked up a slim airline envelope from the side table and opened it.

"London to Aruba at 08.45am. I do hope you make it"

Laughing as she tossed the ticket onto the floor and continued to smoke. She raised a perfect eyebrow at the man's obvious desperation.

Dripping with sweat his whole body trembled.

"Please Mistress, can I come Mistress?"

Not able to wait for a reply, he gave his cock a final few fast jerks and ejaculated over his pot belly and half way up his chest. She released the metal clamps from his sore and burning nipples. Exhausted, the man collapsed onto the floor, panting as the waves of ecstasy swept over him.

Smiling she said, "Now there's a good boy, lucky I didn't say no."

"Yes Mistress thank you, Mistress," he said through strained gasps.

After a few minutes, he dragged himself to his feet, walked over to a corner cabinet and placed his collar neatly on the glass shelf. He took a robe from the ornate hook and wrapped it around his tender, throbbing body. With head bowed, he waited for the woman to finish her cigarette. He then followed her up the large iron spiral staircase to the upper floor drawing room. She seated herself on the large curved suede sofa. He poured her a glass of chilled champagne, then waited to be excused to shower, dress and prepare to head into London.

Twenty minutes later, as she sat with her eyes closed listening to classical music, she felt a gentle kiss on her forehead.

"I am leaving now." he whispered.

She didn't open her eyes but smiled as he refilled her champagne glass then turned and left the room.

When she heard the heavy oak doors close, she walked

across the drawing room and out onto the balcony. She watched as the handsome man dressed in a grey suit and perfect white shirt strutted across the stoned driveway to the waiting Bentley. Before he climbed into the back seat, he looked up, smiled, and blew her a kiss.

She waved until he was out of sight. She loved her husband so much.

This would be the last time she saw her husband

Anthony Fielding alive.

Chapter 1

Dawn was just breaking over Hounslow in west London, promising yet another grey and damp day. The streetlights flickered off. The only sign of life was from a ground floor window in a street of older style terraced houses. The thin and faded floral curtains were closed over old sagging nylon nets. Inside, the room smelled of heady testosterone and stale sweat. It was dimly lit by the blue glow of a large Apple computer monitor. The screen displayed fuzzy snow, and a colourful beach ball icon was spinning as the internet feed buffered.

Dominic Clayton sat hunched in a high-tech computer gaming chair, his right hand covered with a net glove. Each fingertip shone with a different coloured LED light. His green index finger lightly tapped the desk, and the screen changed to an image of a young white man lying naked face down. A thick leather collar restrained his head and his wrists and ankles tied to a brown leather padded bench. His long greasy fair hair was trailing across his nervous looking face. He was positioned facing a video camera, and a powerful overhead light made his glistening skin look sickly white.

A tall, mature dark-haired woman, dressed in a black leather Basque, black stockings and thigh-length boots walked into view. Her long hair was pulled up into a high ponytail held by a silver spiked hairgrip, her well applied heavy makeup giving her a severe and dynamic look.

She placed the end of the silver handled crop on the young man's cheek, brushing away his sweaty hair. He didn't move as the crop moved slowly down the centre of his spine but flinched as it neared his naked buttocks. Without warning the woman suddenly raised the crop high above her head and brought it down across the young man buttocks with tremendous force. The man bucked and strained against the restraints, screaming out as the pain surged through him. Raising the crop a second time the woman looked directly at the camera laughing wickedly.

As Dominic watched the screen went blank displaying a caption that read, 'To subscribe to this service text 9789 and the word Slave." Cursing, Dominic shifted in his chair, his gloved hand twitched causing the LEDs to flash. A second large monitor came to life. It showed a girl hanging upside down by her spread ankles. A man in a monk's habit slowly lit tall white tapered candles.

Chapter 2

The summer had been disappointing. An early warm spell had raised everyone's expectations for another hot and dry summer, but it had transpired to be grey and uneventful. It was now mid-September, and the cool, rainy autumn weather was setting in.

Lucian Palmer Jones sat at his desk scanning a new housing development brochure that had arrived in the mail that morning. The property market had been flat for the last two years with stagnant forecasts and slow house sales. Lucian had chosen to go it alone in the estate agency business in the winter of 2007, just six months prior to the financial crash. His ambitious plans to have four branches within five years seemed like a distant dream now.

The small office, located in Twickenham, south west London, was in need of repair, and his meagre savings were just supporting him in a basic lifestyle. Christina, Lucian's marketing assistant, emerged from the kitchen with a mug of steaming coffee in each hand. She placed one on Lucian's desk.

"No milk" she stated and turned away.

Lucian took three sugars. Christina refused to put more than one and a half teaspoons of sugar in his hot drinks. When challenged she would say, "It's not good for you, sugar gives you cancer; I heard it on the radio."

Lucian had tried all the sweeteners and sugar substitutes, but the Aspartame in the sweeteners made his tongue fizz. He avoided all diet drinks for the same reason.

Times were tough, and the banks were reluctant to start lending again. Politicians kept raving on about the green shoots of recovery being just around the corner. Lucian knew that behind the banks were corrupt and greedy men, who would keep the masses down. The government would never go after the offshore billionaires that exploited the UK tax systems. Whichever party was in power would make no difference, as they were all corrupt and worked for the same unseen hand. Lucian had read the Queen of England earns £8 million a year and yet her workers are on zero hours contracts. She gave a speech about being careful with money, and how austerity measures were a good thing while wearing her million pound crown.

Lucian Palmer Jones is 46 years old, standing 5ft 10 with a slim but toned build. He had been likened to

Daniel Craig without the piercing blue eyes. Lucian's eyes were green, and his slightly crooked nose had spoilt what many would say were handsome features.

After an average schooling at the local comprehensive, he did various jobs before joining a large estate agency firm.

After nine years he had acquired enough knowledge to set up his own estate agency. Lucian worked hard and took care to ensure each sale was followed through, battling against the poor reputation that many estate agents had at that time.

Lucian's taste in women had always been very precise; His preferred taste was a darker, slightly harsher looking woman. He fantasised about movie stars such as Joan Collins and Elizabeth Taylor.

One day merged into another and one uneventful week flowed seamlessly into the next. Little did Lucian know something was about to happen that would totally change his life.

Chapter 3

A tatty passport lay open on an unmade single bed. The photo showing a bald headed man around 48 years old. His name was Dominic Clayton, born in Hounslow London, to Mary and Cyril Clayton. What his passport didn't say was that he had been diagnosed at the age of 9, with multiple personality disorders. The result was afrightened and very confused little boy.

Dominic found sports challenging and as a teenager carried lot of puppy fat, which made him slow and un-athletic. He had faked stomach pains and sickness to avoid sports lessons. In school, Dominic struggled and had the humiliation of having to attend special classes for reading and math. On leaving school, he went from one menial job to another. He worked for a few months at a motorway service station. Dominic's job was scraping plates and feeding them into a huge Hobart dishwasher. The machine ran eighteen hours a day taking in the soiled plates and dishes one end and turning them out clean and steaming at the other. Dominic was too shy to ask for a better or different job and the other staff always put him "on the shitty end."

His apron was heavily stained and caked in grease, but he put it away in his locker at the end of each day. If another member of staff left their cleaner one behind, he would take it. A stash of filthy, stiff aprons lay hidden in an unused cupboard.

The months past and Dominic's hatred for the staff, particularly the management, grew to a burning rage. One Friday evening, after a long and busy shift, the manager called a team meeting. It was summer time and the night trucker's take away van needed staffing.

She asked if anyone wanted that job, someone jokingly shouted out, "Dominic will!!"

Everyone laughed, the Manager had seen how hard it was for Dominic to fit in and had noticed he was always on time for his shifts and worked hard.

"Ok," she said, "Dominic, would you like to work the truck stop?"

To everyone's amazement, he spoke up.

"Yes Madam".

"Ok," she said, "Start tomorrow 7 am to 3 pm."

"Yes Madam," Dominic said again avoiding eye contact with her.

The other members of staff were left speechless until someone whispered loudly, "Don't eat all the pies, Dom!"

Everyone burst out laughing. Dominic fumed inside but said nothing. He swore, if he got a chance, he would break that boy's fingers, one by one and cut them off like twigs with pruning shears.

Working the truck stop was better than the giant dishwasher; the truckers were friendly and sometimes gave him old porn magazines from their trucks.

One evening a little boy went missing at the service station. It was the high season with thousands of cars and caravans in the car park. The alarm was raised, and a team of security staff searched the car parks, outbuildings and surrounding grassland, but to no avail.

Dominic had seen a little boy fitting the description, being led away by a man. He wasn't sure, but he reported it to his managers. Dominic was taken to the police station and interviewed for several hours. They asked him lots of accusing questions almost blaming him for the boy's disappearance. When the police had finished with him; he went back to work to find he had been fired. On asking why the service station area manager said he shouldn't have said anything. People wouldn't stop at these services with children if they thought paedophiles preyed there. They paid him his wages for that day and sent him home.

Dominic was so upset he walked into the woods near his home. He caught small animals, then tortured and killed them slowly, imagining they were the service station managers.

Dominic liked to torture animals. Once, a pigeon got into the attic above Dominic's room. He spent days coaxing the frightened creature into a cage with food. Dominic slowly tortured the bird, burning it with long lighted matches. He stabbed at its eyes with sharp pins, cello-taped onto long knitting needles.

When a neighbour's cat got trapped in their garage, Dominic took his time torturing the poor creature. Enjoying the struggle to hold it tight while he shaved its fur off. Dominic received several deep claw wounds, which only served to excite him more. Dominic broke each leg in turn, and squeezed the cat's ribs until they snapped; he then cut its ears off with a pair of scissors.

Finally, after several days he strangled it.

Chapter 4

The recession had taken its toll. Lucian sat at his desk and opened a pile of red bills. The in-tray held a complete set, the telephone company, mobile phone, council tax, electric, gas and water. Luckily he owned 50% of the building; the mortgage was modest and the rates reasonable due to the square footage. The offices consisted of a small square room for Christiana, a toilet, kitchen area and a larger main room that Lucian used.

The last nine months had seen little return from Lucian's business. He had cut Christina's time down to five hours a day. She had agreed to work 10 am to 3 pm then collect her young daughter from school to save on childcare.

Lucian couldn't see any sales coming up this month. A young couple was buying a house in Greenwich, but this was several months away from completing. He had joined an online property investment group and had attended one of the group's social gatherings. He had gone along and listened to speeches by experts, giving advice to the members.

Lucian had found it a frustrating evening, as the groups were made up of successful property owners who took delight in sharing how many properties they owned in the UK and abroad. Without exception, they all had become successful from buying cheap property in the last recession and selling or renting in the boom times.

None of them seemed to be investing in the current market. Although some were asking if anyone had any older relatives, who might want to release the equity from their homes.

As Lucian was leaving, a man called Haroon Ahmed asked for his business card. He was from Saudi Arabia and was new to the UK property market. Mr Ahmed needed someone experienced to guide him on building a portfolio over the next five years. He was looking for a modest development up to £1 million. Lucian didn't pay much attention but took the man's card and gave him his in exchange.

Lucian went to sleep that night with a heavy heart. He hoped that in the coming weeks and months, sales would improve, and he wouldn't be forced to close his business.

Chapter 5

After leaving the motorway service station Dominic spent most of his time at the local library computer club, learning about computer programs. He quickly found he had a natural talent for programs, searching and navigation came easily to him. It wasn't long before he discovered a whole new exciting world of possibilities at the click of a button.

One afternoon Dominic was caught viewing "Adult" material and was asked to leave. Keen to pursue his new found interest Dominic found a recently opened cyber Internet Café, close to the local shops. The young Pakistani men who owned it paid little attention to the quiet boy, sitting right at the back for hours on end.

One Saturday, Dominic saw a sign in the café window advertising an HP Laptop for Sale for £150. Dominic asked to see it, and the young man produced the laptop from under the counter. Dominic, had £50 stashed away in his room and asked if he gave them the £50, could he use the laptop in the café until he paid off the rest?

The young man agreed, and his older brother asked if Dominic could do them a favour in return.

"What was that?" asked Dominic.

The elder brother looked at Dominic's face and said, "Would you be able to frighten someone for us?"

Dominic laughed and said, "Mate for that laptop I'll break some fuckers neck."

"No!" the Pakistani men said. "We only want to send a message."

"Ok who, where, and when?" Said Dominic

They explained that their cousin was seeing a white boy, from the local college and they didn't like him. Their cousin was already promised to have an arranged married when she graduated. This white boy was seeing her and distracting her from her studies. Dominic grasped what they meant instantly took the boy's home address and the times he was likely to be going home.

The following afternoon, Dominic headed off to the lad's address. He waited in the dark shadows of a derelict warehouse opposite the boy's house. Around the expected time Dominic spotted the boy coming along the road holding a bag of groceries and eating chips wrapped in newspaper.

Dominic approached him shouting "Oi".

As the youth turned around Dominic, without any warning, smashed his forehead into the boy's face.

Blood exploded from the young man's nose and mouth, and he went down hard. Dominic, excited by the reaction, grasped the heavy shopping bag and battered the boy with it. Kneeling down by the boys destroyed face he said, "Oi, I'm speaking to you."

The boy struggled to his knees and through broken teeth, spluttered, "Who are you? What do you want"?

Dominic bending forward yelled in the boy's face.

"If you ever go near that Paki whore again, I will fucking kill you! Do you understand?" screamed Dominic.

The boy reeled back in horror and realising what Dominic had said, answered quietly.

"OK."

Dominic kicked the boy full force in the ribs yelling, "Pardon… I didn't hear you!"

"Ok!" the boy replied a bit louder.

Dominic kicked him again and said, "Ok, what"?

The boy clutching his ribs gasped, "Ok, I won't see her again."

Dominic stood back and said, "That's better? But if I hear you have been fucking that Paki cunt again! I'll be back!"

Dominic turned and walked away, taking the boys shopping and eating the still-warm chips. Arriving home, he called upstairs to his mother.

"Do you want some cake or biscuits mum? I have been shopping."

The following day, the word had got back because as Dominic entered the Internet café. The owner pushed the laptop at Dominic and said, "Take it, take it, and go! We don't want any trouble."

"Cheers mate!" Dominic walked away with the laptop under his arm.

When he got home, Dominic set up the laptop and cleared all the previous data and passwords. He knew from research at the library how to create a new Internet connection. Dominic could see his neighbour was with Virgin.net. He quickly hacked in and logged into the neighbours broadband. No longer limited to the library or the Cyber café, Dominic had the online world at his fingertips.

Most people are not aware that there is more than one Internet and that the most valuable information isn't always on Google.

Within weeks Dominic had joined many online groups and created profiles in the most secret website communities. He created multiple fake online personalities. Dominic could switch from being male or female, white collar professional to bricklayer or barrister. Dominic befriended other hackers and security geeks and learned from their collective knowledge. A group called The Chaos Computer Club, one of the world's largest and most respected political hacking groups accepted Dominic. He was challenged to prove himself as a hacker; he impressed and surprised the guardians of the dark chat rooms. For the first time in his life, he was liked and respected for being odd.

After several months Dominic found himself a job in a call centre; telephoning customers at home in the evening selling credit card Insurance Protection. Dominic hated the job and the boring written scripts but learned how to extract customers secure information. Often they would give bank details, pin numbers and a host of personal information that Dominic would save and store away. As the weeks past he copied over a 1000 UK customer records. Selling them on the Internet to cloning companies in Africa and South America.

Part of his training was to work with IT systems and Digital security. His natural talent for networks meant that others in the teams, including the IT manager, would come to him for help.

After several months the IT manager called Dominic into the office and asked if he knew anything about CCTV and security.

Dominic replied, "I don't know much about it, but I am interested".

The IT manager said he had a friend in the business that was looking for someone to take on and train, he thought of Dominic because of his IT knowledge. The manager said he had arranged an interview.

Dominic went along on his day off and met the guy who owned the CCTV Company.

The day of the interview came, and Dominic was nervous. Dominic knew nothing about CCTV, although he was an accomplished Internet hacker

The IT Manager had explained this was Close Circuit TV and in-house private security systems. The stuff MI5 and the CIA use for spying and surveillance. Dominic spent an hour with the CCTV guy, who showed him the latest technology in webcams and Internet security.

The company's equipment was state of the art, and they had many very high ranking and important clients, some of which were celebrities and footballers. Dominic was so excited by that thought; he pushed aside all nervousness and asked the man for the job.

The man considered the request then told Dominic to wait while he made a phone call. He called the IT manager, and on his return, he said that Dominic could start after serving out his notice at the call centre.

Dominic was delighted and went home to study the CCTV world and learn all the dark secrets.

Chapter 6

The next morning, back in his office, Lucian's phone rang. Christina was out reviewing a property, and Lucian was tempted to let it go to the answering machine.

"Good morning Palmer Jones and Associates."

The voice on the other end was female and spoke with a possibly South African accent. She asked if she was talking to Lucian Palmer Jones."

Lucian said, "Yes."

"My name is Mary Phillips I was given you name by Giles Maconnally, he said that you might be able to assist me?"

Lucian had worked with Giles before he set up on his own. Lucian hadn't spoken to Giles since he left over seven years ago.

"Well yes, how can I help you," Lucian replied.

"I understand that you were at a property meeting last

night. You were speaking to Mr Haroon Armed?"

"Yes, I was," Lucian, replied

"Mr Haroon has had to return to Saudi as his father is unwell, but he would like you to attend the next property auction. To look at some properties, that might be a suitable investment."

"I'm sorry to hear that, when would Mr Haroon like me to start? " said Lucian

She paused and then stated, "Mr Haroon would like you to attend an auction on the 24th. To see if there is anything suitable?"

Lucian turning over the blank pages in his diary and said

"The 24th let me see? Ah yes, I can attend."

"Good, Mr Haroon is looking for a reasonable property say around the £1million pound mark. He is willing to pay up to 3% finder's fee."

"Very well, the 24th then," replied Lucian

The lady thanked Lucian and hung up.

At that moment Christina walked in.

"How did it go?" Lucian enquired

"The traffic was a nightmare, the prospects were twenty minutes late, and the place is a pile of shit."

"I take it that's a no sale then?" Lucian said with a smile. Christina didn't reply; she disappeared into the small room that doubled up as a kitchen. Lucian got to work researching the market to see what was properties were coming up before attending the auction on the 24th.

He spent some time studying the lists and saw a suitable property that was listed at offers between £750,000 and £1.1million. It seemed perfect. He hadn't attended a property auction with any decent money behind him for some time, and this could be the start of something that was much needed.

Dominic showed a surprising talent for gaming. One gaming website carried a competition for the highest scorer to win the chance to be a program tester for Sony Games. Dominic won by such a large margin that the head of Sony Games invited him to receive his award in person at Sony's head office in London.

After working for Sony for several months, he was suspended for selling secrets to the underworld community. By then Dominic had formed a ruthless reputation in the sub-internet as an accomplished hacker.

Dominic frequented BDSM websites, forums and extreme portals. To make money Dominic downloaded short clips of extreme fetish sessions. Then using editing software made up longer films to the customer's individual tastes. There was no shortage of willing takers, who didn't have the time or were simply too frightened to risk putting their credit card details onto sex sites. He posted clips on his own website offering "Search and find services."

Dominic knew the shortcuts; he could access photos or videos without having to go through the frontend password protected gateways.

For his own pleasure, Dominic made up films of dark haired women with red lipstick, smoking and being involved in intense and cruel BDSM sessions. Dominic longed to have the attention of the one those women. He spent many hours online to the point his health would suffer. Often urinating in empty coke bottles, he would order take away food and fall asleep exhausted after not leaving the house for days on end. Dominic's relationships with women had always been complicated. His profiling on dating sites got him dates but after a short time he would either frighten or insult the woman and it would always end badly. Dominic found that he had a deep and dark need to suffer and be hurt. He would search endless BDSM dating sites dreaming that one day he would be able to meet and have a session with a REAL Mistress who would make him pay for his guilty fantasies.

Chapter 7

The morning of the auction had arrived; Lucian drove
to Tetbury, past Prince Charles's walled Highgrove
house and followed signs for Westonbirt School. He
passed the famous arboretum and arrived at the school
entrance at 12.15pm. Lucian parked in the car park and
looked up at the impressive stately building. He
scanned the expanse of well-kept grass and playing
fields. Lucian was looking up at the steps leading up to
the main hall when his phone rang. It was Mary
Phillips, checking he had arrived ok.

"Mr Haroon is very excited about the prospect of you
finding a property for him, so good luck."

As Lucian listened to Mary Phillips, a powder Blue
Bentley Turbo R pulled into the car park. The car
stopped, and a silver-haired chauffeur in a grey suit
and peaked cap got out. Opening the rear door a
woman dressed in a long fur coat and red high heels
got out. She pulled her coat around her curvy figure
and adjusted her dark designer sunglasses. Lucian was
mesmerised.

As she carefully ascended the stone steps in her high heels. Lucian was suddenly aware that Mary was still speaking

"Mr Palmer Jones are you there...?"

"Mr Haroon will Skype you on Saturday morning at 11 am..."

"Hello.... can you hear me, did you get that..."

"Mr Palmer Jones are you there?"

Lucian regained his composure and said, "I'm sorry Mary the signal is bad, but yes, Skype call Mr Haroon at 11 am, Ok got it.... I will call you later."

Lucian hung up.

The school was used for antique fairs twice a year, but on this occasion, the prestigious property firm Gillesby and Hogget from Gloucester were sponsoring the event.

Lucian locked his car and headed up the stone steps collecting an auction brochure on the way into the grand entrance hall. Through the tall oak and glass doors, Lucian could see that a light lunch was being laid out by G&H for the guests. Lucian looked at the schools dark wood panelling and high ceilings. There was a wooden plaque on the wall stating that the school had

240 girls: 90-day pupils and 150 boarding. As Lucian was reading the plaque, he caught a glimpse of two women, standing outside the patio doors smoking and who appeared to be deep in conversation. He couldn't see her face, but he knew from the fur coat and red shoes it was the same woman he had watched entering the school.

As they stood speaking, a man in a suit approached, he passed the woman a business card. Slipping the card into her fur coat pocket, she turned and looked directly at him. Lucian was caught blatantly staring at her. He shuffled his feet awkwardly and quickly looked down at his program. When he looked up again, she was gone.

Lucian went through the large decorative high doors, into another panelled room. It had crystal chandeliers hanging over tables, neatly laid out with plated food, presented in a buffet style. Thirty or so people were standing and talking in small groups. Lucian hadn't eaten that morning and taking a small white plate, he passed along the buffet selecting a few items.

As Lucian did so, someone called his name. He turned around he saw Rupert Anderson, who was one of the senior negotiators, in the prestigious estate agents, Alfred and Harrow.

"What brings you here Palmer Jones?" said Rupert,

vigorously shaking Lucian's hand.

Lucian said, "Hello Rupert long time no see?"

Rupert smiled, "Bit out of your league here isn't it old chap?"

Laughing Lucian replied, "I was hoping to meet one of the investment clubs and make a few contacts."

"Ok, anyone in particular?" smiled Rupert.

Lucian was about to answer when Rupert said, "Well hello, ding dong."

Turning Lucian saw the woman in the fur coat talking to the G&H auctioneer.

"How about her?" smiled Lucian.

Rupert laughed out loud, in his deep booming voice, said: "Dream on, that's Debra Fielding, she is a major player."

Lucian explained to Rupert that he was looking at a lot for a possible investor from overseas.

Rupert said, "The smaller lots are starting in thirty minutes, just time for me to hook you up with a couple of my investment club chums."

They walked through to an elegant dining room, where

another fifty to sixty people were sitting at tables, eating their lunch and drinking wine.

Lucian followed Rupert to a small group. He introduced him to a lady dressed in a pink-checked suit. She had terrible teeth wore shocking pink smeared lipstick and blue eye shadow. She resembled an inferior version of the author Barbara Cartland. Rupert left Lucian listening to the lady. She told him how she had made over £200,000 on her first investment and then lost £300,000 on her next one. Then how she was hoping to meet a bigger investor and go in with them this time and get a better deal.

After listening to her for ten minutes, Lucian finished his glass of wine and on seeing the woman in the pink check suits glass was empty. Said

"Shall I get you another drink?" he asked

Then taking her glass from her bejewelled fingers, he headed for the bar. Once out of sight he dropped the glasses onto the first available surface. Careful not to touch the sticky pink lipstick impression left from her ugly silicone implanted lips. Having escaped, he headed for the auction room.

Debra Fielding walked across the chamber to join Rupert Anderson, who was speaking with a young petite Chinese woman called Helen Chow.

"I hope you are not taking advice from this scoundrel."

Debra smiled, and Rupert faked indignation and laughed.

Rupert and Debra air-kissed on both cheeks, careful not to get her red lipstick on the collar of his perfectly pressed white shirt.

"Debra, you know I always give first class advice and my knowledge is second to none."

Helen smiled and nodded several times not seeming to understand the conversation.

Debra said, "As you appear to know everyone Rupert, who was that gentleman who you were speaking to, is he a serious buyer?"

Rupert laughed again and replied, "Oh no no, that's Lucian Palmer Jones, great name but sadly poor as a church mouse. Hardly your taste Debra, I would have thought unless you fancy going down market."

Debra smiled and said nothing.

Rupert continued, "He is an estate agent and worked for Giles Maconnally years ago now, deals in the lower end of the market. Since he left Giles, he has fallen on hard times due to the old credit crunch."

"He is here to buy something for one of his few clients with means and is looking at lot 293."

Debra opened her program and read the details but didn't say anything in reply.

Debra thanked Rupert and shook Helen's small delicate hand and headed for the auction room.

Chapter 8

In the auction room, the lower lots were already well under way. Taking a seat on one side, about two-thirds of the way back Lucian studied the upcoming listings. There were several small leaseholds for sale; a few pre-agreed planning applications and some NHS commercial lots located in North Wales.

Lucian saw a house in Hampshire that looked promising; he had a buyer on his database that might be interested. If he could secure it today at the right price, he could sell it on at a good margin and make some much-needed money. The next lots were for five to twenty-acre plots, as these began, the room began to fill up with the serious buyers. He sat and listened as the other lots went through and waited for his lot number. The Hampshire property came up next the starting price was £122,000 several buyers got into a price war, and it quickly went up to £175,000. Lucian let it pass without bidding.

The crowd were noisy and boisterous as they entered the room. The auctioneer stopped and announced in a deep, gravelly voice.

"Ladies and Gentlemen we have started the auction so please have the courtesy to take your seat quickly and with as little noise as possible."

The arrogant "big time" investors had little interest and even less respect for the lower priced lots. The lady with the Pink Suit entered on the arm of an older gentleman, with a Bart Simpson waistcoat and a green check jacket. Lucian looked down at his program again to avoid making eye contact.

The auctioneer paused a moment longer and then tapped his wooden gabble.

"Ladies and Gentlemen we are now about to start the next collection of today' lots. Please take your seats so we may begin."

At that point, Debra Fielding entered the room with the other woman. Several heads turned to watch her as they walked past Lucian, her red high heels clicked on the stone floor. Lucian caught Rupert Anderson's eye, and he mouthed "Ding Dong" Lucian couldn't help but suppress a smile as Debra took her seat a few rows in front of Lucian to his right.

Lucian's lot was up next; he focused on the program, as the auctioneer read out the details. The opening bid was £475k, an Indian gentleman and a scruffy farmer immediately expressed their interest. Lucian listened carefully as the price rose to £595k; He gave the auctioneer the nod at £625k. The Indian buyer countered at £650k Lucian knew Mr Haroon could go to £950k. He went again at £675k, to be upped again by the farmer to £700k.

The Indian man indicated he was out. Lucian was just about to respond when suddenly a bid came in at £750k. The farmer countered with £775k the new bidder went to £800k. The property bids were getting close to Lucian's ceiling, but he raised his program and went to £825k. The farmer dropped out at that point, leaving the current bid with Lucian. The crowd gasped as a bid for £1.1 million came in. Lucian was shocked too.

The auctioneer looked directly at him and said any further advances on £1.1 million for lot 293? Lucian shook his head.

The auctioneer looked around the crowded room and confirmed.

"Lot 293 is going for £1.1 million pounds, do I have any other takers... going once, going twice, and sold."

He banged his gabble onto the lectern.

"Ladies and gentlemen there will be a short recess and comfort break before we proceed to the next lot. Please be back in your seats in fifteen minutes. Thank you."

He stepped down from the lectern and began speaking to a woman in the front row.

Lucian got up and headed for the reception room, he collected a coffee from the table as Rupert Anderson approached him with a Chinese woman.

"Lucian, let me introduce Helen Chow."

Lucian took the ladies delicate hand and shook it.

She bowed her head slightly as Rupert spoke in Mandarin and said something that ended in "Lucian Palmer Jones" which Lucian assumed was who he was in Mandarin.

The Chinese lady in broken English said, "Please to veet you."

She was attractive with long straight black shiny hair and classic features. Lucian knew it was a cliché but had always liked dark-haired women in martial arts films

Rupert turned to Lucian and said in his booming voice, "Tough luck on that property old chap. It went for well over the expected value; I think you bailed at just about the right point I wouldn't have paid a million one for it."

Lucian sipped his coffee then asked, "Do you who bought it?"

Rupert replied, "No, might have been a phone in, I couldn't see who was bidding against you."

The auctioneer came into the room, and Rupert went over and spoke to him. Returning he said,

"The Property you were after was bought by a representative of the Quindici Group."

Helen Chow smiled and said, "Quindici Group, Yes, Yes!"

Rupert spoke to her, and he translated to Lucian.

"Helen says that the Quindici Group is a firm based in New York, she thinks Debra Fielding is on the board. Helen's father did business with Debra's husband, Anthony Fielding, and a man called Charles McCready? They were developing a couple of high-end exclusive hotels in Aruba."

"Aruba?" Said Lucian "Where is Aruba?"

Rupert replied, "Aruba is a small Caribbean island in

the Dutch Antilles. A few years ago, Helen's father and Debra's husband were negotiating with the local government officials. They were opposed to anymore all-inclusive hotels being built. Mr Chow and Debra's husband were on the island to secure a large hotel deal and were flying to Venezuela when their small private plane crashed, and they were both killed."

"Oh My God," said Lucian "I'm so sorry for your loss."

Rupert explained, "Helen had taken over her father's business. With interest rates being so flat, investors like Helen could get a better return by investing in property."

"I see," said Lucian "Do you think that's why Debra Fielding is here?"

Rupert smiled "Probably looking for another rich husband!"

Lucian laughed and sipped his now cold coffee.

The auction was over, so they made the way to the exit as the schoolgirls cleaned up the empty coffee cups and stacked the chairs. The woman with the pink suit and lipstick came over to Lucian. She spoke to Rupert and then turned to Lucian and said

"We don't think it's fair when big players swoop in and steal smaller deals, it's disgusting that an unknown property firm from New York can buy up decent houses in England. Don't you think so Rupert?"

Rupert agreed. At the top of the stairs, Lucian shook hands with Helen and Rupert and said goodbye to the lady in the pink suit.

As they parted, Lucian could see the Blue Bentley parked off to the left. Sitting in the back with the window down was Debra Fielding. She was smoking, wearing dark sunglasses and talking on the phone. As Lucian watched, he could see her red lips moving and they formed a slight smile. From his viewpoint looking down at the car, she seemed to be watching him. But with her dark sunglasses shading her eyes it was impossible to tell.

As he descended the school steps, the Auctioneer came out and called after him.

"Mr Palmer Jones, would you come back in I need to speak to you in private."

Lucian was surprised at this request and went back up the steps saying, "Yes, of course, is anything wrong?"

The auctioneer met him at the top and said, "We have a situation, come with me please."

He took Lucian in a side office, sat down behind the desk and made a pyramid with his fingertips. Sitting opposite the auctioneer, Lucian felt a slight pang of nerves as he recalled being called to see the headmaster in his old school days.

The auctioneer spoke, "The property that you were interested in has a problem. As you know at an auction when a buyer agrees to a sale it's a legally binding contract."

Lucian knew this and nodded his head. The auctioneer continued,

"The property was purchased by the Quindici Group. Their representative no longer wants the property and wishes to sell it to you."

Lucian laughed and said, "Oh OK, for twice the asking price I suppose?"

The auctioneer remained deadly serious.

"No that's where we have the problem. The buyer wants to sell it back to you personally for 10% less than your last bid; they will pay for all the fees and want you to have the property signed over to you."

Lucian looked stunned.

The auctioneer asked, "Do you know Ms Debra Fielding?"

Lucian was taken aback.

"Well No, well yes I know who she is. But not really."

The Auctioneer looked stern and said, "If you do know her Mr Palmer Jones then I can't let the transfer happen as it's illegal and highly irregular."

Lucian didn't say anything.

The Auctioneer sat back in his chair and asked again "Have you ever met Debra Fielding Yes or No?"

Lucian spoke openly and said "Look the truth is I don't know Ms Fielding. I have never met her or talked to her in person. I had no idea who she was before today!"

The auctioneer looked serious but said nothing.

Lucian continued, "I was asked to come today to look at properties for a potential client from Saudi Arabia. I'm afraid I just don't have the money to pay for that property personally. If that is what Ms Fielding is suggesting?"

The auctioneer looked at Lucian very intently he didn't speak for a few minutes then said, "I see, it's because Ms Fielding is such a good client that I would even consider this."

"Consider what?" Said Lucian

The auctioneer didn't seem to hear and continued, "If I allow this to go ahead you will need to do the transaction away from here and in private. I will hold up the purchase papers to the seller until your name is on the deeds and the money has been transferred from your account."

"Wait," said Lucian "You don't understand. I don't have a million pounds, and the funds are not my money. I have a buyer that I was purchasing it for."

The auctioneer didn't seem interested anymore and rose from the desk saying "That's your problem to sort out with Ms Fielding."

He led Lucian back to the stairs he shook his hand and turned and walked back into the school. Leaving Lucian totally confused. Had he just bought a house from Debra Fielding?

Descending the steps, he saw that the Blue Bentley had gone and apart from a few staff cars, the car park was now deserted.

Lucian couldn't believe what had just happened. He called the office and left a message to ask Christina to call Mary Phillips in the morning and to let Mr Haroon know that he had managed to get a property for him.

Lucian drove back towards London; his thoughts filled

with images and questions about Debra Fielding.

Chapter 9

Dominic ate the last piece of his large meat feast pizza and tossed the empty box onto the floor amongst the crushed coke cans, chocolate wrappers and crisp packets, then turned to face his monitor again. Dominic was searching through the endless internet live chatter, when he came across a young man's voice repeating the words "Yes Mistress" Dominic's attention was immediately focused on finding the feed and zooming in on this verbal exchange.

Twenty-three miles away in a London house, a woman in leather boots dropped her cigarette and crushed it out under her four-inch platform shoe sole. Turning to the tied down young man she said:

"Enough of your fucking time wasting, you are going to get it now!" The boy moaned again and pulled against the straps that held him down.

She laughed.

"Struggle all you like you filthy pig; you get no mercy from me today."

He moaned again as she positioned herself up against his reddened arse and put the tip of a rubber cock against his asshole.

"Ready Slave," she asked and slapped his bare cheeks.

"Yes Mistress" he replied

"Good," she said, "Because you are going get fucked like you have never been fucked before."

"Yes Mistress." The boy panted dropping his head.

"When I'm finished with your asshole, you won't be able to shit for a week."

The young man moaned as the woman in the boots checked the monitor, noting the pledges were in excess of £1,300. She drew her hips back ready to thrust the large black rubber cock deep into the young man's asshole.

At that point, the feed went dead, and the screen showed a simple box saying "Feed disconnected bandwidth exceeded, please try later."

It took Dominic only ninety seconds to locate the source somewhere in north London. He like the other punters had been drawn in by the live session. Dominic's cock had gone hard in his jeans as he watched the action.

He spent the next ten minutes working his software tools until he accessed the feed again. With the lapsed time the scene had changed. The bed was empty, the trestle removed. The woman had shed her "Mistress" outfit and was now smoking. She was drinking a glass of white wine dressed in a dirty off-white towelling dressing gown.

The young man, now released, was sitting in a blue tracksuit, chewing gum and texting on his phone.

Dominic quickly realised that they had been working a scam. It was obviously a well-rehearsed act and had been tailored to encourage viewers to spend money. Dominic was impressed that a show lasting less than 11 minutes had probably earned the actors over £1,000.When it reached the required level they had stopped the show and cut the punters off.

There would be many frustrated punters sitting in front of laptops, tablets, or home PCs with their cocks in their hands. Having just been taken for potentially £100's of pounds.

Dominic took control of the webcam and scanned the room looking at the red and black painted walls. He zoomed into the various whips and crops hanging on hooks along one wall.

Dominic then focused on the woman and studied her

face and body. She was unconscious of the webcam, but a couple of times she looked directly at the tiny camera. As if somehow sensing someone was watching. He watched her as the young man kissed the woman's cheek and said, "See you later babe."

Dominic was furious; he would never disrespect a Mistress, even a fake one by calling her "Babe."

He could quite easily trace the young man's phone and have something very unpleasant happen to him if he could be bothered.

Right now he was interested in the fake Mistress. He continued to watch her, reaching into his jeans to rub his cock, as she lit another cigarette. She was alone now, and he was fascinated by her stillness and calm posture.

Her scruffy bathrobe was wrapped around her busty frame; she still had her high boots on. She had removed the corset and the strap-on harness. Watching this woman caused Dominic's hard on to return. Dominic found she had something that excited him.

Dominic watched as she picked up the laptop and walked with it still open out of the playroom. She went down some stairs into a lounge area with contemporary furnishings and sofas. The woman, still unaware that Dominic was watching, her sat with the laptop on her knees. She started to press some keys on the keyboard and was looking directly into the webcam. Dominic opened another tool on his desktop and was then able to see the woman's screen.

He could see her accessing her Pay Pal account; the account balance was £17,000. There was a new entry of £1,200 that they had made from tonight's online live session. Dominic clicked few keys with his gloved hand mouse and captured the woman's keystrokes. It was going be so easy to hack and clear her account out later.

She placed the laptop on a wooden coffee table giving Dominic a perfect view of her face and shoulders. She sat back on the couch pulling off her shiny black straight-haired wig, revealing a mop of short dirty blonde hair. Despite the well-preformed act on the live cam, being a blonde shattered the illusion. Dominic knew then this woman wasn't right for him.

Chapter 10

Two days after the auction, Lucian had an appointment with a young couple looking to buy a property in Greenwich south east London. The houses were ex NHS homes near to the Cutty Sark and the Greenwich Observatory. The traffic had been bad getting out of Greenwich as he returned to the office.

Christina was tastefully dressed in her dogtooth check coat and shiny knee-length boots. She washed her coffee cup in the sink packed up her purse and then prepared to leave for the day. Lucian suspected that the 1960's had had a real influence on Christina when she was growing up in Poland. Christina often sported a sixties style of dress and was prone to doing her hair like Audrey Hepburn in Breakfast at Tiffany's. She even had the cat called "Cat".

She was halfway out the door when she shouted back, "Did you get that call this afternoon?"

Lucian sat down at his desk and saw a post-it note stuck to his screen. It read, "Debra Fielding called" His heart stopped.

"When did she call? What time, did you take a message?"

Christina called back, "It was her office, and the lady asked for your mobile number, I gave it to her, didn't she ring you?"

Lucian took his iPhone out of his jacket pocket. It showed no missed calls. He dialled his voicemail and the recorded message said, "You have no new messages."

"Damn it," said Lucian tossing his phone onto the desk.

Sensing his disappointment, Christina called back.

"Do you want me to stay?"

Lucian looked up and said, "No it's Ok, you can go, and I'll see you in the morning."

That night he sat watching TV. Arsenal was playing Bayern Munich in the Champions League semi-finals. The game was slow he was fidgety and lost interest after twenty-five minutes. Taking his IPad from the side table, he searched for random items on eBay. He couldn't find anything interesting and turned to his email. Opening his personal mailbox, he saw there was a new message from the Quindici group. His heart started to beat faster as he read it.

It was a single line message "Mr Palmer Jones, please call Carol at the Quindici Office at your earliest convenience" and gave the number.

He checked the time it was 9.45 pm. He picked up his mobile and called the number; it rang three times. He suspected this time of day the answering machine would be kicking in on the next ring.

As he moved the phone away from his ear, someone answered. He put the phone back to his ear he said "Hello?"

A slightly camp voice said, "Can I help you?"

Lucian asked if Debra Fielding was available and the voice said, "I'm terribly sorry Ms Fielding is out of the office on business."

Lucian explained he had been asked to call this number, and his name was Lucian Palmer Jones.

The voice on the phone said, "I'm sorry, I suggest that if you call back in the morning and speak to Carol, Ms Fielding's PA, she will be able to help you."

Lucian thanked him and said, "I'm sorry I didn't catch your name?"

"I'm Marcus, Ms Fielding's housekeeper" he announced and hung up.

The next morning, Lucian was in early and busied himself doing the follow-up paperwork for the Greenwich job. He figured that Debra Fielding's office would not be receiving calls before 9 am.

At 8.45am Christina arrived, wearing a black and white mod mini dress, black tights and white kitten-heeled pointed sling-backs. Her hair was tied back in a bun, and she was sporting a headscarf and large oval shaped sunglasses.

"Good Morning Christina," said Lucian. She smiled but didn't say anything and disappeared into her office.

At 8.55am Lucian's phone rang and Christina announced that he had a call. Lucian asked who it was, and Christina said it was Arthur Parkinson from Greenwich county council.

Lucian checked the time and said, "Ok thank you, Christina, but when you have put him through could you call Mary Phillips. Please let her know I have found something suitable for Mr Haroon. Could she let him know and that I will be in touch."

After forty-five minutes, Lucian had finally put the phone down and sat back in his chair with his hands behind his head. He had met and spoken to Arthur Parkinson several times, and that man could talk for England. Lucian wished that he had dodged the call, but he did need to get the Greenwich project moved along.

Checking his diary, he saw he had another viewing at 12.45pm. It was in North London.

The project was near completion. Lucian was meeting some buyers that were interested.

He checked his watch; he should have left twenty minutes earlier if he was going to get there on time.

Lucian called Christina and asked her if she could go in his place? But she told him no because her boyfriend was taking her out for lunch.

As Lucian couldn't get cover for the meeting he resigned himself to a drive across London. As he picked up his keys the phone rang again, Lucian could see that Christina was on the other line.

He picked up the phone on the fourth ring.

"Hello, Palmer Jones associates."

A well-spoken female voice spoke up and asked, "Is that Lucian Palmer Jones?"

Lucian replied, "Yes can I help you?"

The voice replied, "I sincerely hope so Lucian, this is Carol Barnes and I work for Debra Fielding at the

Quinidci Group."

Lucian took a breath releasing it wasn't Debra but her PA calling.

He continued, "I got your message yesterday. I called back late last night and spoke to Marcus."

"Yes, Marcus told me you called."

Lucian said, "Carol, I'm sorry, but I will have to call you back this afternoon as I'm leaving for a meeting right now."

Carol spoke quietly and said, "I think you will find your meeting has been cancelled. I was hoping to catch you before you left for North London."

Lucian sat down again.

"I'm sorry what did you say."

Carol repeated, "The reason I called you yesterday, was to advise you that the meeting you were going to in North London was with one of our people. Unfortunately, they had to fly out of the country early this morning."

Lucian put his keys back in the draw and said, "Ok, well thank you for letting me know."

Sitting back in his chair, he prepared to end the call and hang up.

Carol said, "There is a matter of the Hampshire Property we need to discuss."

Christina and Lucian had tried several times since his return to contact Mary Phillips and Mr Haroon, his potential buyer, but despite leaving several voice mails and email messages had had no joy.

Lucian explained to Carol that he didn't have the funds personally, and he was there to buy a property for someone else.

Carol said, "I really couldn't comment on that. Ms Fielding would like to conclude this as quickly as possible. I suggest you meet her to discuss the transfer and how you are going to fund it."

Lucian felt his heart begin to beat faster in frustration, he said, "I have to say, Carol, this is all rather strange, I keep saying, I wasn't there to buy anything for myself on that day."

"Well, you will have to take that matter up with Ms Fielding, Lucian."

Carol continued, "Ms Fielding will be in Southampton this week attending the boat show. She would like to have a meeting with you on Monday."

"Very well" Lucian sighed.

"We will send a car to pick you up at 6.30pm, at your offices."

"That's late!" Lucian said, rather louder than he intended.

Then reluctantly, Lucian said, "Ok, the address is… "

Carol interrupted, "We have the address, just don't be late, Ms Fielding deplores lateness."

Chapter 11

Dominic's father had died from a prolonged and painful illness that the doctors couldn't identify. One doctor suspected he was suffering from mercury poisoning but could never identify the source. His job at the silkscreen printers was blamed for his constant stomach pains and problems with his toilet functions.

He died one night after violent vomiting and bleeding from the bowels and nose. The doctor who examined the body signed the death certificate as liver failure. Dominic remembered his mother giving his father a tablet every evening for "Gout" which seemed strange looking back.

After his father's death, Dominic stayed at the Hounslow home at his mother's insistence. He lived in a terrible environment of constant criticism, ridicule, and humiliation. In his father's absence, his mother would make Dominic her personal servant. She demanded meals and drinks at all hours of the day and night. She would call him at work and demand that he come home immediately to make her cups of tea or collect shopping to satisfy for her liking for chocolate biscuits and Twiglets.

The daily ritual of mental abuse continued well into his adulthood. His mother would accuse him of looking at filthy sluts in dirty magazines. Constantly berating him for not having a girlfriend and that he must be turning into one of those Bum Boy queers, she was a heavy smoker, and Dominic would watch his mother lying in bed or in her armchair smoking continuously. Dominic cleared away her fag ends after each day when she went to sleep.

He was desperate to leave home, preferably to another country away from his miserable life in Hounslow and his overbearing mother with her acid tongue. She would tell friends that he couldn't leave his "Willie" alone and what a "Dirty, disgusting perverted little boy." he was.

He sat listening to her verbally abuse him, reminding him of his every failure and mistake. She would constantly compare him to a bright boy who lived across the road. Ridiculing Dominic about how proud the boy's parents were of their son's academic achievements.

At 5.9ft Dominic was not physically large, but was very intimidating to look at with a shaved head and a face deeply lined with internal mental pain and suffering from years of abuse.

When Dominic's mother finally died of stomach cancer, Dominic was relieved. He did not feel sad at her passing, and he felt free, probably for the first time in his life.

He was now able to live his life; he set about cleaning up and redecorating his parent's old and dated house.

Late one evening Dominic built a huge bonfire in the back garden. He burnt every single thing that reminded him of his mother, the old wooden furniture, tatty curtains, her clothes, her bed and every trinket that she had kept. He burnt all her paperwork and every single photograph.

He was going to destroy the miserable memories once and for all. Dominic sat on an upturned log. The air reeked of smoke and the fumes from burning plastic. He watched as the last remains of his parent's life turned to embers and the grey ash floated up into the night sky.

He poked at the remains to make sure nothing had survived the intense heat before returning to the almost empty house. Dominic opened all the windows, some he had to use brute force or snap the handles as they had jammed shut for years. The fresh cold night air blew through the house as Dominic peacefully slept.

Over the next few months, Dominic worked in the evenings painting and decorating. He bought new furniture and enjoyed browsing magazines for the latest trendy designs. A new high gloss kitchen was installed with a range of modern appliances; blue marble worktops and a cream tiled floor. The lounge area was now a state of the art office filled with expensive computers and an array of technical equipment, including a massive wall mounted 80-inch flat screen TV.

Dominic's single bedroom was now a modern black and cream en suite bathroom. Connected to what was his mother's bedroom, her room was completely unrecognisable now, with its king size leather bed and a whole wall of mirror wardrobes.

Next door to Dominic's room was a 3rd bedroom, which Dominic kept continuously locked.

Chapter 12

Lucian woke before the alarm and lay in bed thinking about meeting Debra Fielding that evening. During the day Lucian checked his watch hundreds of times. As the hours crawled past Lucian tried again to contact Mary Phillips without success. He dealt with a few emails from Mr Parkinson about the Greenwich project, Christina noticed he was on edge and didn't bother him with any invoice or accounting questions. Finally, it was time to go home to get ready for his meeting.

Arriving home he stripped off his work clothes, he carefully shaved and stepped into the shower, letting the steamy hot water warm his shoulders and body. As he soaped his body, Lucian imagined Debra in her fur coat and high heels smiling at him. Turning the tap to cold, he rinsed himself off quickly and got out of the shower.

Wrapping a large white fluffy towel around his waist draping a smaller one, boxer style, over his head Lucian went back to his bedroom.

Opening his wardrobe Lucian scanned his clothes. He

had rebuilt his wardrobe with the essentials for gentlemen after he had left his wife. He now had a working wardrobe, two well-cut business suits, one black, one blue, a quality black dinner jacket, a couple of pairs of jeans, one faded and one smarter dark denim. His shirts were all designer branded and were pressed and on coat hangers fresh from the shirt laundry service. He had a selection of casual jackets including corduroy and a linen fabric. He also had a heavier black dress jacket, a leather jacket and a quality wool overcoat. His shoes were all neatly lined up beneath.

He selected a good shirt and a pair of cream chinos with polished brown brogues and stripy socks. Lucian dried his hair adding a pinch of hair gel, dressing carefully to not crease his shirt. He crossed the bedroom went to his cherry wood bureau and opened a thin drawer. It contained several watches and pairs of designer sunglasses. He picked a gold Rotary watch, the expensive timepiece felt good as he fastened the strap to his wrist.

Once dressed he looked at his reflection in the full-length mirror did the classic James Bond double finger gun pose.

"Ok Mr Palmer Jones" he mused,

"Your mission, if you choose to accept it is to go and

meet the lovely Debra Fielding."

Lucian had been waiting behind the office doors for ten minutes when the blue Bentley Turbo R pulled up. Christina had left a few minutes before, after commenting on how smart he looked and asking him who the lucky lady was.

He had smiled and said "its just business."

She shot him a look and said "Really? Just business?"

Lucian approached the passenger door, which was locked. The window lowered, and a chauffeur in a grey peaked cap said, "In the back, if you please sir."

As instructed Lucian opened the back door fully expecting to see Debra Fielding waiting inside, but it was empty. The car pulled away as Lucian fastened his seat belt and looked around the car. He remembered watching her sitting outside Westonbirt School, speaking on the phone and smoking. There was no trace of smoke or any scent at all, apart from the lovely smell of leather and the fresh coolness of the air conditioning.

He touched the polished gold ashtray and it flipped open making him jump. He pressed another button and a small compartment opened to reveal drinks holders, with two stylish cut glass decanters and four matching tumblers. He fiddled with more buttons and a small TV opened up. He could imagine Debra sitting smoking catching up on the stock market or reading her emails.

The driver caught Lucian's eye in the driving mirror, "Having fun sir?" he said with a slight smirk on his face.

Embarrassed Lucian shut the TV flap and looked out of the window.

The car picked its way through the outer suburbs and joined the M3 at Junction One. The big car accelerated smoothly up to eighty-five miles an hour.

Lucian asked the driver, "Where are we heading and how long will it take." Feeling slightly childish asking such obvious questions?

The driver didn't make eye contact.

"We are going to Southampton, Sir it will take about fifty minutes this time of day."

Lucian nodded and said, "Ok, thanks, do you know where in Southampton? "

The driver appeared to not hear said nothing and ignored his question.

Lucian looked out of the window at the evening sky as

they speed past Fleet, Basingstoke and onwards towards Winchester.

Leaving the M27, the Bentley headed smoothly towards Southampton docks and city centre. As the car purred along the long inward road called The Avenue

Five minutes later the car pulled into the front entrance of the De Vere Grand Harbour Hotel.

The driver turned in his seat and said, "We are here Sir. Please go to the bar and wait, someone will be with you in due course. Lucian thanked the driver and made his way through the glass revolving doors. Once inside a pleasant looking young girl with a strong eastern European accent asked him if he was checking in. Lucian explained he was meeting someone and could she direct him to the bar. Taking her directions, Lucian went to the well-appointed bar. The bar area was surprisingly noisy; the three barmen were busy making up drinks orders and cocktails.

Lucian went to the bar and waited, scanning the room for a spare seat. A barman finished a large order and turned to Lucian, who was looking around the room for signs of Debra.

"Yes mate, tell me what's your poison" he spoke with an Australian accent,

Lucian smiled at the barman's approach and ordered a small bottle of Budweiser beer.

"Glass," said the barman

"Yes please," he replied.

"That's £7.70 please."

Lucian took a deep breath at the high price, and handing over a ten-pound note said,

"Is it cheaper without the glass?" said Lucian

The barman didn't say anything just took Lucian's £10 note putting the change into a small silver tray. Lucian swept up the coins, noticing the barman's disappointment at not leaving it as a tip.

Lucian saw a small group stand up and vacate their seats he headed over to sit down before anyone else at the bar noticed. He sat sipping his expensive beer, it tasted warm and flat; disgusted he got up to take it back. As he approached the bar, a hotel bell boy tapped him on the shoulder and said

"Mr Palmer Jones?"

Lucian turned and said, "Yes."

"There is a call for you sir."

Placing his warm beer on the table, Lucian followed the bellboy to the service phone at reception, checking his mobile as he went. It had full signal showed no missed calls or text messages. When he reached reception, he picked up the house phone receiver.

"Hello, Lucian speaking."

The voice on the other end was the same calm, efficient lady from the other night

"Mr Palmer Jones it's Carol Barnes I have a message from Ms Fielding. She has been called away on business and won't be meeting you at the Grand Harbour Hotel this evening as planned...."

Lucian couldn't hide his frustration interrupting Carol he said, "Great, it's nearly 9 pm! How the hell do I get back to London now!"

Carol spoke again, If you would allow me to continue Mr Palmer Jones! Debra would like you to join her on her trip."

Carol was silent for a moment as if reading something then said, "Debra leaves Southampton on a cruise at 10.15pm tonight. Arrangements have been made if you agree to join her on board?"

"What!" Lucian replied.

This was surprising, as he hadn't even met Debra yet. Now he was expected to go on a cruise with her at the drop of a hat. He also noted Carol referred to "Ms Fielding" as "Debra."

Carol spoke again in her soft efficient tone.

"There is a cruise ship representative at the hotel who will take you on board. Have safe trip Mr Palmer Jones."

Before Lucian could object Carol hung up on him. Replacing the handset and shaking his head in disbelief, he walked back towards the bar to be greeted by a young lady, accompanied by an older man in a blue suit.

The man approached and said, "Mr Palmer Jones? I'm Alex Knightley. I'm the chief personal officer; this is my assistant Juliette Harding. We are here to escort you to the ship. Come this way please."

Lucian lost for words followed Juliette and Alex out of the front entrance to an awaiting golf buggy. Alex jumped in next to the driver.

"Hold tight," Alex said as the golf cart launched off down the ramp across the road heading towards the port entrance. It was a bumpy ride, several times Juliette was pressed up against Lucian's hip. At one point they raced over a ramp, and Juliette nearly ended up on his lap.

"I'm so sorry Sir," she said, Lucian just smiled

"How long is the cruise and where is it going?" Lucian asked

Alex turned to him.

"It's eleven days, first stop is Madeira then onto Miami then last stop is St Lucia."

Lucian said, "Oh, ok thanks."

But in his head, he was screaming, what the fuck! Eleven days! I can't do that! What about Christina! This is insanity!

"If I pinch myself I will wake up," he mumbled to himself as he sat next to Juliette.

As if Alex Knightly had read his mind he said, "Everything has been taken care of Mr Palmer Jones and your luggage is already on board."

"Oh really?" Lucian replied in a sarcastic tone, wondering if they hadn't picked up the wrong person from the bar.

The golf buggy bumped its way to the cruise port

reception then drove straight past the check-in booths and down a covered walkway. It drove into a service lift, which raised swiftly, the buggy then drove into the hold of the ship parking by a second lift.

Alex jumped out and said, "This way please, Mr Palmer Jones."

Lucian blindly followed.

They entered the elevator and ascended coming to rest on level 4. Lucian and Alex exited, but Juliette stayed in the lift and said, "Nice to meet you I hope you enjoy your cruise Mr Palmer Jones" and she gave a shy smile.

As the elevator doors closed, Alex indicated they go into an office to his left. Sitting behind a desk, Alex opened a folder and read the details on a piece of paper then passed it to Lucian. Alex then explained he was a temporary guest of Ms Debra Fielding and would be accompanying her to Madeira, which was the first stop in four days' time. Lucian signed the temporary visa, Alex asked for some ID. Lucian showed him his driving license that Alex photocopied and placed in the file.

"Don't I need a passport or something?" asked Lucian Alex just smiled and said,

"It's all been taken care of Mr Palmer Jones."

Lucian couldn't think straight, was this is just some

crazy dream or a ridiculous joke.

Alex stood up and said he would accompany him to the dining room where Ms Fielding was waiting for him. They got back in the lift and went to the dining level, as they exited the mirrored lift Lucian asked if he had a cabin to stay in?

Alex gave a slight smile.

"This ship doesn't have any cabins, other than for staff. We only have suites; as you were a late addition I haven't been told what your sleeping arrangements will be yet. I will, of course, let you know as soon as I get the details."

Great, Lucian thought, I haven't even got a bed!

Lucian was feeling very stressed, totally confused and annoyed at the fact that everything had been so-called "arranged" without even asking him!

Alex took Lucian through to a private dining room, a table for two was beautifully set with tall flickering candles, fresh flowers, and gleaming silver wear.

The cut glass wine glasses shone in the soft candlelight. Sitting at the table with a glass of red wine in her hand was Debra Fielding.

Chapter 13

Dominic opened his email and saw he had a new message. He was surprised to see the mail wasn't from one of the Pro Dom's replying to the various requests he had made in website chat rooms. It was from a woman called Carol in Hampshire enquiring about installing a full CCTV security network.

"Hmmm," Dominic thought out loud.

Before responding Dominic checked the email address header, he set his specialised tools to do a quick search for more information. The results were minimal with some news posts on the Quinidci Group and several links to a man called Charles McCready. Dominic did a subsequent search and found the Quinidci Group email was on PRQ hosting company. Dominic knew all clients using their hosting services were protected under Swedish privacy laws.

Dominic's inner mind began to stir; he wondered if the email could be a trap. Was someone checking him out or testing his ability to perform searches? He decided that he would play it straight, for now, assuming Carol was genuine and did require his CCTV services. Dominic replied using his work email writing a simple response. Minutes later he received a response to say Carol would like Dominic to do a site inspection at the Hampshire property. Dominic typed an email back confirming he would be available next week.

Dominic had to be careful, as he had installed live feeds and cameras in the places like London's Dolphin Square apartments. Some very influential people had commissioned this specialised equipment. These specially equipped rooms allowing politicians to offer visiting wealthy businessmen the opportunity to watch the abuse of young boys and girls. Dominic was horrified at the length these sick men would go to be involved in these child abuse rings. He was often called back to Dolphin Square to fix or improve and enhance the equipment in these places. Despite his extreme tastes, Dominic was sickened by child abuse. He hacked and destroyed child porn sites whenever he came across them, then anonymously reported the IP addresses to WikiLeaks.

The clients asked if he would like to be rewarded for being discreet with sexual favours. With Dominic's particular sexual tastes he had no interest in the young boys and girls these old men preferred. So instead he would ask for access to specialist software tools used by the security agencies and not readily available to the public.

Despite not finding much information on the lady from Hampshire he got the visit confirmation. Dominic decided he would find out more once he was down at the house.

Chapter 14

"Hello Lucian". Debra smiled and extended an elegant hand with red painted nails that matched her lipstick. Lucian's stress and annoyance melted away immediately at such beauty.

He approached the table took her delicate hand; he had an overwhelming urge to kiss it. As he bent slightly, she moved her hand indicating him to take a seat at the table.

Debra looked towards Alex, and he approached the table. "Would you be a sweetheart Alex and bring another glass of wine."

Without speaking, Alex bowed his head indicating his understanding and went to get the wine. Lucian sat and looked at the woman who had dominated his thoughts from the first time he had laid his eyes on her. She was dressed in a long emerald green evening gown with a plunging neckline.

Lucian struggled to keep his eyes above the diamond necklace she wore around her neck.

She had a cashmere wrap draped loosely around her shoulders, fastened at the front with a gold chain. She wore diamond earrings with a blue sapphire in the centre.

On the table next to her was a gold cigarette box with an inscription engraved with some words in flowing script on it. The box was turned towards Debra so he couldn't read it, but she noticed he was looking at it. By way of explanation, she said, "A present from my husband, before he died."

Lucian's heart was beating fast, and he felt his palms sweating. He still hadn't spoken a word and almost felt he couldn't talk.

Alex returned with the bottle of wine pouring Debra a taste which she declined passing the glass to Lucian. He took the long stemmed wine glass feeling awkward, as he didn't know anything about wine.

He simply took a sip and said, "It's fine."

Alex poured two new glasses. Debra raised her glass and with a smile said, "I'm pleased to meet you, Mr Palmer Jones."

They spent the next hour chatting about Lucian's business and Debra's travels. He found once he started he couldn't stop telling this gorgeous woman about his life. Lucian told Debra he been married, They had two children, a son thirteen and daughter eleven who still lived with their mother in a beautiful house. He said he had always worked hard, tried to be a good and devoted husband. He explained that his wife had had an affair and he was devastated when he got divorced. Debra was an excellent listener interjecting from time to time to keep the conversation flowing. After a while she suggested they go up on deck where she could smoke. They took the lift, and Lucian felt slightly uncomfortable but also strangely excited at being in such close proximity to this incredibly beautiful woman.

They stepped out onto the upper deck the night air was cold and damp. A chilly wind swirled around the deserted decks. Far below the cold Atlantic Ocean looked dark and uninviting. Lucian could hear the distant sound of music coming from the sky-lounge bar above. To the rear, the massive propellers caused a ten-mile wake pointing back towards Southampton. Lucian's work and his home all seemed a million miles away now.

Debra watched as Lucian turned his collar up and rubbed his hands together to stay warm.

"Lucky you don't have to sleep up here tonight Lucian."

Lucian laughed, and when she didn't laugh, he said,

"No, I think it's a little cold for camping."

This time she did laugh and walked to the side of the ship. Debra pulled her wrap closer around her shoulders, opening her handbag took out her gold cigarette box and her gold lighter. Passing them both to Lucian, she leant on the highly polished rail and let the night wind blow her long dark hair.

Lucian fumbled with the gold box taking out a slim cigarette then struggled to light it in the wind. Debra ignored his efforts when he did manage; she still made him wait for another few seconds. She spread her arms across the rail and raising her chin indicating him to put the cigarette between her red lips.

Lucian turned the filter towards her mouth holding it gently within her reach. Debra reached forward never breaking eye contact and took the cigarette into her freshly painted red lips. Drawing on it hard it flared up in the cold night air, as she did so a small flake of ash fell into her cleavage and rested on her breast. Smiling she looked down at the ash then looked at Lucian with a questioning look in her eyes.

Lucian shuffled his feet slightly not knowing quite what to do. Should he use his finger to flick it away or should he try to blow it away?

Debra clearly was enjoying his discomfort and said,

"Show me your tongue Lucian."

Shocked by her directness again he stammered, "What, sorry, er."

"Your tongue Lucian, you do have one don't you?"

"Yes," said Lucian and pointed his tongue out.

Glancing down she looked at the cigarette ash on her cleavage. Then reaching behind his head pulled his face towards her breasts. Lucian could taste the ash, as it clung to his outstretched tongue.

Debra released his head; he could taste a mixture of bitter ash and the sweet tang of Debra's perfume. Tossing the cigarette over the rail Debra pulled her wrap around her shoulders and headed towards the doors

Debra waited for Lucian to hold the door open for her.

The warmness of the ship was a relief after the coldness of the open deck. Lucian and Debra walked to the ship's show bar, which was full with passengers enjoying a female jazz singer and a small three-piece band. The singer had a good voice, and they paused to listen as the singer did a cover of a popular modern jazz track. Debra stood close to Lucian and swayed slightly to the lively rhythm. She linked her hand through Lucian's arm and rubbed her hip against his.

He coughed, and she smiled at his obvious discomfort.

As the singer started another song Debra said, "It's getting late, I have some calls to make, and then I will retire for the night."

"Ok," said Lucian unsure as to what would happen next?

Debra took her hand from his arm smiled and said "Thank you for this evening I have enjoyed your company. Will you meet me for breakfast?"

Lucian replied, "Yes, of course, what time and where?"

Debra smiled.

"8.30 at the Coffee Connection café bar on the sixth deck. We can look over the property papers while we eat?"

Lucian replied "Yes Debra, thank you and goodnight. "

Lucian watched her evening gown swaying as she walked towards the lift. He noticed the red soles of her black Louboutin court shoes. As she drew close to the mirrored elevator doors, a man in a dark blue suit joined her. Lucian felt a slight pang of envy as the man pressed the shiny button while gently placing his hand on Debra's lower back as they entered the lift.

Lucian returned to the bar and sat listening to the jazz singer as she went into another upbeat number. Several passengers got up to dance one couple did a spectacular jive routine, and the crowd applauded as they finished their dance. Lucian began to relax as the singer delivered an Adele song, Lucian remembered hearing it had been written by Bob Dylan originally.

Sitting at the bar Lucian reflected on the evening. It was strange that only after a few hours with Debra how she made him feel so special. As he sat there deep in thought, the barman approached and said, "What would you like to drink Sir?"

"Oh yes, a large scotch and coke please," said Lucian.

As his drink arrived the barman said "Which suite sir?"

Lucian smiled "I don't have one. Can I pay cash?"

The bar paused and replied,

"I'm sorry Sir we don't take cash, all purchases are billed to the suits."

Just then a female voice said "Mr Palmer Jones,"

Spinning around at the mention of his name he saw Juliette Harding standing there.

"Oh hello," said Lucian.

Still, in her work suit, Juliet smiled.

The barman gave a light cough Lucian turned to Juliette and asked:

"Would you buy me a drink I'm afraid I don't have a room or cabin to bill it to?"

"Of course, put it on 927."

Lucian took a long sip from his drink as Juliette sat down next to him he looked at her over his glass.

Juliette had on a white blouse that was tight across her front. He could see she had a deep cleavage in a light blue lace push up bra. Her slim and rather a girly frame were a complete contrast to Debra's full and womanly figure. Juliette's shoes were flat leather pumps, her skirt was just above the knee. She wasn't wearing stockings, as Debra had been, only beige coloured tights. Juliette's hair was still up, and her lipstick was pale pink.

Juliette noticed Lucian checking her out and said, "Where is Ms Fielding? Is she coming back to meet you?"

"No," said Lucian, "She has retired for the night, did she leave any instructions as to where I'm sleeping?"

Juliette thought for a second then said, "Alex has gone

off shift for tonight, but I will check with reception, wait here, I won't be long."

"Thank you" replied Lucian

Lucian ordered another drink the barman put it on Juliette's tab. He felt the scotch taking effect and all of a sudden felt incredibly horny. Lucian ordered a second and then a third, which slipped down very well after the other two have paved the way. After twenty minutes Juliette returned holding a gold plastic card. Having downed the third drink, Lucian was feeling rather dizzy.

Holding up the gold card she announced, "This is a key card for the Grand Suite, you are in the adjoining guest bedroom."

Lucian smiled.

"Oh ok, thank you, Juliette! I think I am a little drunk, so I'm going to go to bed."

Juliette held onto the card.

"Do you know where the grand suite is?"

Lucian swayed as he slipped off the bar stool laughing he slurred:" I really have no idea?"

Juliette took his arm and said, "I had better show you

then."

They walked to the lift Lucian felt the effect of the scotch more with every step.

"Have you eaten tonight?" asked Juliette

"Tonight!" said Lucian." I haven't eaten all day."

Instead of going to the lifts Juliette led Lucian to the stairs, and they descended one floor to the deck below.

As they headed towards the all night buffet restaurant, they passed the nightclub Lucian saw a sign for the Cigar Lounge. As he walked past he made a note to ask if Debra had been in there.

She had found it rather cold on deck she might prefer the smoking lounge until they got across the Atlantic into warmer climes.

Lucian stumbled slightly on the shiny marble flooring as the thick carpeting gave way.

Juliette caught him, holding him up as they entered the restaurant.

They went to the buffet, Lucian selected a few items, and Juliette poured him a large fruit juice.

Sitting at a table, Lucian ate in silence, while Juliette

checked her phone. Realising he hadn't checked his, Lucian did the same. Lucian saw several from Christina? Deciding he was far too drunk to respond tonight, he swiped the phone off.

After eating a plate of food, they left the restaurant and headed for the lifts. Juliette selected the right floor, swiping the gold card through the reader to access the top deck's Grand suite. After a short ascent, the doors opened to a plush hallway with ornate decorations, plants, rich wood panels and chandeliers.

The walls were decorated with original art, and the doors were all painted in high-lacquered gloss and had what appeared to be real gold door furniture. With Juliette holding Lucian's arm, she led him past Grand Suite door to the adjoining door. Swiping the gold card through the door reader, she opened the door, and Lucian fell in landing on the floor.

Juliette helped him up, ushered him to the bedroom and placed him on the bed.

Her hair had come down on one side, and her top was now untucked, she removed his shoes and put a cashmere throw over him.

Tossing back her hair, Juliette tucked in her blouse and turned to Lucian who was already fast asleep and snoring lightly.

Heading for the door, she said to herself, "It's ok. You are welcome Mr Palmer Jones."

After getting no reply, she closed the door behind and headed back to the lifts.

Chapter 15

Dominic's childhood was difficult his father was a quiet and reserved man. But whenever he was alone with the young Dominic, would take on the role of a strict Victorian father figure.

One of the chores Dominic was forced to do, was to bring in coal from the coal shed.

This task is especially horrid for the youngster, as the coal shed was little more than a concrete block bunker with a slatted wooden lid. It had a small access hole to allow the coal to be shovelled out.

Each evening his father would send him out to the yard with a large tin bucket to get the coal for the living room fire. If he weren't back in few minutes, he would stride outside in his vest and braces to see what was taking so long. As the coal pile decreased and the coal was too far back for the shovel to reach his father would order Dominic into the bunker. Dominic with the large tin bucket had to venture further and further into the dark bunker. He would stifle screams as his face went through cobwebs, the spiders crawling down his neck and on his hair.

His father would berate him for his non-manliness and shout at him saying, "Hurry the fuck up, or I will make you sleep in there you little faggot."

His father would not accept that Dominic had an irrational fear of spiders and dark, cramped spaces. He believed he could cure the boy's fears and slowness by beating him with his belt.

With the large heavy bucket in his hands, Dominic would carry the coal inside. Often covered in soot and crying, the boy would be sent upstairs to be faced with a cold bath to wash the black powder off with.

His mother would call up the stairs to make sure he didn't make a mess in her bathroom. On occasions when the weather was freezing his father would place the young Dominic in a hot bath to scrub the dirt and filth off him. If he complained it was too hot, the next time would be ice cold and the scrubbing harsher than before.

His mother would scold him for taking too long and accused him of touching his filthy little cock while washing with the stinking Coal Tar soap.

His mother had fluffy soft pink bath towels, but Dominic wasn't allowed to use these. He had to use a hard worn out and threadbare towel, that had been left behind by a visitor. Straight after his bath, he went to his bed and tried to warm up by snuggling down under the covers on the hard lumpy mattress. His pyjamas were his father's old ones his mother had cut off the legs, and the sleeves to make them fit. The waist was held up with a thin dressing gown cord.

His bedroom was always cold in winter, and he had to sleep in his socks to keep his feet warm. His father refused to fix the broken radiator valve. Turned down low, it gave off precious little heat as Dominic got dressed for school in the mornings.

These days he slept on a memory foam king sized bed with electric heating embedded in the mattress. Dominic's house was always warm and a far cry from his terrible upbringing with his now dead parents.

His pyjamas were pure Chinese silk and the sheets 1000 thread count Egyptian cotton. When alone in bed at night he would fantasise about a dark haired harsh Mistress treating him badly. When Dominic got excited, he would get up and increase his imaginary session by sitting on a large rubber butt plug, taking clothes pegs or clamps and applying them to his nipples and balls until he could take no more. Dominic longed to be slapped, scolded and told off by a beautiful woman. What he desired was a woman who could treat him harshly, and for that, he would willingly give everything he owned.

Chapter 16

The slow hum of the ship's massive propellers invaded Lucian's consciousness waking him with a start.

He looked around the luxurious cabin not knowing where he was for a second or able to get his bearings.

It was evident he wasn't in his apartment or his bedroom. Lucian's head started to thump as he remembered last night's events. How he had boarded a cruise ship, met Debra Fielding and had a few too many drinks in the bar.

He turned around quickly to make sure he hadn't slept with the young Ms Harding. Thankfully the bed next to him was empty. He checked the time it was 7.55am his thumping head reminding him he had been drinking whisky.

Dragging himself to the bathroom, he looked at his tired face in the mirror. Turning on the hot tap, he splashed his face with warm water rubbing his eyes and running his fingers through his hair. Facing the mirror, he cracked a smile and mimicked into the mirror

"So Mr Bond, not looking so pretty this morning."

He quickly showered dressing in the same clothes he has on the night before.

Brushing his hair with his fingers, he headed for the restaurant to meet Debra for breakfast.

As he arrived, Debra was already there, talking to two smartly dressed men. Smiling, Lucian headed towards the table, a third man, in a dark suit blocked his way.

"Go and get a coffee, take a seat Ms Fielding will be with you shortly." Debra didn't look at Lucian

Lucian looked over to Debra, but she was deep in conversation. They were too far away to hear what they were saying. Debra was smiling and shaking her head, the men were not smiling but gesturing with their hands.

Lucian went to the breakfast buffet then taking fresh coffee and toast to a table. He checked his phone and saw he had a missed call from Christina. Swiping the screen he dialled up the voicemail to hear Christina's voice saying she was sorry but she wasn't well and wasn't coming in today.

"That makes two of us," Lucian said smiling to himself.

He watched Debra as she continued her meeting, slowly drinking his coffee and eating his toast. Lucian looked out of the ships picture window they were clearly far out to sea, with no sign of land only grey sea and sky for miles.

As Lucian was sat gazing at the sea, he saw in the window reflection that Debra was getting up from the table and was walking towards him.

Debra wore a black dress with white piping along the edges. She had on red stilettos and carried a matching red handbag. Her hair was up in a red sparkly clasp, and her makeup looked fresh. Her red lipstick looked perfect. Over her arm, she carried a dark fur coat. Swallowing toast with a sip of coffee he looked up as Debra approached.

Before he could speak or say 'Good Morning' to Debra, she walked straight past his table. As she passed she dropped her fur coat in his lap and said, "I need to smoke, come with me, Lucian."

Lucian quickly got up following Debra out of the restaurant out onto the deck. The day was grey and cool and, although not raining, the sea air held a slight dampness.

Debra walked to the rail. Lucian quickly helped her on with her fur coat, which she pulled close around her body against the stiff sea breeze.

"Did you sleep well, Lucian?"

Lucian replied, "Yes thank you, Debra, I think the lifeboat would have been rather cold and uncomfortable."

Debra smiled

"Yes it would have been, but I might have quite enjoyed you being uncomfortable Lucian."

Lucian waited for her to say something else. She seemed lost in thought, as she looked out over the grey sea. Lucian checked his watch it was 8.45am.

Debra said, "Do you have any plans for today Lucian?"

Lucian looked at Debra and replied, "I am on a ship in the middle of the Atlantic. Not quite what I had planned for today."

Turning to face Lucian, Debra laughed.

"So if you weren't with me today what other exciting projects would you spend your time on?"

Lucian grinned and said, "Oh, I have a meeting with some important people, then lunch with some even more important people. Then a date with a woman who likes to take trips on cruise liners, but apart from that I was free."

Debra laughed again and handed Lucian her cigarette case and lighter.

She didn't say anything as Lucian took a slim cigarette from the box and put it to his lips.

As he had done the day before, he attempted to light it for her. Debra didn't help him and seemed to enjoy his fumbled efforts to light the cigarette. When he had managed to get it to light, she took the cigarette from his lips and asked, "Have you ever smoked?"

Lucian replied, "No, I tried it with my mates when I was very young, but it always made me feel dizzy and sick, so I never took up the habit."

"Oh," Debra said, "I love smoking! It's such a pleasure; it's such a shame smoking has got such a bad press these days."

Then she asked, "So if you don't smoke what other vices do you have Lucian?"

Lucian didn't reply straight away, so Debra continued, "Do you masturbate in the shower Lucian?"

He couldn't answer straight away he was shocked by Debra's directness then mumbled, "I play golf, and I like movies?"

Debra threw her head back and laughed.

"Golf oh my god that's hardly a vice. Movies that sounds a little better. What sort, serial killers and gay porn?"

Lucian was again embarrassed and blurted, "No, no nothing like that!"

Debra laughed drew on her cigarette then she flicked the butt out into the sea air.

She looked at Lucian straight faced and said, "Did you enjoy kissing my tits yesterday?"

Despite the cold air, Lucian's cheeks flushed, he felt speechless and couldn't reply.

Debra laughed harder, she stroked Lucian's red face and smiling said, "I'm teasing, let's go in I am freezing."

As they entered the landing area again, Lucian saw the men in the dark suits waiting for Debra by the lifts.

Turning to Lucian, she said, "I'm sorry I have some meetings today, but you can take me to dinner tonight, and we can discuss the property then."

"Of course," said Lucian.

"Where shall I meet you and what time?"

Debra said, "Well as you are staying next door, knock for me at 6.30."

"Ok," said Lucian.

Debra looked him up and down.

"And Lucian.... wear something nice?" She walked away not waiting for an answer.

Lucian headed back to his cabin and called his voice mail, no messages. With Christina off, he probably wouldn't get any calls today.

Sitting on the bed, Lucian tried to understand everything that had happened. With Debra, he felt comfortable yet not in control, he liked the sensation of being all at sea. He smiled at his obvious pun.

After a few minutes, he recalled Debra's last words.

"Wear something nice."

Leaving the cabin, Lucian went to the reception and asked for Juliette Harding. The girl on reception said Juliette wasn't on duty until 3 pm and could anyone else help?

Lucian said no, but could Juliette contact him when she came on duty. The receptionist agreed to pass on the message.

Chapter 17

Back in his cabin, Lucian stared at the ceiling while he listening to the gentle hum of the ship. After a few minutes, he was surprised by a knock on the cabin door. Jumping up off the bed it made him feel slightly dizzy.

Opening the cabin door, he expected it to be the maid service to clean the room, but standing there was Juliette Harding, dressed in jeans and a jumper.

She smiled and said, "I was just checking you were ok after last night?"

Lucian said, "Yes I'm fine, come on in."

Juliette entered the cabin and seeing the unmade bed she said playfully, "Sleeping it off today?"

Lucian pulled the cover up and said: "No I have already been out but came back for a rest."

Juliette said nothing just smiled.

Lucian continued "Look, I have to get some new

clothes, I don't have anything nice enough with me, and could you help me please?"

Juliette smiled again and said, "Yes, I'm not on duty until 3pm, that should be plenty of time."

They spent the next two hours in the ship's boutiques, selecting day and night wear.

Lucian tried on several different causal outfits Juliette sat and waited as he came out of the changing rooms in various outfits. Juliette squealed with delight and clapped her hands as Lucian paraded about in Hawaiian shirts and hideous checked golfing jumpers. He modelled pink Bermuda shorts with white tennis shoes and a Panama hat. On seeing some of the choices she put her hands over her eyes and shook her head saying he looked like her Dad.

After several hours Lucian returned to the suite with arms full of carrier bags.

Sitting alone with his parcels, Lucian started to unpack to find something to wear that evening. Later dressed in a cotton shirt, dark blue trousers and new shoes, he checked himself out in the mirror. Lucian put on a designer linen jacket and a new Omega watch that Juliette had chosen for him costing over £200.

He gave himself the thumbs up and left to go next door.

He knocked and waited. When there was no reply he knocked again, a buzzer sounded, and the door opened. Entering a large spacious room, with expensive gilt mirrors and velvet couches, the Grand Suite certainly lived up to its name.

Debra called through from the adjoining room.

"Hello Lucian, help yourself to a drink and mine's a gin martini."

"Shaken not stirred," he replied not being able to resist the irony.

"What did you say?" asked Debra.

"Nothing" replied Lucian still smiling as he poured himself a scotch with ice and then prepared to make a gin martini. He knew what was in a gin martini but had never actually made one before. Having made the drinks he called out to Debra "Where do you want yours."

She called from the other room.

"Bring it through I'm just getting ready."

Lucian went through the large double doors into another large room with a four-poster bed, two large couches and a dressing table with a three-sided mirror.

Debra was sitting on the dressing table stool in a Versace evening gown; her hair elegantly clipped back, and she was applying her makeup.

Lucian paused in the doorway "Oh I'm sorry, I didn't realise you weren't ready."

Debra looked at Lucian in the dressing table mirror as she applied dark eye shadow to her eyelids with a small sable makeup brush.

"It's ok. Bring me my drink, and come and sit with me."

Lucian took over Debra's gin martini,

She turned towards him and took it from his hand with bright red painted fingernails.

"Thank you, Lucian," she said as they touched glasses.

The cut of the evening dress created a deep plunging cleavage; Lucian couldn't help but to look at Debra's breasts. He recalled how he had tasted the bitter ash on his tongue and the sweetness of her perfume.

Debra put the glass to her lips taking a sip of the drink. She licked her lips, and then placed the glass on the glossy dressing table. She went back to applying liquid eyeliner, to enhance the false eyelashes that she was wearing.

Lucian had a fascination with makeup, as a youngster he would sometimes go to Boots to watch the girls on the makeup counter. There were countless makeup artists on YouTube giving demonstrations on creating certain celebrity looks.

He sometimes went to the department store where the girls looked like models, with heavy makeup that was expertly applied. He recalled how Christina often did her make up in the classic sixties style, but with too much massacre and eye shadow, she sometimes looked like Count Dracula.

Debra was clearly an expert in applying makeup. She did it with great skill, making the eyeliner flow across the edges of her eyelids into bat shaped wings at the side of her shapely dark eyes.

Debra then blended it in with more dark tone. She worked in silence, and he couldn't take his eyes from Debra. Lucian felt awkward standing next to her holding his drink. She watched him in the mirror as she applied blusher to her high cheekbones.

As she worked, Debra said, "You can bring my lipstick and pencil, they are in my evening bag."

Eager to have something to do Lucian crossed the large room and collected Debra's Gold clutch bag from the sideboard. Lucian felt a little uneasy going through a ladies handbag and held the bag out for her.

She didn't turn around while doing her eyebrows but said, "It's in there somewhere Lucian, a red lipstick but give me the pencil first please."

He knelt on one knee, balancing the bag, found the red pencil and lipstick; he handed Debra the lip pencil.

He watched fascinated as she outlined her perfect lips with a thin bright red line. Giving back the pencil, Debra indicated the lipstick was next. As he passed her the lipstick, she frowned at Lucian and tutted. He realised she wanted him to take the top off and turn the bottom to expose the pillar-box red shiny lipstick.

Corrected, he passed her the prepared lipstick.

She turned away and carefully applied the red lipstick to her sensuous mouth doing the top and bottom lip in turn. Lucian stared wide-eyed at this erotic act and without realising ended up on both his knees watching as Debra took a tissue and kissed it leaving a perfect lip mark. She handed the used tissue and lipstick back to Lucian and he replaced the cap.

Checking the finished look in the mirror, Debra stood up and smiled at Lucian on his knees as she walked towards the couch. With her back turned to Lucian, she adjusted her lace-topped stockings. Picking up a hairbrush she began to brush her beautiful long dark hair.

Glancing at Lucian who was still on his knees, she said: "Can you brush my hair for me?"

Standing up again Lucian took the hairbrush from her and started to comb out Debra's long black hair. He ran the brush from the crown of her head right down her back almost to her waist. Lucian thought how beautiful this woman looked. As he brushed her full, shiny straight hair, she closed her made-up eyelids. Lucian could see the blended eye shadow, her perfect eyeliner, and the long flowing eyelashes.

She clearly was enjoying the sensation.

Lucian was lost for a moment in perfect calmness, as he continued to run the brush through her hair from tip to tail until it hung perfectly straight and shiny down her back.

She opened her eyes sensing he had finished and said: "Fetch my gold sandals would you Lucian."

She watched him as he went to the wall closet and opened it. Inside were rows of designer dresses and underneath dozens of high heeled sparkly sandals.

Lucian asked, "which ones?"

Debra said, "You choose they are all lovely."

Picking a pair of Jimmy Choo's designer slingbacks, he took then over to Debra. She extended a stocking clad foot and pointed her toes. Lucian without thinking dropped to his knees again in the deep pile carpet and carefully put on Debra's right shoe. She smiled raising her left foot so Lucian could repeat the act.

Debra stood up in her heels, Lucian's face was at her waist height, as she walked past him she stroked his head making him feel dizzy. Staying on his knees, he looked after Debra and was amazed by the beauty of this woman. She was so glamorous and sexy, yet she had an aloof air that he was finding irresistible.

Gathering her wrap she came and stood before Lucian looking down at him. She paused as if waiting to say something or for something to happen. Then she turned and said,

"We should go, the Captain is waiting."

Lucian rose from his knees, breaking the spell.

He followed Debra across the room, opened the door and they left.

In the lift, he could smell Debra's perfume, and it dawned on him that he was in a situation that he had no control or resistance over.

After dinner, Lucian offered to take Debra to the Cigar Smoking Lounge. She agreed and as they walked along the passage Debra slipped her hand into Lucian's arm. She walked at a leisurely pace her high heels making her hips sway slightly against him. He could feel her closeness, and he liked it.

She casually asked Lucian, "Did you like watching me earlier and putting my shoes on for me?"

Lucian remembered kneeling at her feet and placing the expensive gold sandals on her outstretched toes.

He said, "Yes it was strange, but I did enjoy helping you with your shoes."

"Helping?" Debra said, "Do you always help people on your knees?"

Lucian was again stuck for words.

"Well err, yes err helping you yes."

Debra smiled as they entered the smoking lounge and said, "Maybe you can help me again later?"

Later that night Lucian walked Debra back to her suite and once inside, he fixed her a drink and sat on the couch while she went to the bathroom.

She was a long time, and Lucian began to wonder what

she is doing and if she was ok.

Calling her name he waited outside the bathroom door and asked, "Are you ok Debra? Do you need any help?"

Debra called through the closed door, "Yes I believe I do, come on in Lucian."

He pushed open the heavy panelled door and saw Debra standing over the sink with her lipstick in her hand, a cigarette burning on the marble sink top.

Lucian turned to go saying, "Oh I'm sorry I didn't realise you were smoking, I will fetch your drink."

She smiled and said, "It's ok the smoke dictators don't work in here, I asked for them to be turned off so I could smoke."

Returning with the drinks, he placed hers on the hard marble sink top and leant against the doorframe.

Debra took a sip of her drink and a long drag on her cigarette;

"There's nowhere to sit in here, and maybe as you did it so nicely earlier you should kneel down again Lucian?"

Lucian looked at Debra, and she smiled a red-lipped smile and said, "Well?"

"Are you serious?" said Lucian.

"Completely serious Lucian" Debra replied no longer smiling at him.

He stood for a couple of seconds watching Debra very carefully, then ever so slowly sank to his knees in front of her. She put the cigarette to her lips drawing the smoke deep into her lungs and then blew the smoke over Lucian's head. Dropping the red lipstick coated butt into the sink, she stepped forward, so Lucian's head was level with her hips.

She walked past him and stroked his face.

"Sort that out for me there's a good boy."

Heading into the bedroom, she sat down in an armchair.

Lucian watched from the bathroom still on his knees, feeling rather foolish. He reached up took the wet cigarette butt from the sink placed in it the bin, running the tap to wash away the ash in the basin.

Debra didn't seem to notice and sat sipping her drink "Will you take my shoes off for me Lucian?"

Lucian went to get up, but Debra pointed with her finger for him to stay down on his knees, hooking her finger to indicate he was to crawl forward to her feet.

He did so and came to a stop at her feet and looked up at her with questioning eyes.

Debra smiled and said again "Good Boy."

She then lifted a gold shoe Lucian carefully undid the strap and placed it on the thick pile carpet. He couldn't help himself and started to massage Debra's stockinged foot. Debra put her head back and closed her eyes. Looking at her, Lucian could see again the amazing well-applied eye shadow and the eyeliner creating a perfect shaped outline. Her fresh lipstick shone in the light as Lucian stroked her toes and rubbed the soft soles of her feet.

After a couple of minutes, Debra placed her foot back on the floor and without opening her eyes raised her other shoe. Lucian repeated the process with her other foot.

Debra opened her eyes looked down at Lucian and said: "You're very gentle Lucian it pleases me to have you around."

"Thank You," said Lucian slightly surprised at Debra's statement.

"But I do have to tell you something?"

"Ok," said Lucian

Debra sat forward giving Lucian a full view of her cleavage. She told him to get up and follow her to the large wall-sized mirror on the left side of the suite.

Standing behind him, she looked over his shoulder "What did I tell you about tonight."

Lucian thought for a moment then said, "You asked me to wear something nice?"

Debra smiled and said, "Yes I did ...and?"

Lucian felt embarrassed and said, "I did try, but apart from what I was wearing and casual things that they sell on the ship there was nothing to wear."

Debra didn't say anything just raised an eyebrow.

Lucian asked, "Don't you like what I'm wearing?"

Debra didn't reply she just kept looking at Lucian in the mirror and appeared to be thinking. After a few minutes, she walked back to the couch, picked up her now empty glass. He looked at himself again the mirror and shook his head. Lucian went over and stood by the sofa. He reached for her glass, took it to the bar and refilled it.

She didn't take the drink, just sat back with her arms resting along the back of the couch, her breasts rising and falling slowly in her evening gown. Raising her hand slightly she gave the slightest movement with her fingers, Lucian looked at her questionably again.

This time, Debra didn't speak just extended her index finger pointing at the floor. Lucian getting the message sank to his knees holding her glass patiently.

Debra took it from him and said: "Do you like me, Lucian?"

Lucian cleared his throat and said, "I don't know you very well, but yes Debra I like being with you."

Debra smiled and said, "Good, would you like to please me Lucian?"

Lucian looked at Debra sitting relaxed and comfortable, he was on his knees in front of a beautiful woman, on a luxury Cruise ship and on his way to the Caribbean.

He lowered his head and mumbled, "Yes."

Debra sat forward again and put a red nailed finger under his chin and said: "Would you?"

Lucian spoke louder and said, "Yes, I would Debra."

Standing up Debra walked to the door and said, "Good, now I have early meetings in the morning, so I will wish you good night Lucian."

Getting off his knees, Lucian walked across to the door, and Debra turned her cheek so Lucian could kiss it lightly.

Back in his cabin, Lucian lay on his bed replaying the evening in his mind. As he thought about Debra he felt his heart beat faster and his cock stiffen.

He realised being with Debra made him incredibly horny and very sexually frustrated.

Chapter 18

Dominic's morning started early, with the ping of incoming mail. Opening the screen, he saw that Carol had sent the address and postcode. Dominic put the postcode into Google Maps, straight away locating the house. By using the street view, he could see that the property was a large private house with a gated wall and a large circular drive.

Dominic could see the property had a triple garage with three vehicles outside. The property was classic in design and judging from the windows on the front could have five or six bedrooms. The satellite view showed a pool, out-buildings, well-kept gardens and a conservatory.

Dominic had been to many such places installing all manner of security cameras both inside and out. He searched for the building particulars on the estate agents house valuing software. The searches came back with estimated value of the homes in that area as being in the region of two million pounds.

Dominic scanned left and right with the Google street

view and concluded that the house he was going to was the largest and the highest value on the road. He always did this search before a site visit, as he had no need to work for money. If the job didn't interest him, the property was too small or was in a bad repair he simply wouldn't bother going.

Dominic was able to zoom in and get the private registration numbers of the three vehicles. One pale blue Bentley Turbo R, a Mercedes soft top, and a BMW X5. Then by accessing the DVLA database he was able to find that they were all registered to the Quindici property development company. The only data available was a link to a law firm in New York called Marcus and Stein. They had a website but gave little away other than they were private investment lawyers and bankers with offices in New York and London.

Dominic was puzzled by the lack of information. Carol probably was a stay at home mum, with children and a husband that works in the City. These woman's husbands often travelled away on business leaving "The Wife" at home to shop for household things and clothes.

The corporate wives get together over coffee or at the school gates and trade notes and gossip.

"Oh did you hear Sarah has a new pool!"

"Did you hear on the school run last week Margaret pranged her new Range Rover Vogue."

These women probably got talking to a neighbour, who knew someone miles away whose house was burgled, so they installed security or bought an expensively trained guard dogs just to be safe.

Dominic didn't like dogs and more often than not, these wealthy type women had dogs. But they tended to buy toy dogs, like Chihuahuas. So they didn't have to walk them, and there wasn't much shit to clear up.

They never seemed to own big dogs, unless they lived in the country and had dogs and horses. The model type women usually couldn't stand to have hairy animals in the house, slobbering on their designer fabrics.

In Dominic's experience, these women often tended to be very house proud and sometimes were OCD, which made them very fussy and difficult to please.

Dominic would see what Carol was like tomorrow. But from the view on Google, the house didn't look like a farmhouse; it had a pool but no stables.

He would get down there early tomorrow and do a recce of the area and have a look at the back of the property and the neighbourhood borders.

Chapter 19

Lucian woke from a vivid dream and realised he had a massive hard on. In his dream had been kneeling at Debra's feet as she looked down at him with wild eyes and slapped him across the face. He was pleading with her, about what he didn't remember. He was on his knees, naked, and he was wearing a leather collar.

Shaken from the dream he went to the bathroom, washed his face, cleaned his teeth, got dressed and left to meet Debra for breakfast.

Debra was waiting for him, alone this time. Lucian went to the buffet and selected a light breakfast.

Debra was eating white toast and drinking black coffee. She seemed to have time this morning and seemed more relaxed as she ate.

After eating they walked up onto the upper deck, the sun was shining, and the sea was a deeper aqua blue. The air was warmer with a lighter wind, and the liner cut an impressive path through white-capped waves.

Lucian spoke.

"Have you thought about what to do with the property from the auction?"

Debra looked out to sea and said, "Yes… you can have it! I didn't want it in the first place."

"What, why is that?" said Lucian

Debra turned and said, "We owned a lot of real estate around the world."

"My husband was killed in a plane crash in Venezuela a few years ago, and I sold off most of the properties."

"He was involved in some deals in Venezuela and Holland. He was on his way to a meeting with a Hong Kong businessman call Martin Chow when his plane exploded killing them both."

Lucian said, "Yes, I met Helen Chow at the auction, she is in the UK looking for people to make investments."

Debra looked back out to sea and said,

"Yes, she is spending her father's money like water."

"I knew Martin well, he was a close friend of my husband."

Lucian joined Debra leaning on the rail; they touched

shoulders, and she made no attempt to move away. After a few seconds, she leant in slightly her hair blowing back, tickling Lucian's cheek and neck. She paused looked at her handbag at her feet on the deck. Lucian didn't need to be asked this time and, reaching into her bag, he pulled out her cigarettes. He lit one with the gold lighter, managing to do it the first time.

Debra took the cigarette from Lucian and said, "I have made you an appointment for this morning."

Surprised Lucian said, "Really where?"

"With a friend of mine, he is a tailor."

"Oh," said Lucian feeling embarrassed about his clothes again.

Debra looked him up and down.

"I would say you might be a 32-inch waist although maybe a 33-inch might be more comfortable for you. I guess a 30-inch inside leg? Do you wear a size nine shoe, Lucian?"

"Yes I do" Lucian replied, surprised at her accuracy.

Debra kept looking at Lucian he could feel her eyes scanning his body from head to toe.

After a couple of minutes, she said: "They are top

tailors and fit men and women all over the world. Usually in hotels but they have set up on the cruise for five days until we get to Madera."

They took the lift to the 5th deck.

Lucian followed Debra to a suite at the end of the corridor. She didn't knock just opened the door and went in.

Three men were standing in front of a full-length triple mirror. One man was standing in a suit jacket, shirt, tie, socks, and polished black shiny shoes, but without trousers. The other two men were looking at him. The taller man was older and had a tape measure around his neck. The younger one was adjusting the shoulders of the jacket.

They stopped when Debra walked in; the older gentlemen acknowledged Debra.

"Hello, Ms Fielding we have been expecting you. Please take a seat in the other room, help yourself to drinks we will be with you shortly."

He completely ignored Lucian and turned back to the men looking in the mirror.

"We think a little more in the chest area to better conceal the shoulder holster?"

The man removed his jacket to reveal a gun in a leather shoulder holster.

Lucian looked away and followed Debra into the adjoining room.

Taking a seat on a velvet sofa, Lucian leant in towards Debra and said, "That man has a gun!"

Debra smiled and said, "Yes I know isn't it exciting?" then laughed at Lucian's apparent shock.

There was fresh tea and coffee on the table. Lucian served Debra a black coffee, which she sipped while watching Lucian add three sugars to his strong tea.

"If you carry on with three sugars in your tea you will need to have a 34-inch waist before long. Don't worry I will ask Angelo and Pepe to put some expansion in the middle for you."

At that point the door opened and the older gentlemen came in. Lucian caught a glimpse of the younger man, who was on his knees with his face close to the man's now bare bottom.

Closing the door behind him, the older gentleman looked to the ceiling, waved his hand and said, "All part of the service!"

Debra stood up laughing and hugged the man.

"Angelo how are you, you old Queen, it's been far too long!"

Angelo smiled a wry smile and said, "It used to be my job to offer the extras, but now Pepe is favoured, such a lovely boy, don't you think." Angelo almost skipped his way over to where Lucian sat.

Debra turned to Lucian and said, "Angelo I want you to meet a special friend, this is Lucian Palmer Jones. He is staying with me for a few days, while we do some business."

Angelo looked at Lucian and nodded.

Debra continued.

"He has nothing decent to wear, can you help this poor boy with a few items."

Angelo took a step forward towards Lucian, took his hand, pulled him to his feet and then walked around him.

Pausing directly behind Lucian he said, "I would say;

Height: 178 cm

Weight: 78 kg

Chest: 119 cm

Bicep: 41 cm

Waist: 79 cm

And Size 9 feet

Dresses to the left, has one leg marginally longer than the other and would have a slightly larger right foot."

Coming around to the front, Angelo dropped to his knees and placed his tape measure inside of Lucian's thigh causing him to jump back.

Angelo looked up at Debra who in turn looked at Lucian

"Stand still Lucian! Angelo won't bite; that is unless I tell him too."

Angelo again placed the tape measure on Lucian's inner thigh; Lucian stood very still staring at Debra the whole time.

Angelo stood up again and said "inside leg 30.5" about right I would say."

Debra nodded her agreement and then said to Lucian "Angelo will look after you, meet me tonight for dinner at 6.30pm in my suite."

Angelo smiled and cooed.

"Who's a lucky boy, dinner with Mistress?"

"Angelo!" Debra snapped

Angelo bowed his head.

"I'm sorry Ms Fielding."

Debra turned to leave and said, "Something for day and evening wear Angelo, plus a dinner jacket for Gala night."

Angelo came to the door and showed Debra out. She kissed his balding head and said, "Don't give all my secrets away Angelo, you naughty boy."

"Yes Mistress" he replied.

This time, Angelo didn't hide the fact he referred to Debra as "Mistress."

When the door opened again the man with the gun was gone, and a flushed Pepe arrived, nodding his greeting to Debra as she left the suite.

Alone now with Angelo and Pepe Lucian said, "I don't know what I'm doing here, so please could you help me."

Angelo raised his arms, looked at the roof and said in a very camp Italian voice said, "You are here, so we can make you look fabulous darling" as he minced over to Lucian.

When Lucian asked about payment for the clothes, Angelo laughed.

"Don't worry Mr Lucian it's all taken care of!"

"Now take off those awful clothes please and let's get to work!"

Lucian slowly undressed under the watchful gaze of Angelo and Pepe.

"I think Ms Fielding has taken a shine to Mr Palmer Jones. I don't blame her. Do you Pepe?"

Pepe blew Lucian a kiss, and they both laughed at Lucian's obvious discomfort.

Lucian stood in the middle of the room, although still in his boxers and socks, he felt naked and just wished the pair of them would stop prancing around and get on with it.

"Lucian, has Ms Fielding asked you about the "red and blue pill yet?"

Angelo looked Lucian up down, and Pepe giggled to himself.

Lucian replied, "What do you mean the red pill or blue pill?"

Angelo laughed and said, "Obviously not? Have you seen the Matrix?"

Lucian said, "Oh Yes, of course, I remember,"

"They talk about Neo taking the red pill and seeing how deep the rabbit hole goes. Or taking the blue pill to wake up the next morning and all of this is forgotten, and he goes back to his ordinary life."

"Yes" Angelo smiled a knowing smile.

"What will you take the red pill or the blue pill?"

"I don't know; maybe I will never get given a choice."

After two and half hours of the Angelo and Pepe show, Lucian emerged from the tailor's suite, holding three suit carriers and several other carrier bags.

His dinner jacket would be ready by tomorrow night, and he was asked to return then.

On returning to his suite, Lucian showered and tried to clear his nose of the strong after-shave both Pepe and Angelo wore. As the water ran over his newly measured body, he reflected on the new experience of being dressed by professional tailors. Now he was away from Angelo and Pepe; he admitted to himself that he had enjoyed it, and it felt very special.

At 6.30 pm, Lucian was dressed in a new handmade shirt; a custom made jacket, perfectly fitting trousers, and a pair of new shoes. He looked at himself in the mirror and liked what he saw, and he felt good.

Lucian stood outside Debra's door and knocked gently. To his surprise, she opened the door and came straight out. Debra took his arm, and they walked to the lifts.

She was wearing another low cut sweeping gown, and her hair was in a very high ponytail held in place by a sparkly crystal collar.

Her makeup was slightly darker than the daytime, and her lips were brilliant ruby red.

"Did Angelo and Pepe look after you? I like the new outfit, you look good."

"Thank you" said Lucian. "But you really must let me buy the clothes."

Debra looked at Lucian directly.

"I won't hear of it, it's a gift, and besides you can repay me for it in other ways."

"Oh?" said Lucian.

After a lovely candlelit dinner, Debra and Lucian went to the smoking lounge; the weather had turned, and it was raining on deck. They had drinks, and Debra smoked as she asked Lucian more about his business and home life. He told her about the estate agency and Christina, his divorce and the type of clients he looked after. Lucian explained that he didn't have the money to purchase the auction house outright and that he could not get hold of his client to let him know he had a suitable property.

Debra didn't seem bothered she just said that he was to rent it out and just look after it for her.

If it turned out to be a sound investment he could sell it on and give her a percentage back. She explained she would rather do that than give her money to the thieving bastards at the banks. Lucian asked why she would do that. He told her that he felt uneasy about taking her house and making money out of her.

She smiled and said, "What was the point in having money if you didn't make it work for you in a fun and exciting way?"

Debra told him that she owned a fur shop in Dubai and a salmon farm in Scotland. She went on to say she had money and liked to use it to fund new businesses and sponsor up and coming designers.

Lucian listened to Debra speak and found he was staring at her face and admiring her hair and makeup again. He couldn't put his finger on why he was so fascinated by this woman. Debra reminded him of a Hollywood actress or the girlfriend of a famous racing driver.

But neither of these women were as real as Debra Fielding or in his opinion, as interesting. As she sat smoking, she told Lucian more about her husband and how they had been together for twenty-six years. She was very young when they met, and he had left his first wife for her.

Debra explained that she suspected that her husband's death was no accident. She thought that it was to stop him from completing a dual hotel complex deal in Aruba. She went on to explain that particular businessmen didn't want the island to expand with more hotel developments. The two new proposed hotels would be near to the recently closed oil refinery at the southern end of the island.

Lucian still didn't know where Aruba was, but he hung on every word as Debra spoke.

After a few more drinks Debra said it was time for Lucian to escort her back to her suite. At the door, he stopped and prepared to wish Debra good night and leave. However, she asked him to join her for a drink, and they went inside. Debra told Lucian to pour the drinks and that she would be right back.

Leaving Lucian, she went into the bedroom and closed the door. Lucian fixed drinks and looked around the beautiful suite with its crystal chandeliers, thick carpets and mirrored walls. He noticed the shiny surfaces and original art on the walls.

Debra entered the room wearing a flowing Liliana Casanova Tuilerie dressing gown and 5-inch red stilettos.

She walked over to the velvet couch and sat down crossing her legs. Lucian took her drink to her and held it out for her. She didn't move just sat with her arms along the back of the sofa, relaxed as if waiting for something.

Lucian felt a panic in not knowing what he was supposed to do. Still, she waited, raising an eyebrow at his questioning face. Debra gave the slightest wave of her finger pointing to the ground before her. Lucian understood and slowly and hesitantly knelt at her feet; she smiled taking her drink from him.

"Thank you, Lucian, you are a fast learner, I like that in man."

Lucian didn't' speak.

"I asked you the other day if you find me attractive Lucian."

Lucian nodded.

"Do you? ... You can tell me, Lucian."

He stammered, "Yes.... I do."

"Yes, I do ...what Lucian?"

Lucian repeated, "Yes, I do find you attractive. Debra"

Smiling Debra sat back and said, "Good, I'm pleased. Now fetch my cigarettes from the other room, they are in my evening bag."

Lucian rose to his feet and went to the bedroom; he found Debra's bag on the chair.

A huge selection of makeup and perfumes covered the top of the dressing table. Lucian picked up a perfume bottle and sniffed the cap. It was the one Debra had worn the first night. He remembered the fragrance and sweet taste when he licked the ash from her breast.

As he held the perfume bottle, a voice came from behind him. "Someone is a nosey parker!"

He jumped nearly dropping the perfume but managing to catch it before it hit the hard glass topped surface.

Red-faced like a naughty child he stood perfectly still.

"Could it be Mr Palmer Jones, I wonder."

Turning he saw Debra standing in the doorway looking at him, red faced he put the perfume back on the dressing table. Stepping past him, Debra came into the room and with a swirl of her flowing nightgown and sat down at the dressing table.

Passing him the hairbrush she said, "Brush my hair for me, Lucian."

Lucian took the hairbrush and began to brush Debra's long and wavy hair. Debra closed her eyes enjoying the sensation.

"My hairdresser told me that he only got into hairdressing to be close to the wealthy women so he could fuck them!"

Lucian didn't reply.

"Does that shock you Lucian?"

Lucian stopped brushing for a second.

"Er, no."

"I guess it was a way to do what he loved; he obviously enjoys it."

"I suppose it's a bit like working in a ladies shoe shop and having a foot fetish."

Debra opened her eyes wide and said in mock surprise "Lucian!! And what do you know about fetishes may I ask"?

Lucian flushed and said, "Nothing!" wishing he had not spoken.

He just kept brushing Debra's long hair.

She continued to sip her drink and when it was nearly gone she asked him to get her another. But before he went to get it she said, "Can I ask you to do something for me, Lucian?"

Without hesitating, he said, "Yes of course."

Debra paused for a minute.

"Did Angelo fit you out with new underpants this morning?"

Lucian blushed and replied, "Yes, yes he did."

Debra laughed and said, "That old queen doesn't miss a trick,"

"Can I ask you something, Debra?"

Debra nodded a slight smile on her face.

"Angelo told me that you would ask me about the red and blue pill, like the scene in the Matrix? Are you going to ask me that?"

Debra didn't say anything just looked at Lucian in the mirror.

After a long pause, she said, "There is no pill Lucian it's just a movie."

"Anyway, it's already been decided I won't need to ask you."

Lucian looked disappointed but said nothing.

Debra turned to look at him.

"Now the thing I want you to do is this...."

"Strip down to your underpants and fix me another drink, will you do that for me, Lucian?"

Lucian looked down and said, "Yes."

"And one more thing, when you come back I want you to kneel down and pass the drink to me. In fact, every time we are alone. I want you to kneel at my feet unless I tell you not to, is that clear Lucian?"

"Yes" replied Lucian.

Placing the hairbrush on the dressing table, he turned

away to make the drinks.

He went to the bathroom removed his shirt and trousers the returned and knelt at Debra's feet holding her drink for her. She took it and passed Lucian the hairbrush again. She had taken her hair out of the high ponytail and it fell in long dark waves down her shoulders and back.

As Lucian was now kneeling he had to reach up to run the brush the whole length of Debra's hair. After a few minutes, Debra turned on her stool and asked Lucian if he was cold? He said he wasn't, she then asked him to come to the side of her dressing table.

She picked up a red lip liner pencil and traced the curves of her lips with a thin red line. Then she made sure Lucian was watching and applied new fresh, bright red lipstick. As he knelt in his underpants, he felt hot and fidgeted slightly as he was watched. Debra noticed and took her time applying a thick red layer to her lips.

Then taking a cigarette from a silver box on her dressing table passed Lucian a gold lighter with the inscription "Mistress D "down the side.

He took the lighter and lit her cigarette, wondering if the smoke detectors were also turned off in the bedroom.

They didn't go off, so he assumed she had requested it for the whole suit. She watched him and blew smoke over his head. The thin white tip of the filter was coated with the fresh red lipstick.

She smiled and said, "I will need an ashtray unless you are volunteering your hand or mouth Lucian."

He saw one on the bedside table and started to rise to fetch it. Debra touched his shoulder and applied a slight pressure to indicate he stay on his knees. He stayed down and crawled over the thick carpet, picked it up and returned to hand it to Debra. She didn't take it from him just flicked her ash into it, turning back to the mirror; she applied fresh blusher and eyeliner to her shapely eyelids.

As he knelt there watching, she continued to smoke totally ignoring him as she retouched her makeup. She periodically flicked ash into the cut glass ashtray. When she had finished her makeup, she took another sip of her drink and finished her cigarette.

She passed the still burning butt to Lucian to put out. Standing up she walked towards the bathroom and said, "Come over here Lucian."

Crawling after her, felt his cheeks flush as he realised he had a hard-on. With just his underpants on it was impossible to hide it.

The bathroom floor was hard glossy marble; it had underfloor heating and was warmer than the large spacious bedroom. Debra checked her hair in the long mirror and watched as Lucian crawled onto the hard polished floor. He stopped, sat back on his heels and bowed his head.

Debra seeing his erection smiled and said, "Well, now that's a pleasant surprise."

He didn't reply, just kept his head down and felt his cheeks flush red. Debra walked past him closing the bathroom door, then lifted her nightgown and sat down on the toilet. Lucian looked up at her and noticed she wasn't wearing underwear.

He said, "Oh, I'm sorry I will wait outside for you."

Debra laughed.

"Don't be shy Lucian, I'm not" and began to pee.

Lucian dropped his head again not wanting to look at a lady peeing.

Debra finished and said to Lucian "Pass me a towel Lucian, I don't like toilet tissue."

Lucian collected a small soft white face towel from the heated towel rail.

He held it out for Debra, who ignored it stood up spreading her legs and said "Clean me!"

Lucian was stunned and hesitated for a second or two; his heart was pounding and his bulging hard on aching.

"Hurry up it tickles."

She held her gown skirt high over her waist and Lucian placed the towel between her legs gently wiped it between her thighs.

Debra smiled, stepped away and said, "Thank you, Lucian."

Debra was still wearing her high-heeled shoes. She walked towards the large bed and dropped her gown. Lucian got a full view of her curvy figure, her naked back, bottom and legs. She drew her long dark hair over one shoulder and looked back at Lucian as he knelt on the bathroom floor trying desperately to hide his aching erection.

Debra didn't speak but ran her shoe up the calf of her leg rubbing it up and down slowly.

Taking another cigarette from the dressing table she lit her cigarette, naked with her back to Lucian, she blew smoke into the air. As he watched, she leant forward very slightly to flick the ash into the ashtray by the bed.

He saw her curvy bottom and shapely legs in the five-inch heels. His hard on was now bursting at the fabric of his underpants, and he felt hot and sweaty as he knelt on the heated tiled floor.

Debra looked over her shoulder again.

"Come here, Lucian."

As he got close, she turned a slapped his face hard with her hand.

He reeled back and held his cheek with his hand, feeling the heat spreading under his palm.

He looked up at Debra with hurt eyes and she glared down at him with her hands on her naked hips and fierce eyes. He could now see her large full breasts and flat stomach and her partially shaved mount of Venus.

She stared down at Lucian.

"Take off my shoes I'm going to bed."

Her voice was even and had no edge of anger or stress.

Lucian fell forward and helped Debra off with her shoes and placed them together next to the bed. She threw back the covers on the large and beautifully dressed bed, lifting her legs and swinging her knees under the covers pulling them under her chin.

She placed her head on the pillow shut her eyes and said "Good Night Lucian."

Ignoring Lucian, she didn't speak again and kept her eyes closed. Lucian's hard on deflated quickly as he rose and he went to collect his clothes. On his return, Debra was breathing gently and was clearly asleep. He quietly left the suite, feeling his red cheek he went to his own suite and went to sleep very confused.

Chapter 20

Day by day Dominic's obsession for finding a real mistress grew. Dominic had a folder on his computer desktop that contained many images and video clips of dark haired ladies wearing heavy makeup and smoking. This was Dominic's favourite folder, and he spent many hours watching slides shows of these bitchy and hard looking women. He understood from speaking with other online fetishists that the relationship between a devoted sub and a Mistress was very special. It was almost a religion and had little to do with sex or the common misconception that you had to "Like Pain." It was more to do with power exchange and literary "Submitting" and "Giving" yourself totally to that person. A survival expert doesn't eat bugs and drink his own urine because he likes it; he does it to survive and to "Beat" the challenge of the desert or jungle. Soldiers don't stand guard or go into hostile environments to past time. They go in with a strong belief they are doing their duty, respecting the Code and are willing to die for Queen and country. The captured terrorist holds out under torture and gives no information because they believe in the cause, and their mission is from God.

The "Code" of a submissive is just as strong, and when tested with torture or deep humiliation they endure for their Mistress; gaining immense pride in "Taking It" and "Pleasing" their dominant partner.

The Dominant also has a code; the relationship will fail if one or both parties are not getting fulfilment from the sessions. A dominant must give the sub what they need while satisfying their own, sometimes sadistic desires. There is no gain in causing permanent harm or inflicting real damage, as the sub will lose faith and the Dom will not have such a willing partner to indulge in sessions.

This was the issue that Dominic had; he was looking for the role-play with a matron type nurse giving out bad medicine. But afterwards to be cuddled and be told what good and brave boy he had been. Dominic wanted the aloof pose of the beautiful rich bitch but then to be smiled at and be noticed. He craved the stern auntie who spanked his bottom for peeping at her through the door. But then hold him to her bosom and stroke his hair, dry his tears and tell him he was a good boy really.

Chapter 21

The next morning as Lucian woke his thoughts was immediately filled with Debra.

Debra hadn't said why she slapped him or if he had done anything wrong. Lucian felt guilty that when she peed in the bathroom, he was ashamed of being so shocked at this simple act. Everyone pees and goes to the toilet, it was just weird that he was watching, and she didn't mind. Debra didn't seem to have any embarrassment; he felt his cock growing hard again, as he thought about Debra, naked standing in heels, hands on her shapely hips with him on his knees.

Unconsciously Lucian touched his cheek where she had slapped him. As he lay in his bed, his cock became harder as he replayed the images of her naked in the bedroom. Lucian couldn't deny it, with her looks, and what she said he had fallen for Debra Fielding.

Lucian felt excited and scared at the same time, it was intoxicating. Lucian had wanted to do things for Debra; he felt he wanted to please her. When she had slapped him he had felt crushed, the rejection hurt him deep inside. Whether Lucian liked it or not this amazing woman was inside his head, he was totally hypnotised by her.

He shook his head and checked the time, it was 7.15am. It was too early to get up. Reaching for the TV remote control Lucian flicked through the channels. He passed over the news and sports channels but paused on an old film when he saw a scene from Samson and Delilah. It was the American romantic religious epic.

The scene on the TV was when the dark haired Delilah went to seduce Samson. She discovers his superhuman power comes from his long uncut hair. She makes him fall in love with her, finds his secret and cuts his hair, stripping him of his strength and then betrays him to the Philistines.

Lucian was mesmerised by the roles and the obsession Samson had with this dark haired beauty, how she was so awful to him but he loved her, and it didn't matter what she did to him. Lucian watched the rest of the movie, then showered and dressed in his new clothes.

He left the suite and searched the upper decks, restaurants, lounges and bars, but there was no sign of her. He had asked the reception to call her suite just in case she was sleeping but got no answer. After an hour Lucian went to the reception to see if there had been any messages left for him, but there was none.

The only message was an email from Christina about a problem with the Greenwich deal. Christina would have to wait.

Returning to his suite, he saw that a gold edged postcard had been slipped under his door. Picking it up and putting the card to his nose, he caught the scent of Debra's perfume. Written with an elegant fountain pen ink was a message from Debra.

Dinner at 7.30pm, collect me at my suite at 7.15pm. Dress formally; see Angelo and Pepe for evening dress code. Don't be late!

D xx

Lucian put the card on the side. Checking his watch is was still only 9.45am. He headed off to find Angelo and Pepe.

He arrived at the suite and knocked lightly on the door; Pepe opened it in a shocking pink waistcoat. He also wore a perfectly pressed white shirt, very tight black trousers and shiny Chelsea boots. His slightly long flowing hair reminded Lucian of a cross between a footballer and a mature Italian gentleman. Angelo greeted Lucian and ushered him through to the dressing area, where a black dinner jacket and trousers were hanging on a suit stand.

Taking off his jumper Lucian went to pick up the jacket, but Angelo swept it away like a professional matador saying

"No, no Mr Lucian shirt first, nothing spoils a dinner jacket more than a tatty shirt and tie."

Taking Lucian to the other side of the suite Angelo opened a double wardrobe. Inside was a full rack of white dress shirts and drawers of bow ties. Angelo started to grab shirts piling them onto Pepe's outstretched arms. When Pepe could hold no more, Angelo began to undo Lucian's shirt.

As Lucian stood naked from the waist up, Angelo started discarding shirts, placing one after the other up against Lucian's chest until he was satisfied with his choice. After much theatrical fussing Lucian stood by the large triple mirror dressed in a dinner jacket, black bow tie, in custom cut trousers and shiny black shoes. Angelo, pleased with his work, stood back, wiping a tear from his eye.

He whispered to Pepe, "Mistress D will be pleased, no?"

Pepe nodded slowly.

Lucian looked at his reflection from all angles and said, "Not bad, thank you, gentlemen, I'm all set for the ball."

As Lucian continued looking in the mirror, Angelo's

phone rang.

"Pronto" he answered in Italian.

He had a heated conservation with the caller and when he ended the call he said

"You must excuse me, Mr Lucian, I have a client that is just too fat. He has split his new trousers and has to have them repaired before the drinks reception tonight. I must go, but before I do, I have something for you."

As Lucian removed the jacket and shirt, Angelo came back into the room carrying a flat wrapped box.

He held it out for Lucian and said, "It's a gift from an admirer."

Smiling he stepped back and watched excitedly with his hands clenched under his chin. Lucian undid the ribbon and took off the wrapping to reveal a gold box.

He opened the box, it contained a solid gold chain collar the sort an Egyptian or Roman emperor might wear.

Lucian took the collar from the box holding it in his hands.

He was about to try it on when both Angelo and Pepe leapt forward like a pair of well-choreographed ballerinas and stopped him. They startled Lucian and made him jump back, Angelo explained it was very special, and he wasn't to ever put it on himself. It had to be placed on him by someone else when the time was right. Lucian put the gold collar back in the box and wondered when he would get to wear it.

He thanked them for their help and left carrying his new dinner suit, shirt, tie, and new shoes.

At 6.15pm Lucian was ready, dressed in his new dinner jacket. He took a final look in the mirror took the gold chain collar from the box and put it in his inside pocket.

He left the room and knocked on Debra's door.

After a few seconds, a tall young man dressed in a brilliant white dress uniform and shiny black shoes approached Lucian and said, "Mr Palmer Jones, the Captain is waiting please come with me."

Minutes later Lucian was in a room full of people; several smartly dressed young men and women were circulating serving drinks and Canapés. Lucian looked around the room and saw the ship's captain drinking champagne. Angelo and Pepe were also there speaking to other guests, but no sign of Debra. A man in white approached Lucian with a tray of champagne. He took one and then heard a voice from behind. Turning he saw Alex Knightley, who had brought him on board the ship.

Alex took Lucian to one side.

"Ms Fielding has been delayed and will not be attending the champagne reception. However, she was insistent that you attend, then to meet in her suite at midnight, after the gala dinner."

Lucian asked where she was, but Alex just said that she had been taken ashore by helicopter, further than that, he didn't know. Lucian wondered what sort of meeting justified a private helicopter at such short notice. Then again he didn't know Debra very well, and she may do this all the time. After an announcement, Lucian followed the crowd making their way upstairs to the main dining room, which was set up for a gala dinner. It was impressive with ice sculptures, exotic fruit, and beautiful table displays. He sat with a group of Norwegian passengers who spoke in their own language all evening and didn't once include Lucian. The night progressed, the food came in several courses but finally dinner was over, and Lucian could now excuse himself and return to his suite.

As he did so, he heard sounds coming from one of the nearby suites. It sounded like furniture being moved around. As he stood in the passage the suite door opened and several men came out of the door carrying boxes and clothes. Through the open door, Lucian caught a glimpse of a bed that had been remade in scarlet red silk and furs. As he peered in, a tall black woman came out of the bathroom. She must have been over 6 ft. tall and wore very high thigh length boots over long slender ebony oiled legs. She wore a leather corset and her large 44 DD breasts were only just covered by the corset top. Her hair was in a high ponytail and her makeup was heavy with very dark eye shadow and scarlet red lipstick.

She stopped and put his hands on her hips.

"So slave, you are early and why aren't you dressed as I instructed?"

Lucian said, "I'm sorry, I think I'm in the wrong suite."

The tall lady smiled and walked with effortless grace in her high heels to the drinks cabinet. Taking a glass of white wine from the side, she said,

"Oh yes, I think you are in the wrong place. I have a client to see, and if I were you, I wouldn't want to stay in here too long, or you may wish you hadn't."

Curious Lucian asked, "Why what is going to happen in here?"

The lady smiled again flashing perfect teeth.

"I am going to torture and abuse a worthless sub, who

is going to pay me thousands of dollars to whip his fat ass until it bleeds".

She laughed at Lucian's shocked face.

"Then he will pay me thousands more and beg me to fuck his ass with a large strap on cock."

Lucian was so shocked he couldn't speak. He felt the blood drain from his face and his stomach tighten with fear.

Lucian hurried to his suite and breathed a sigh of relief. What had he got involved in? It was all too weird and getting weirder by the day.

He spent the next couple of hours surfing the Internet to find out what a Mistress was? He read several articles and found it didn't just refer to a girlfriend or lover of a married man, as he had always thought. A Mistress was a term used to describe a Dominatrix or a female who plays a dominant role in a relationship.

A "Dom" was also referred to as a "Top".

He also read about "Collaring" and what it meant, how a submissive would wear a collar to signify their servitude and submission to a Mistress. A Mistress or a Master may own that sub and consider them as their property. Much as Slavers would collar slaves to keep them in servitude. The collar in a BDSM relationship was both a physical and a mental condition. When a Mistress or Master collared a sub, it was like a marriage or bond that couldn't be easily broken. Lucian looked at the solid gold collar and wondered if this was to be his collar.

Was Debra going to make him her sub?

He thought about this and although it was a scary he didn't baulk at the idea of being special to this amazing woman. He found an article called "Love me? Prove it!" It was a story of a US Marine who had been trained to be a Navy seal. He had years of combat experience, had been shot twice and was hard as nails. This big man was married to a younger petite wife who was his Mistress. He told the magazine he would do things for her and endure all manner of humiliations if she required it. He explained his Mistress was like the Marine Corp, that he had taken an oath, the Marine code is so strong that he would gladly die rather break the code.

Similarly, he would do anything to please his Mistress. They had a loving and close relationship and had been happily married for nine years. He said if he could endure a session with his Wife/ Mistress, it gave him the strength to go to war and do his job in Afghanistan and Iraq.

His wife was only 5 ft. Tall and slim, she would make

him kneel kiss her feet and slap his face and spit at him. He would gladly endure these humiliations for her. The marine was over 6 ft. tall and heavily muscled like a weight lifter, but he would take this from her, as she was his Mistress.

Lucian read of another case where a city broker in London earned over a million pounds a year in bonuses and spent over £25,000 a year on seeing a professional Mistress. He described how with the credit crunch, the brokers and bankers were highly stressed.

He had tried all sorts of drugs including cocaine and heavy drinking, but nothing worked to allow him to sleep. A fellow banker had recommended finding a Mistress, the broker had laughed at first but found one online went to visit her, paying over £1,200 for a two-hour session. He explained she would take away all his stress, even though she made him do some degrading tasks. He found it an enlightening experience, and he had been going back every month. He claimed he would now be lost without the Mistress in his life.

Another Managing Director of a well-known large airline wasn't gay but would submit to his long term Mistress. He would be slapped and caned, made to kiss and lick the woman's ass hole while she drank champagne that he had brought along.

Lucian found these stories unbelievable and read case

after case of successful men, who liked to be dominated by female Mistresses. Why did these, successful people crave the cruelty and harsh attention of these Mistresses?

Lucian couldn't get his head around the idea of liking pain? Yet these men and woman didn't like pain, they just endured pain or discomfort to show that they were worthy.

Lucian thought about how Debra had slapped him and how it had felt. He had learnt from the articles that a "Sub" isn't a wimp. In fact, the things that some of these "subs" were taking weren't anything to do with being weak. Lucian suspected that it took incredible trust, and great mental will power, to submit to a Mistress in this way.

Checking the time he saw it was now 11.50pm, he went to the bathroom washed his face and went next door. Looking around the suite, he saw drinks had been set on the side, and a white robe lay on the chair. On the robe was a hand written note, he picked it up, and it read

"Go to the bathroom strip naked, put on the robe, make me a drink bring it out to the balcony. Do not speak, kneel at my feet and wait for further instructions."

D XX

Lucian's mouth went dry as he looked at the closed door to the balcony, knowing Debra was standing behind those flowing curtains and waiting for him to kneel at her feet. Suddenly he felt sick as fear gripped him, Lucian turned to bolt out of the suite when he felt the gold collar in his pocket. This gave him some strange comfort, so Lucian went into the bathroom, stripped naked and put on the white robe.

Lucian went to the bar and fixed Debra a gin martini. He placed it on a silver tray and headed for the balcony. Stepping out Lucian saw Debra leaning on the rail to his left. With his heart pounding, he took a deep breath and carefully knelt down.

Debra was smoking looking out to sea and seemly oblivious to his presence. The weather had warmed up as they had neared Madeira and the sea breeze was light and warm. He was completely naked under his bathrobe and yet still felt flushed and warm being in Debra's presence.

After a couple of minutes, she turned and passed the nearly burnt out cigarette butt to Lucian, who stubbed it out on the decking floor. Without having anywhere to put it, he placed it in his pocket.

Debra looked on amused.

"Next time you don't remember the ash tray, I shall

make you eat it!"

Laughing she took the martini from his outstretched hand, walked on her high heels past him stroking his head as she went. The mere touch of her fingers felt wonderful, he closed his eyes at the sensation. Staying on his knees Lucian crawled after her. Once inside he knelt on the thick carpet and looked at Debra.

She was dressed in a long floor length flowing black lace see through nightgown. She had on lace topped stockings and a black satin corset that pushed her full breasts up. Around her neck, she wore gold and jewelled studded collar. Her makeup was perfect her hair was down but clipped up from her face with a sparkling hair clasp. Her lips were perfect red; Lucian noticed she had outlined them before applying the lipstick as she had the other evening. She saw him looking at her and walked over to where he as kneeling.

She put her finger under Lucian's chin raised his head, so he was staring directly into her beautiful eyes. Looking down at his naked chest she stroked his hard nipples.

He gasped, and she laughed.

Sensing his nervousness, she said, "Do I scare or excite you Lucian?"

He swallowed hard and said, "Both I think."

Debra suddenly reached down pinching both his nipples and twisting them hard. This caused Lucian to take a sharp intake of breath, but he didn't speak or cry out. He gritted his teeth remembering the articles on "Taking Pain".

Debra let go and said "Good Boy."

She walked in her high heels to the bathroom indicating Lucian follow her. He crawled on all fours to the hard marble floor of the bathroom.

"Shut the door and take off your robe."

Lucian pushed the heavy door closed, and then took off his robe, placing it on the hook on the reverse of the door. Falling to his knees again Lucian watched Debra as she applied fresh red lipstick. As Lucian watched, he felt his cock begin to harden. He shifted his position Debra looked at him in the mirror.

"Problem Lucian?"

Lucian flushed but said nothing.

Debra took a makeup brush, pursing her lips applied blusher to her cheeks. Satisfied with her look, she turned, walked to the small couch against the bathroom wall and sat down.

Debra signalled for Lucian to crawl towards her, he did as he was instructed, coming to kneel before her. She lifted her foot poking the thin high heel into his hard on. The metal tip pressed hard against his private parts. She smiled pushing the heel tip into his balls making him squirm. This made her frown, so she pushed harder still. But this time, he stayed still and took the pressure.

She stopped pressing down and said, "Good Boy... learning fast."

She stood up walked to the toilet and stood by the bowl.

She looked over her shoulder at Lucian and said, "Come here take down my panties, so I can piss."

Lucian didn't speak he just crawled on the cold hard tiles and nervously reached up under Debra's nightgown. He reached past her stocking tops until he could feel a thin cloth piece that was Debra's black lace panties. He carefully pulled them down over her stockinged thighs, down past her knees to her high heels. She lifted one heel, then the other so Lucian could remove them.

Once off Debra sat down and peed noisily into the bowl. When she had finished, she stood holding up her nightgown and waited. Lucian looked at her enquiringly.

She looked down at him.

"You know what to do Lucian dry and clean me."

He flushed and reached for a white towel, rose briefly to run the water in the sink until it was warm. Dropping to his knees, he gently ran the warm wet towel up inside Debra's legs. She spread her legs slightly rocking back and forth on the warmed towel, pressing down on Lucian's hand.

Debra looked down again and said, "Where are my panties?"

Lucian had dropped them on the floor when he rose to get the towel. He picked them up again and showed them to Debra. She took them off him, opened them up and put the crotch over Lucian's nose and mouth saying,

"Can you smell my pussy Lucian?"

Lucian drew away, Debra just laughed at him.

She screwed the panties into a small ball and raising Lucian's chin said, "Open your mouth."

As he did, she said "Wider."

He did, and she pushed the panties into his gaping mouth making him gag slightly. The lace fabric caressed his tongue and roof of his mouth. She opened the bathroom door walked into the main reception area and across to the balcony. She opened the balcony door, picking up her cigarettes from the table.

She called to Lucian.

"Came and keep me company while I smoke."

Lucian was still naked and with the panties in his mouth, crawled across the carpeted floor onto the polished wooden deck of the balcony. Debra stopped, took the panties from his mouth and passed him her cigarettes and the gold lighter. He managed to light the cigarette first time. Debra congratulated him on his improvement in cigarette lighting. As she smoked she didn't look at Lucian and said:

"If I asked you to do something for me would you do it without question?"

Lucian thought for a minute and said," I think I would."

Debra said, "Are you sure? You don't know what I want yet?"

Lucian replied, "I know but that's the fun isn't it?"

"Fun?" said Debra "What makes you think it's anything

fun?"

Lucian fell silent, dropped his head looking at his now deflated cock. The cold air and kneeling in the open had killed his hard on. Debra finished her cigarette and said,

"Is that a yes then?"

Lucian looked back up at Debra.

"Yes Debra."

Bending forward to make eye contact Debra said stated, "Whenever we are alone, I wish you to refer to me as Mistress is that clear."

"Yes." replied Lucian

"Yes what?" said Debra

"Yes Mistress." corrected Lucian, thinking how easy it was to call her Mistress

Walking away from Lucian, she opened the patio doors calling back.

"Get up Lucian and come inside."

Rising from his knees he followed her into her suite.

Once inside Debra sat on the couch and said, "Pour me

another drink, have one yourself, get your gown and come and sit with me."

Lucian went and retrieved his bathrobe from the bathroom, fixed Debra another martini and himself a large gin and tonic. Taking a large swallow, he went to sit with Debra on the soft couch. Debra reached over and pulled the robe apart slightly and said, "Let me look at you."

Running her eyes up and down his chest she said, "Did Angelo take care of you today, did he give you anything?"

Lucian replied, "Yes he did, but I didn't get a blowjob from Pepe."

Debra laughed out loud.

"I can arrange it if that's your thing Lucian, but I suspect it's not."

Then casually she said, "Have you got any money, Lucian?"

"I have a few quid in my wallet if that what you mean."

Debra smiled and said, "No, I'm talking about some real money."

"I'm afraid I don't Debra, sorry Mistress, and I actually

can't pay for the house you want to sell to me."

Lucian was silently worried when Debra didn't reply straight away but eventually said, "Look I have money, and it's not everything you know."

Lucian smiled.

Debra continued, "What if I loan the house to you then you could rent it out until you have made some money and then buy it off me."

Hasn't she made this offer before?

Lucian didn't answer he just took a sip of his drink and looked at the floor.

"Think about it, and we can talk again."

Lucian nodded and then blurted out, "Do you like me, Debra, I'm sorry, Mistress?"

Debra looked at him with a raised eyebrow and said "Like you? Yes, I do, but I hardly know you, Lucian."

"I have been reading up on this sort of thing, and I'm really not sure it's for me."

Debra stared straight at Lucian.

"This kind of thing, is what exactly?"

Lucian looked at the floor and said, "Well you know all this Dom, Sub stuff, all that whipping, spanking, and all the kinky sex."

Debra laughed out loud again and ruffled Lucian's hair in a playful way.

"I think you are getting too much sea air or watching too much porn."

"I'm tired now, so will you go into the bedroom and prepare my bed for me."

Lucian rose and said "Yes Mistress."

He turned down the covers and switched on the bedside light as Debra came into the bedroom. She dropped her gown and went towards the bed, she had taken down her hair, and it flowed over her shoulders covered her now naked breasts. She slid in under the covers and pulled them around her chin.

She said, "It's cold in here, there is a hair dryer in the dressing table drawer please warm me, Lucian."

Lucian went to the drawer found a hair dryer. Plugging it into the socket by the bed and turned it on to blow hot air. Debra lifted the covers so Lucian could move the hair dryer back and forth under the covers giving Debra a warm air massage.

Then turning away she pointed her shapely bottom at Lucian as he held up the covers and continued to move the dryer up and down her body.

Debra turned over and passed him a gold coloured leather cock strap. He picked up the strap looking at it as he held it in his hand. She said

"That is for you Lucian, whenever we are alone, you must kneel at my feet. I expect you to wear it around your cock and balls."

"Yes Mistress"

Debra didn't reply, and after a few seconds, Lucian sensed that Debra was asleep.

He turned off the hair dryer, unplugged it and returned it to the draw. Checking that Debra hadn't moved, Lucian went to the reception area dressed and left, taking the gold studded strap with him.

Once in his own bed, he played with it, rotating it between his fingers. Lucian then realised his hard-on had returned. Taking the strap, he unfastened it and wrapped the strap around his cock and balls. Using the popper Lucian fastened it, the tightness made his balls ache. Lucian took his cock in his hand surprised how hard he had become. He had seen cock straps before but never experienced the feeling first hand. His mind was flooded with thoughts and images of Debra, she really did excite him.

He found her behaviour shocking, like peeing in front of him, yet it really turned him on. Before Lucian knew it, he was rubbing his cock, the more he thought about Debra, the harder he rubbed it until with a gasp Lucian came all over the bed covers. Lucian recovered, feeling guilty and embarrassed, he realised he hadn't done that since he was a teenager. Lucian went to the bathroom and cleaned himself up and got back into bed. Lying there looking at the ceiling he realised the gold cock strap was still wrapped around his cock and balls, but now it felt comfortable, so he slept with it on.

Chapter 22

Dominic sat in the South London traffic, cursing the queues of cars and lorries inching their way forward through the contraflow.

Dominic had a meeting with a fat seventy-two-year-old man who owned a warehouse storing sex toys and fantasy costumes. He had a Donald Trump style comb over style, a wispy moustache, and smelled of stale sweat and piss. He said he had made his fortune by selling lubricant to sex shops all through the 1980's. He had sold literary millions of sachets of lube to the gay and straight market by mail order. It worked brilliantly until the Internet came along and all the large sex retailers opened their own online shops and took away that market.

The premises had been broken into, with thieves taking over £50,000 of stock. He was underinsured, and he now wanted to add cameras to prevent it happening again.

Dominic banged the steering wheel violently with his palms. He was in a hurry to get home and back in front of his screens. He had been following a thirty-eight-year-old gay man who had a new twenty-three-year-old boyfriend. The older man was into fisting. The young man was due to get his first experience of taking the man's whole fist.

Dominic was also following a seventy-year-old retired Sea Captain, who discovered on a trip to South Africa, that he enjoyed having very rough anal sex with black women? On his return, the captain was asking for contacts for a willing black woman? Dominic had thought.

"Good luck with that Captain!"

Dominic glared intensely at a nervous looking woman in the vehicle beside him. She watched as he slowly ran his tongue up the glass of the van's window. In horror, she screamed, looked away and wouldn't look back at him. Dominic laughed then leaving the frightened woman behind; he pulled the van into the faster-moving lane.

The drizzling rain slowed the traffic, and the contraflow was miles long. There was no visible activity, other than two men smoking by a single yellow JCB. Dominic raged at the inefficiency of the British motorway workers.

Dominic drove alongside a man in a 500 SL Mercedes.

The man was speaking on the phone, sitting in the comfortable leather interior of his car. Dominic stared at his bright blue tie and white shirt he noticed his expensive looking watch. As the Mercedes pulled forward, Dominic took a photo of his license plate on his phone. If he could be bothered, he would get into his world and see if he had any dirty secrets. Dominic could find out if he was cheating on his wife, fiddling his tax return and what he looked at late at night. Dominic had many ways to spy on strangers. He was able to tag any online polls and load it with a cookie. That would activate a program when the questionnaire was opened or forwarded. He had found out dirty secrets of well-known celebrities, successful businessmen and officials in this way.

Dominic banged the steering wheel violently with his palms. He was in a hurry to get home and back in front of his screens, where he could entertain himself online.

Chapter 23

10.45am. Lucian had overslept for the first time in years. Dressing in another new set of clothes he went to breakfast. After eating, he went outside and sat on the sun deck. The weather was warm, the sky was blue, and the sea had changed to a dark aqua blue as they neared land. Finding the sunlight a bit too bright he went inside headed to the shops. With a pair of designer sunglasses and a classic design Panama sun hat, he returned to the upper deck to take in the approaching land and harbour. From his position, he could see the port workers preparing to make fast the massive ship's moorings. There were several "Lucky Boys" on the quayside with bundles of items to tempt the wealthy passengers with fake designer towels and trinkets.

With no money and nowhere to go, Lucian watched the cable cars run up the side of the mountain. By shading his eyes he could just make out the botanical gardens at the summit. Across from the cable car, Lucian could see the winding cobbled streets that led down from the village at the top. He had read about the famous

Madeira sleighs as they steered their thrilled passengers safely down the smooth, shiny cobbles back towards the harbour area.

A steward in a white uniform approached Lucian with a card, this time in an envelope. He quickly opened it and saw it was from Debra. The envelope contained not a postcard as before but a hand written letter. In a classic flowing style written with a fountain pen, it explained she had left early that morning. She was going to Dubai and would be back in a few weeks. She thanked him for his company and that she would be in touch at some point regarding the house details.

Lucian read and reread the letter unable to believe what he was reading, was this some sort of joke or a test of his loyalty? Has she actually left him on the boat and gone to Dubai without him.

Lucian put the letter in his pocket, sitting in the warm Mediterranean sun he suddenly felt cold, alone and completely devastated.

Lucian was replaying the previous evening, trying to figure out what went wrong? Maybe he wasn't "Submissive "enough or maybe he wasn't bold enough? Should he have tried to get into bed with her? Lucian wasn't sure what to think, but he had to face it she was gone, and he had nowhere to go. He surely couldn't stay on the boat all the way to the Caribbean?

Leaving the deck, Lucian headed back to the shops and purchased a medium sized suitcase from the luggage concession. Returning to his cabin, he packed his clothes then went to the reception to ask for Alex Knightley.

The young lady on reception said, "He hasn't come on shift today as he was unwell".

Lucian asked if anyone had seen Ms Debra Fielding, the receptionist stated that they hadn't. Lucian explained he had to leave the ship and return to the UK.

The receptionist asked Lucian to wait while she made a call, shortly after a manager came out of the inner office. The gentleman's name was Harvey he asked Lucian to accompany him into a small room adjacent to the reception desk.

Once in the office, Harvey asked if Lucian was Debra's personal assistant or manager?

Lucian explained he had been a guest of Ms Fielding, and he had been staying in the suite next door. Harvey looked concerned and said it was highly irregular for guests to have extra guests other than staff or assistants.

Lucian laughed at the idea of being Debra's servant.

Harvey didn't see the funny side.

He looked seriously at Lucian and explained there was a large bill against his suite number.

It contained several onboard services such a tailoring, duty-free shopping and bar tabs.

Harvey explained that the bill would need to be paid in full before he could leave the ship.

Lucian asked how much the bill was?

Harvey replied, "It was $9,750.86."

Lucian felt faint, "Nearly £7,000!"

Lucian was shocked he had just assumed that Debra was paying for everything.

"There must be a mistake?" said Lucian

Harvey looked to see if there were any notes on the computer then turned to Lucian and said, "I'm very sorry Mr Palmer Jones, but there are no instructions on the system. Therefore you will need to settle the bill before we can allow you to leave the ship."

Lucian said nothing his mind reeling with the shocking information.

Harvey asked, "Did Ms Fielding say when she would return and if she would be re-joining the ship on the way to the Caribbean?"

"No," Lucian said, "She didn't and I'm embarrassed to say I don't have any money?"

Harvey raised an eyebrow.

"I see?"

Lucian continued, "I really need to leave today, and fly back to the UK."

Harvey said he would make some more enquiries and asked Lucian wait for him in the bar on the top deck.

Relieved Lucian agreed.

Back in the bar, the ship seemed less busy as many guests had gone ashore. After four days at sea, they wanted to visit Madeira and see the sights.

Lucian had a coffee, sat watching the passengers as they made their way up the port at Funchal.

As Lucian waited the time dragged, he asked the barman if he could make a telephone call. The barman agreed and lent Lucian his iPhone. He called the office Christina answered ranting at Lucian for not being in touch.

She told him in her heavy emotional accented English

how worried she had been. She told Lucian that everyone thought he had been abducted by aliens or taken by the East London Mafia.

Lucian told her to claim down and explained he had met a potential new client and was working on an exciting opportunity.

He was on his way back now so could she arrange a flight back from Madeira to London Heathrow as soon as possible.

"Madeira! I thought you went to Southampton?" Christina screeched at him.

"It's complicated Ok just book me a flight would you please!"

Lucian really didn't have time or inclination explain it all to Christina.

"Ok," Christina replied sensing that she wouldn't get any more information from Lucian.

After several minutes she called back to inform him she had managed to get him on the 6 pm flight from Madeira to London. He thanked her for saying he would be back in the office in the morning to sort out the other problems. She told him off again and then hung up, he handed the phone back to the bartender thanking him.

He took a sip of his coffee and looked up when a voice said:

"Not going ashore, Lucian?"

Standing there was Juliette Harding, who smiled and said, "Where is Ms Fielding today? Is she away doing business again?"

Lucian just stared at the floor and shook his head. Juliette sensing something was wrong asked Lucian if he was all right.

He explained that Debra was gone and that he had a difficult situation now with paying the bill and getting home.

Juliette listened and , seeing how worried Lucian looked asked, "Maybe I can help?"

Lucian forced a smile back "You are very kind Juliette, but I don't think you have $9,000 spare on a marketing assistance wages."

Undeterred Juliette said, "Let me see what I can do, I know one or two people on board. Maybe I could get them to waive the fees."

Lucian was surprised and laughing said, "You are joking, who do you know, the captain or the owner or something?"

Juliette looked serious for a minute.

"Actually, as a matter of fact, the captain is my uncle."

Then smiling broadly she announced, "And this ship was built by my grandfather."

"Ok," blurted Lucian who was taken aback by another crashingly embarrassing assumption.

Juliette left to make some enquiries. Lucian watched her rounded bottom in her knee length skirt and flat shoes. He couldn't help imagine her in a pair five-inch heels with red soles like Debra wore.

STOP IT! STOP IT! He told himself.

He felt like he was going slightly crazy. Since meeting Debra he was turning into a sex maniac.

A while later Juliette returned and announced

"It's all taken care of Lucian, as it happened Ms Fielding did leave instructions."

"Really" Said Lucian

"Yes," Juliette said

"Alex Knightley was supposed to update the system, but was taken ill in the night and didn't turn up for his shift this morning."

"Has she paid for everything?"

"Yes the bill has been paid, and you are free to go."

Lucian was speechless. He couldn't believe his luck. He thanked Juliette and apologised for assuming her lowly rank was a reflection of her abilities and apparent good connections.

She smiled and said, "You know that assumption is the mother of all Fuck Ups."

Lucian laughed and gave her a quick hug. Stepping back he smiled thanked her again. Taking his new suitcase full of lovely clothes, he disembarked without any fuss.

Lucian found a taxi driver that spoke English and made his way to the airport to check in. He boarded the plane still in disbelief at the events that had unfolded over the last five days.

Lucian sat sipping whisky to numb the whirlwind in his head.

As the plane flew towards London, he reflected on how he had been swept along with Debra and her high-level world.

His world was so different to Debra's.

In his world he had never been involved in that level of

lifestyle, it was something he only dreamed about. He was surprised how upset he was feeling about being dropped out of it with such speed and how he missed Debra's company. He would return to his modest apartment and do some serious thinking about the BDSM world that Debra had briefly shown him.

As the plane descended into Heathrow airport, he took out his phone from his top pocket and began flicking through the many photos he had taken over the last few days.

In each one, they were both smiling and looked happy, At the sight of Debra a lump swelled in his throat and tears burned at the back of his eyes. Staring out of the plane's window, he let them flow down his cheeks.

He knew he was in love with her.

Chapter 24

Dominic had set up a program to capture online polls sent from Yahoo email addresses. It was common to cut and paste these online questionnaires. He found all manner of subjects, from UFO sightings to extreme sexual fantasies.

This is how he came across a woman named Debra and her new submissive trainee called Lucian. She had sent Lucian an online questionnaire that morning from Dubai. Dominic had tagged and captured the details.

The man was easy to hack, his name was Lucian Palmer Jones, and he was forty-six years old.

Dominic remotely accessed Lucian's computer and sent a spying program hidden in a video of a mouse eating cheese. The program swept through the hard drive and displayed some interesting and annoying facts.

Lucian's emails showed that he had recently flown back from Madeira having been on a cruise for 5 days. Dominic could see the details of his return flight to the UK.

He spent the next thirty minutes viewing photos and watching videos that showed that Lucian had encountered a dominant woman on the cruise. It would appear from the videos and pictures this was not staged or acted out. There was one scene where Lucian was brushing Debra's silky hair. Dominic had always longed to perform this simple, pleasing task.

Dominic was instantly jealous of this man. He had been looking for a real Mistress for many years. Feeling the fury rise in his chest, he raged why wasn't it him, kneeling brushing her beautiful long hair. Dominic knew this estate agent was nothing compared to him. In his mind, Dominic was much more worthy than this fucking wimp.

Slamming his fists on the desk, he exploded, "How did this fucking dull, boring man who didn't even have a fucking Facebook page, find a real life Mistress!"

Dominic sat forward in his high-tech chair and began to work his tools. Dominic now wanted to know everything about this man. One of his software packages allowed Dominic to watch Lucian via his webcam. He would see what this man did and get into his life big time.

Chapter 25

It was 8.27am; Lucian pulled up outside his office. A cold rain fell, and the temperature was only seven degrees. It felt cold compared to the twenty-seven degrees in the Madeira sunshine the day before.

Lucian sat at his desk looking at the stack of overdue bills and letters, but he was not in any mood to deal with money issues today. The last few days had left Lucian in a daze; he felt like it had been all some weird and wonderful dream. Lucian wondered if he would ever see Debra again.

Switching on his computer, new emails flooded into his inbox. He ignored the requests for holidays, cheap flights, and sexual dating with Russian brides. As he scanned the entries, he noticed that his personal email had received three messages. Clicking on the first message Lucian saw it was from the auctioneer. Thanking him for attending and giving the date of the next auction. The second was from the Audi garage, he passed over that one and opted for the third email.

Opening it, he saw the email was from Debra.

Lucian's heart missed a beat.

"Hello Lucian, I trust you got back to the UK ok? I'm in Dubai, and the weather is hot. Log onto Yahoo Live chat at 9.15pm tonight, tell me how much you are missing me."

"Mistress D XX"

Lucian was shaken from his thoughts as Christina burst into the office. Soaking wet in her red and white plastic mac finished off with bright red wellingtons. She ran around the desk and gave Lucian a massive damp hug, leaving a wet patch on his blue shirt.

"Oh, I didn't think I would never see you again!" she squealed.

Lucian wiped the water from his desk and said, "It's Ok Christina, I'm here."

"I thought you had run off with dat rich biatch" Christina gushed.

Lucian smiled.

"No don't worry, I'm back in one piece, broke, and still single."

Christina smiled as she hung her wet coat on the hook and swapping her wellies for a pair a navy blue Dolly pumps.

"Any news on the Greenwich project,?" Lucian asked.

"Yes they called a couple of times, and there are a lot of emails for you to reply to."

Lucian thanked her then asked for a cup of tea with three sugars.

Tutting as usual at the amount of sugar, Christina left the room. She returned a few minutes later with a steaming mug of tea and gently placed it down on Lucian's desk. With the sweet tea drunk and emails read, the day dragged on.

Lucian passed the time with replying to emails, making a few calls to apologize for his sudden absence. Saying his diary was now clear, and he would be attending all meetings from now on.

As closing time neared, Lucian told Christina to lock up. He packed his laptop in his bag, picked up his keys and headed out of the door.

Once home Lucian fixed himself some quick stir-fry food. He spooned the noodles and peppers into his mouth as he sat at his laptop checking his personal mail again. He was disappointed to see there was nothing else from Debra.

He logged onto the BBC iPlayer and watched a rerun of the football from the weekend. Lucian enjoyed the match and time passed quickly, looking up he realized it was just after 9 pm.

It took a frustrating few minutes of logging in and out repeatedly to get his Yahoo mailbox to open. When he finally did get access, he spent a few minutes deleting all the junk mail.

As the trash bin filled up, his messenger pinged with the words

"You're late!"

Checking the time it was 9.16 pm. He had been distracted by deleting emails and missed Debra logging on. After typing a brief greeting, Lucian waited for Debra to respond.

The reply was short and to the point.

"Are you kneeling?"

Lucian immediately fell to his knees a flush rising on his cheeks as he typed.

"Yes, Mistress."

There seemed to be a delay in the connection. Lucian had waited for another forty seconds before the next message came through.

"Are you at home?"

"Yes Mistress" he replied

"Good boy" Debra typed.

"Wouldn't want you caught by your cleaner kneeling by your desk. I don't know what she would think?"

Lucian typed back, "Sadly I don't have a cleaner. I can't afford one."

For the next few minutes, the conversation flowed. Lucian felt happy and excited chatting to Debra.

Debra asked, "Did you get home ok?"

"Yes Mistress" Lucian typed.

"Have you decided if you want the house or not."

"I would love to take it, but I really can't afford it. It's just not right to give it to me free of charge."

"I believe you would "Take It" for me, Lucian. And the house."

Even though it was just lettered on a screen Lucian flushed at the thought of "Taking" things for Debra Fielding!

He managed to compose himself and typed,

"Where are you, what is the time in Dubai?"

The reply came back after another short delay,

"I'm in bed its 2.30 am, Dubai is five hours ahead of the UK."

"Are you not tired Mistress"?

"No, I have something for you to fill in for me?"

"Oh ok, what is it?"

"Check your emails, fill it all in, send it back soon as you can."

Lucian wondered what it could be. Maybe it was a loan contract for the house. Debra didn't give any further information and her last message read:

"Log on again tomorrow at the same time and Lucian, Don't be late again!"

Lucian sent a reply, "Yes Mistress, thank you Mistress, and good night Mistress."

She didn't reply, and he felt foolish typing so many Mistresses in one sentence!

As he waited on his knees for one last reply, he was

thinking about the cruise and what they had done in Debra's suite. After a minute he clicked on his personal email and saw two new messages. He could see Debra's mail with the attachment on it and another unknown email.

He clicked on the unknown mail first and saw a screen shot from a video that showed a man on all fours. He had a large red ball gag in his mouth and a chain attached to his collar. Standing close behind him was a woman with long dark hair, dressed in a leather corset. He clicked on the close button and instead of it closing, the laptop went black, and an electronic laugh filled the room. The screen then flickered, came back to life with a picture of a real mouse eating cheese. Lucian clicked his mouse, hit refresh and after a few seconds, the screen returned to normal. He then went back to his inbox deleting the strange email leaving Debra's.

He opened the attachment and waited for the document to download, and saved it to his desktop it read:

Submissive Application Form.

The pages were filled with a selection of yes no and multiple choice questions. Lucian scanned down until he came to a list which had tick boxes next to it "Into" "Not Into" "Would Like to try" "Would not like to try."

The list was long and contained some things that Lucian could only assume, were types of fetishes or sexual activities.

Including,

Knife and Gun Play

Burning Branding and Fire Play

Foot hooking – feet fetish

Breath play – suffocation and strangulation

Lucian read the whole list then sat back in disbelief at some of the titles and explanations that were listed by them.

Who in their right mind would want to put a live animal, like a hamster or rat inside their anal passage with a tube? Who would get off on having the genitals brushed with stinging nettles or having deep heat put down their pee hole?

Lucian shuddered at the thought.

Kneeling down kissing Debra's feet was one thing, but stinging nettles on his nuts! No way.

He completed the questionnaire saved it to his personal folder on the desktop, then logged back into

Yahoo.

He typed in Debra's Email and attached the survey.

Typing a brief message he wrote:

"Interesting stuff but a bit extreme for me, I think."

He pressed send but the mail didn't go, stalling in the Outbox.

Lucian tried again, but it just wouldn't send. He cancelled the message, redid it attaching the questionnaire again. Pressing the send button again nothing happened.

Then as Lucian watched in amazement, a message flashed across the screen

"Foolish is the man who plays with fire, for certain he will burn."

After three seconds the message disappeared, and Lucian was left with the Yahoo screen again. He tried to send the email a third time and this time it went out straight away? Shaking his head, Lucian shut the laptop and got into bed, taking his phone with him.

Lucian's phone beeped with an incoming text. It was a number he didn't recognise, it said:

"Sleep well D x."

He picked up the phone to reply, but a message under the text stated that this number does not receive incoming calls or texts.

Smiling slightly to himself he closed his eyes and fell asleep thinking of hamsters running through nettles!

Chapter 26

The next day Lucian was busy with phone calls and emails. He kept checking his Yahoo messenger every hour or so to see if Debra had been in touch. By the time Lucian got home, he was desperate to message her again. She was three thousand miles away and any contact, even if it was just typing on a screen, meant he was in touch with Debra.

Lucian cleared away his supper dishes and poured a glass of red wine. He noticed his computer was on. Lucian thought this was strange, as he was sure he shut it down before going to sleep last night.

Firing up his messenger he checked his mail. One made no sense at all. It was from someone called Furious Boy. The message was just two lines, and it read,

"Those who are of poor seed will never claim immeasurable pleasures or riches."

It was signed by Furious Boy.

Lucian deleted it and went off to Google and out of

curiosity typed in a single word "Mistress." The first two references were from Wikipedia. The first read

"A mistress is a relatively long-term female lover or companion who is not married to her partner, especially when her partner is married."

The second reference from Wikipedia was:

Mistress may refer to:

• Schoolmistress, or female school teacher (also called a "schoolmarm"); see school master

• A dominatrix into BDSM

• A female owner of a dog

As Lucian was reading his laptop screen went blank.

A small red dot started to move around in the centre. As he watched, it grew from a pinhead to the size of a penny. Then it moved randomly around the screen growing in size until it reached the size of a tennis ball. It stopped directly in the centre again and began to spin. The red ball increased in speed until it was spinning at a tremendous rate. Then all of a sudden it exploded filling Lucian's screen with what look like blood, it ran down the inside of the screen.

This startled Lucian, it looked so real, Lucian almost

expected it to leak out of the laptop screen onto the keyboard. It didn't, of course, so he sat back and watched until it suddenly disappeared and the screen returned to the Wikipedia references

Then another email came through; he opened it and was shocked to see in massive 78-point type.

"Beware the desires of the unworthy!"

 The sign-off was Furious Boy again.

Lucian immediately deleted the email and blocked the sender.

He was staring at the screen as his Messenger pinged and Debra typed:

"Hello, Lucian."

Excited he replied, "Good evening Mistress."

She typed a smiley and then:

"Have you worked hard today, did you miss me?"

Lucian explained that his day had been quite dull, and he had been thinking about her all the time.

He then asked Debra what was she doing.

She told him was sitting in an Italian restaurant, on the

balcony overlooking the synchronised water fountains at the Burg Kalifa. The night was still hot, and the fountains were performing to Whitney Houston's song "I will always love you."

Lucian replied, "That's sounds lovely, I have always liked that song."

He then asked, "Where are you staying?"

"Burj Al Arab" she replied.

"I've heard that's one of the best hotels over there, is it as expensive as they say?"

Debra ignored the question and asked if he knew of a man called Charles McCreedy.

Lucian said he didn't.

She explained he was an English multi-millionaire property developer and that she had had a meeting with Charles's assistant, a man called Adam Bennett earlier.

Debra went silent for a few seconds then typed,

"Can I ask you something, Lucian?"

Lucian typed: "Yes Mistress."

Debra explained she was going to ask Lucian a series of

questions and he was not to lie or say don't know.

He must answer each question by single keystrokes, typing letter Y for yes and N for no.

Lucian found this bit strange, but he understood and agreed to answer.

She asked the first question. It shocked him and sent blood rushing to his head and his cock at the same time.

"Did you have a jerk off after putting me to bed on the cruise?"

His finger hovered over the N key then typed Y, as he couldn't lie.

This set the tone for the next few questions.

She carried on asking questions for the next twenty minutes. Lucian was surprised how easy it was to tell almost a virtual stranger about his most dark sexual desires.

He told her that he liked to watch her doing her make-up and he found kneeling at her feet exciting, and it had turned him on.

He answered all her questions and then typed:

"Please, could I ask you a question, Mistress?"

He waited, and she didn't reply.

He asked again thinking the connection had dropped, but she typed,

"Are you kneeling Lucian."?

He typed:

"N."

"Are you naked Lucian?"

Lucian typed:

"N."

"Well get naked and kneel down for me Lucian."

"Yes, Mistress."

Then quickly stripping he knelt on the carpet and typed again:

"Can I ask you the question now Mistress?"

He smiled as she typed:

"Y."

"Why did you slap me, I thought you liked me?"

He hesitated before pressing send and glancing up he saw the tiny red light of his webcam was on!

Shrinking the Yahoo messenger screen, he saw that his Skype box was open and showing him as being "available." He appeared to be connected with someone, but there was no name. He typed "Hello" in the message box.

There was no reply, but the red light suddenly went off.

Lucian returned to Yahoo Messenger and hit send to Debra.

Debra's response came back, and it surprised him.

"I slapped you because I do like you Lucian."

Lucian went to reply, but Debra was no longer online. However, he had received two emails from her.

The first one gave instructions telling him to strip naked to kneel down.

"I am already naked, Mistress," he said to himself.

The next part of the email said he was to go and find a few items before opening the next email.

He ran down the list with curious excitement.

- The gold leather cock strap

- Two wooden clothes pegs

- A needle

- A black permanent marker

- A face cloth or small towel.

After a quick search, he found all of the items. Lucian picked up his laptop and took it through to the bedroom. He put the laptop on his bed and knelt down with the towel between his knees. To his surprise, he had a hard on, and his balls were starting to ache.

He opened Debra's second email. Debra stated that if he was to have her attention, then he must pay for that privilege. Not in money terms, but he must sacrifice certain things if he was going to be allowed to be in her presence. Be it in person or online.

He read the next set of instructions. They were more exciting; Lucian's heart raced faster, and his cock throbbed with anticipation.

Debra had instructed him to put the gold strap around his cock and balls. What she stated was that under no circumstances was he to touch him self. Reading these words he felt as if could cum without a single rub!

She then instructed him to put a wooden clothes peg on each nipple. Lucian hesitated, feeling slightly foolish.

He picked up the clothes pegs and tried them on his finger testing how much they pinched.

He read the next line.

"Lucian, get on your knees! Get the pegs on your nipples for me, Now!"

He flushed as if she was in the room standing over him and had seen his hesitation. Lucian put the pegs on as she instructed. He gasped as one then the other pinched his nipples. The pinching pain made him feel tense and horny.

The next instruction was to take the black marker and to write an "M" on the inside of his wrist. Lucian did this and looked at the M he had written. Lucian smiled; it was like writing the name of a girl you fancied in school on your pencil case.

As he knelt there with the clothes pegs on his nipples, his feet started to go to sleep. Finally, he was to take the needle and press the sharp point into his thumb.

"Oh My God, she wants him me to draw blood!"

"Ok well here goes," he said out loud,

He gritted his teeth and jumped as point pierced the skin of his thumb.

He watched as a small drop of blood appeared. As the droplet grew Lucian took a tissue and made a bloody thumbprint on the surface.

He was to show her this as proof he had obeyed her wishes and that he was worthy of her time.

Lucian looked up and in horror realised that the webcam light was on again!!

"Fuck! Someone's watching me!" he shouted.

He jumped to his feet and slammed the laptop lid down. Still naked and with the clothes pegs hanging from his nipples, Lucian ran into the bathroom. He pulled the pegs from his nipples tossing them into the sink. The pressure hadn't been much at first, but as the blood flowing back into them, they throbbed and burned. He wouldn't have thought that so little pressure would cause such an intense sensation and hurt that much.

Looking at himself in the mirror he said out loud "What the fuck am I doing!!"

Returning to the bedroom, he didn't fire up the laptop again for fear of more instructions or unwanted webcam intrusions. As Lucian lay in bed, he was in turmoil with his mind flashing with images of Debra, her smoking, her ruby red lipstick, and her high heels.

The invasion of the laptop was very scary he didn't know who it was. Who would or could do such a thing?

Was it Debra? Lucian seriously doubted it was her. He would ask her next time, but he had a feeling it was something far more sinister than just Debra checking her instructions were being carried out properly.

Lucian had to admit that he really liked Debra but was freaked out by the research he had done. He was deeply unsettled by the thoughts of getting further involved and starting to want, or worse still, need this type of sexual excitement.

He tossed and turned in his bed unable to sleep or get his mind to rest. At 2.30 am Lucian got up made a coffee and nervously approached his laptop.

Thankfully it was blank and the small LED camera light was black. Opening up a word document he began to type:

Dear Debra.........

An hour later he had written a long rambling letter, starting with his regret that he couldn't accept her offer of the house.

He told her he had completely fallen for her. He

admitted he was scared of this new sexual excitement; but was worried he wouldn't be able to stop if she asked him to do more extreme things.

He was flattered of course, but he felt he just couldn't be her submissive.

Finally, he wrote he thought it would be best if they didn't carry on seeing each other anymore.

He pressed the send key then immediately regretted posting the email. He should have slept on it!

Finally, he went to sleep half wishing he had not sent the email letter, but the other half pleased he had acted before it was too late.

Chapter 27

A short distance away, but a million miles in cyber connections, Dominic sat reading Lucian's email grinning to himself.

So he doesn't want a Mistress! Well, I do! If that's the case, he won't have her, and I will.

Dominic rewrote the rambling email, changing it to read that Lucian didn't want anything to do with Debra and her freaky sex life or her money.

He pressed send sitting back smiling, pleased with his handiwork. Dominic would, of course, monitor the response and intercept that too.

The following morning Dominic was preparing to go to work and after showering and shaving, he dressed then checked his email.

There was an email from Debra to Lucian.

He quickly read Debra's eloquent reply to Lucian's attempt to break off the relationship.

For some strange reason, Lucian's original email had got through, even though Dominic had replaced it with his own. He didn't understand why and would need to investigate later.

Dominic didn't have time to do it now, so he quickly set a program up from Furious Boy. He sent a set of photos to Lucian's phone and laptop.

Chapter 28

A young couple were purchasing a rundown fabric mill on the outskirts of Reading in Berkshire. The couple were going to refurbish the building into business units for rental.

Lucian spent a good part of the day on the phone with the planning department.

As Lucian waited on hold, he clicked on his Yahoo messenger, in the hope Debra had responded to his email letter. There were no messages or emails in his inbox. He now regretted sending it and was nervous about her reply.

Later that evening, Lucian was watching TV when his phone pinged with an incoming text message. Swiping his iPhone, the number was withheld, but he opened the message.

It showed a picture of a dead bird, its neck was broken and its head twisted at an impossible angle. There was no caption or message, just the bird.

Lucian deleted the message, sat back to resume watching TV when the text alert went again. Opening his phone the bird photo was back. Then a series of texts came in all at the same time. He counted nine new messages, all identical containing the dead bird. Lucian began to delete them, but as quick as he did they popped up again. Thirteen more texts arrived. He just couldn't get rid of them fast enough, so in frustration, he turned his phone off.

He went over to his laptop and opened the Yahoo email. There were seventy-two emails in the inbox. Opening one he saw the dead bird again. There was no message and no return address. Lucian suddenly felt scared. This was so weird.

He checked down the inbox, highlighting the emails. Lucian was just about to "delete all" when he saw the sixty-seventh email was from Debra.

He opened her mail, deleting the others.

Dear Lucian

Thank you for your email. I think we need to discuss this in person when I return to the UK, meet me at my house in Winchester.

Kindest Wishes

Debra

That evening Dominic sat at his computer watching the mailbox remotely reading the email from Debra.

He hadn't managed to intercept her mail or send his adapted email from Lucian.

His well-worded email saying that he (Lucian) didn't want to be involved with a freak like Debra and her sick twisted world had been returned.

This meant Lucian's original mail had got through, and Debra had received it. This was very strange, as the mail server seems to detect his bogus IP address and blocked it.

Dominic was livid.

He clicked a few commands and easily got back into Lucian's computer. He activated the camera on Lucian's laptop then sat back to watch him as he sat typing. He had managed to disable the red LED light on the laptop's webcam after Lucian's reaction the night before.

He moved remotely into Lucian's pictures finding some of Debra and Lucian having dinner and Debra smoking on a large ship's deck. He also saw photos of a jazz singer in a bar. And two camp looking men dressed in suits and Lucian dressed like James Bond.

To Dominic's delight, there were also some of Debra dressed in stockings, smoking on a balcony. Her hair was blowing in the wind. Her eye makeup was heavily applied, and she was wearing extremely high-heeled shoes. These were obviously from Lucian's iPhone, so Dominic quickly copied them onto his hard drive for closer analysis later. There was a short eight-second video with Lucian kneeling in what looked like a bathroom, presumably from the same place others had been taken.

Dominic started to import the photos, as he did so he felt his cock stiffen. He decided when he had finished he would get his black leather pouch that contained his favourite set of pegs, clamps and his leather cock ring. Tonight he would do one of his own unique "Self-abuse Sessions."

It was evident that Debra was still in Dubai.

Dominic had plans for Debra's return and the removal of Mr Palmer Jones.

Chapter 29

The day of Debra's return couldn't come quick enough. Lucian moped about doing simple tasks and working late into the evening to pass the time.

He hadn't heard anything from Debra for a few days, and his email box was empty.

Thankfully Lucian hadn't received any more dead birds or emails from "Furious boy" on his laptop. Although the other evening, he couldn't put his finger on it, even though the webcam light wasn't on he had a strange sensation that he was being watched.

Debra had said they were to meet upon her return to talk about his letter. He still regretted sending it but looked forward to seeing Debra again.

Lucian was sitting watching TV when his mobile rang with a "Withheld number." Lucian didn't answer it and let it go to voice mail.

It was Marcus calling to say that Lucian was to attend a meeting on Friday at Debra's Winchester House. He said he would email the time and address. Lucian listened to the message again and then deleted it.

Before going to bed, Lucian checked his computer but there was nothing in the inbox.

The next morning Lucian got up early, as he had to attend a meeting in central London. On his return to the office, Lucian checked his email again.

There was a message from the Quininci Group giving the date for this coming Friday and the address in Winchester with a postcode reference.

Lucian made a note of the details but failed to see that there was an attachment to the email.

Later that evening he opened the email again at home, this time seeing the attachment he quickly opened it.

It read as follows:

My Dear Lucian

I have the need for a submissive to be my partner.

I find you very attractive, and you seem willing to please me. I am returning to the UK in a few days and wish to see you again, but only if you are willing to obey my wishes, consent to my desires and be worthy of my time.

My husband was my devoted submissive and my life partner. We had been together for over twenty-five years, enjoying many years of sessions and sharing many wonderful experiences.

I believe you would enjoy the lifestyle, but you must enter with a clear understanding of what is required of you.

To get started you must agree to my rules:

If you accept these, then I will see you on my return and begin your training and initiation into the Lifestyle. I will be your Mistress and help you embark on your journey to becoming my collared submissive.

These are my Mistress Rules. There are no exceptions or flexibility; they are absolute for you to be my submissive.

Must do's

1. Text your Mistress every morning without fail.

2. When Mistress wishes to smoke, you will light cigarettes holding an ashtray for your Mistress.

3. You will serve The Mistress her food, wine and coffee on a silver tray.

4. When required you will Worship your Mistress on

your knees while she smokes.

5. You are required to shave your pubic hair when you are with your Mistress.

6. You must text or email your Mistress at the end of every day.

7. When taking pain from your Mistress, you must never complain or say NO.

8. You will not have intercourse with The Mistress unless she wants you to please her.

9. Mistress will expect you to wear a collar and a cock strap when pleasing her.

10. You will not come or masturbate when not with The Mistress.

11. When travelling, you will drive the Mistress and may be required to dress in a suit and peaked cap.

12. The Mistress will need to have food prepared and served to her.

13. Your asshole will be abused and subject to pain with dildo's and strap-ons.

14. You will be required to take abuse in the form of being slapped and spat at.

15. You will be required to kneel and be humble before your Mistress.

16. You will be required to take canes, crops and whips to carry marks for your Mistress.

There is no alternative or negotiation on these rules and if you do accept them it will be unconditional and without question. It is a form of moral contract, and it is a commitment of the heart. But it involves your mind, body and soul.

Read it again carefully Lucian and text me your reply.

If you agree and consent to my rules, I will see you at my house when I return to the UK. If no, then have a nice life.

I await your decision.

Kindest Regards

Debra (Mistress D)

Lucian read it, then read it twice more, hardly believing what it was saying.

What was he was supposed to do?

If he chose to not go, he was to send a simple text "N" message by midnight. This would mean he would never see Debra again; he would carry on with his life never knowing what might have happened. If he agreed and turned up at the appointed time, he would be accepting his fate giving up his choice. He would become involved with a lifestyle that would mean his life would never be the same again.

He lay awake thinking about what Debra had written, he wondered if he could handle it. Sleep suddenly claimed him, the text message with the capital "N" written on his phone was never sent.

Dominic downloaded Debra's attachment and printed it out. Then with a scalpel, he sliced neatly between each one of Debra's rules until he had a pile of thin strips. Dominic then slowly set light to each piece. He ignored the pain as the flame neared his fingertips. Dominic lit each piece in turn until he had a pile of ashes on his desk. When Dominic had burned the last one, he stood up raised his hands high above his head. Then slammed them down onto the table, sending a cloud of ashes into the air; the force caused his computer monitor to topple over.

Chapter 30

It was Sunday morning and the roads were clear as Debra's driver drove her back from Gatwick.

The return flight back had been comfortable, and Debra had managed to sleep for some of the journey. She had taken a light breakfast as the aircraft made its descent to Gatwick airport. The trip had gone well and Debra had enjoyed the sights and smells of Dubai with its incredible wealth and splendour. She had felt safe in the old Gold Souk and wandering the markets in the old city. Debra shopped, attended some meetings and spent a day at the Grand Prix.

While in Dubai, Debra viewed an apartment complex, owned by an English multi-millionaire named Charles McCreedy. Charles was keen for Debra to invest in the new development. Charle's right-hand man, a smooth talking, good looking Australian called Adam Bennett, showed her around. But after only a few minutes, Debra informed Adam she was leaving, she loved Dubai and its culture, but she felt no passion for this sterile building. Even with its glamorous reception areas and high specification finish, she was not impressed.

Debra preferred Venice and would travel to Italy in few weeks to look at a property there. She loved the old city and had visited many times. Debra felt more inspired there, as the refurbishments of old palaces were far more exciting than the rather souless Dubai projects. If Lucian passed his first initiation session, she might take him with her. Lucian said he had never been to Venice.

Debra checked her phone for messages, ignoring the usual bullshit requests that charity organisers send to wealthy people. She was regularly invited to attend this, sponsor that. Debra despised all mainstream charities, preferring to donate to causes she felt strongly about. Knowing her money would make a difference, not just line the pockets of the charity founders. One leading "Charity" announced a £3million profit the previous year. She was disgusted that a "Charity" could make "profit" The money was supposed to the causes and not the shareholders.

As the car headed towards Winchester, she made a couple of calls speaking to Marcus and Carol to ensure everything was set for her return. Carol mentioned the CCTV man. Debra thought for a moment then recalled, she had asked Carol to find a CCTV contractor who could fit a new security system to the house.

Her husband had installed state of the art Internet

servers and encrypted email to prevent spying. Her husband had pleaded with her to install more security, but she never did.

Debra's thoughts turned to Lucian.

If Lucian accepted her rules, she would show him the "Red Room", where he would be tested to see if he was worthy to accompany her in more intense sessions and sharing the intoxicating feeling of "The Lifestyle."

Lucian had shown signs of being very submissive, obeying her simple wishes. He also confessed to having a massive shoe fetish.

Debra had smiled at this as she had over two hundred pairs of shoes, ninety per cent of them were high heels.

He had been very honest and frank, saying he had had fantasies about dating rich, classy women, with long dark hair. Lucian also said he favoured femme-fatale women, in high heels who wore red lipstick and smoked. She loved to smoke often finding it sexy and was delighted that Lucian had said he liked it too.

Debra would make Lucian get heavily involved in her smoking fetish. She would see how he would take to being made to kneel and do the duties her husband had found so difficult to perform. Debra had no intention of giving up even though she knew it was socially unacceptable. Her husband had never smoked and disliked the fact Debra enjoyed it. Knowing her husband disapproved she would torture him by making him watch her smoke, holding her ashtray in his cupped hands while kneeling before her. Debra would occasionally flick ash onto his chest or onto his hard cock. If she were feeling cruel, she would make him open his mouth and tap ash onto his tongue. She delighted in his reaction of disgust and would get him to open his mouth again showing her his blackened tongue and spit into his mouth to help the ash go down. He would groan and plead, she would laugh, and although nearly sixty-seven years old she would call him a "dirty little boy."

There were other duties and tasks that Lucian would be introduced to, and some were quite extreme. Debra would enjoy seeing where his limits were and how far he was prepared to go to please her sexually. Debra had sent the rules and given him the chance to say he couldn't handle it. Lucian hadn't texted her to say No, so she was preparing to have a session with him to see if he had what it takes to be her sub.

Debra and her late husband had been involved in many sessions. It had taken years for him to completely submit to her. Once he had given up his body and mind to her, she had total control over his sexuality. Right up to the day of his death he was totally devoted and worshipped her every move. He had said he had no desire for it to be any other way. If he couldn't have Debra as his Mistress and be involved in sessions, he didn't want to have sex at all.

Debra had sent Lucian a set of rules and would later send him instructions for when he arrived. She was planning to introduce Lucian into the world of submission and train him to worship and adore her. Of course, he had the option to opt out and return to his normal life. She hoped he would give himself totally to her desires and wishes.

The car took the Winchester exit, and Debra texted Carol to let her know of her imminent arrival.

Chapter 31

For several months now Dominic had been seeing a counsellor. He would have to cancel his appointment as it clashed with the day and time he was due to visit the house in Winchester.

He had been attending the sessions each week in an attempt to decipher his mixed up mentality. Dominic got days of deep dark depression he found it difficult to snap out of. As he got older, he decided there may be some value in seeing someone.

The first meeting was awkward as the counsellor was an attractive woman in her mid-fifties with dark shoulder length hair. She had classic good looking facial features. She dressed smartly and wore light but well-applied makeup. Dominic was instantly attracted to her.

She was calm, supportive and listened to him recalling accounts of his abusive father and constantly criticising mother. Once he relaxed in the councillor's company, Dominic would relate stories of how his father and mother would mistreat him as a young boy. He explained his sleep was haunted by night terrors and he found it hard to relax and sleep deeply without the aid of sleeping pills. The counsellor told Dominic these were the result of all the years of abuse. And he would have to deal with the issues one at a time and his recovery may take years.

At a later appointment, she asked Dominic about his fantasies and if he masturbated often. She also asked if he had he ever had sex with a prostitute. Dominic was reluctant to speak about his sexual preferences and despite the counsellors prompting, he didn't answer her questions. She didn't push the subject and tried on several occasions to explore the sexual side of his mind. On one occasion she mentioned, "Mother Complex". Dominic, had read about Oedipus and the obsession with a mother figure. He was fuming and told her he didn't want to fuck his mother and anyway she was dead!

Dominic didn't seek a mother replacement, he just wanted to find and spend time with a full-grown woman, not a girl or a trophy wife. Dominic told the counsellor after a tearful session that every day he lived with firm belief he would find the perfect woman.

What Dominic wanted to say was he believed if he could find a woman who could be a "Mistress" to him, he would free himself from these feelings. A Mistress would make up for all the love and attention he had been deprived of all his life. Finally, after months of counselling, Dominic admitted he sought a confident woman who was preferably wealthy, well-bred and educated.

Dominic explained how difficult it was to meet a real woman. Most women who he came in contact with were either young women with a footballer's wives mentality or grey haired older ladies with ageing husbands. These older types gave all their affection to their cats, dogs or horses, while their husband had sordid affairs with boys or young gold diggers whose only interest was in their money. Dominic had no idea that by going to Winchester he would encounter the woman of his dreams.

Chapter 32

The electric gates swung open and the car pulled into the driveway, gliding to a stop in front of the house.

The driver opened the car door for Debra who was greeted by Carol and Marcus. She hugged Carol and patted Marcus's pert bottom. Carol smiled saying everything was prepared, and asked if Debra would like some lunch. Debra said she would like something light. As they walk up the steps to the house, Carol reminded Debra about the fund raising dinner that evening. And as Debra was the primary sponsor she must attend.

Debra thanked her and asked what time she needed to be there, and Carol replied "7.30pm".

As she sat in the kitchen eating, Carol informed Debra that she had had found a recommended CCTV security contactor. Carol had checked that the website reviews from his customers were positive. He was expensive, but then Carol didn't think that was a problem. Debra thanked Carol and asked Marcus if he had managed to source the equipment they would need.

Marcus said it had taken some time, and he had been forced to go several different suppliers to get the exact specification. But he had managed to source all of it as instructed. Debra thanked him and asked where the equipment was. Marcus said it was all stored inside the roof space of the Pool House.

Debra said "Good Boy". Marcus smiled but said nothing.

She then asked Carol when the CCTV man was coming to do the installation, as she was going to be busy for a few days.

Carol said "The CCTV man is due on Tuesday at 11.30 am, is that convenient? I can change it if not."

"No it's fine" Debra smiled

After lunch, Debra said she was going to take a nap then get ready for the evening dinner engagement. She asked Marcus if the Red Room Chambers were prepared. He confirmed that he had got them ready the day before, and they were waiting for her inspection.

Debra asked if Judge Roberts had been to visit, and if had he enjoyed his stay. Marcus confirmed that the learned judge had spent a good two hours in a gold cage in room 1. He had eaten his all of his cold porridge from the dog bowl and sobbed like a child to be released.

"Good, I will send him some harsher instructions for next time," said Debra

"Also, I am seeing Lucian on Friday and possibly again at the Cottage shortly after."

Marcus then asked, "Will anyone else being joining you on Friday?"

"No, it will just be Lucian and I."

Marcus and Carol exchanged glances. Marcus couldn't help but snigger behind his hands. Carol dug him in the ribs. Debra noticed and placing her hands on her shapely hips. Addressing them both and firmly stated,

"Look you two, I want complete privacy for the weekend no interruptions under any circumstances. Is that clear!"

Marcus and Carol both as one said, "Yes Mistress."

Finishing her lunch, she asked, "Anything else?"

Carol informed Debra of a few other messages and calls to the office. Marcus, serious now, said there was something she should be aware of. The security system had been alerted to a couple of attacks, someone was doing some deep searching for Debra's profile.

He said that PRQ in Sweden had emailed to say they

had been contacted too, but they couldn't trace the source. Debra thanked them both and went upstairs.

The meeting with the CCTV guy was on Tuesday and although tired from travelling she thought it was important to have the work done. It had been her late husband's wish that she would be safe, and the house would be secure at all times. She would speak to the IT guys at PRQ tomorrow and see what they made of these personal profile searches.

It might have been that smooth-talking Australian Adam from Dubai. He had clearly had an eye for her, wanting to take her to dinner in Dubai after the condo complex viewing. With Debra cutting short the viewing he probably was trying to find her number.

Other than that she didn't know.

Chapter 33

The night before the Winchester meeting, Dominic went to bed at 10.30 pm. On this occasion, he slept well and awoke before the alarm at 6.20 am to a bright and sunny morning. Dominic dressed in his black combat trousers and steel toe capped army boots. He selected one of the many branded polo shirts with a square company logo on the breast.

His van, a silver Mercedes Sprinter, had blacked out windows, reinforced floors, chrome wheels and enhanced suspension. The signage and number plates were interchangeable. The dashboard console was GPS satellite connected, with a high-speed mobile 4G network. The alarm system was connected to his phone allowing him to access the mini cameras on the van.

Leaving London, he travelled down the M3 motorway listening to a local radio station. Dominic liked music and had been sent to piano lessons as a child. Due to his dyslexia, he could not retain the sheet music or remember the scales from one week to the next. His mother would scold him, making him practice for hours after church service on the old out of tune piano they kept there. His music teacher was a horrible woman, a friend of his mother's who believed that she could force him to learn by applying punishments.

Arriving outside the house, Dominic activated a tiny microdrone. He did a quick sweep of the house, pool and the grounds. Dominic sent the drone high over the roofline, stopping when he noticed a small grey metal box half hidden by the chimney breasts. It was not an alarm casing or a relay telephone box. This type of box indicated the property was on a private and secure network.

As Dominic checked his watch, he recalled the message "Don't be late". At 10.58 am he pressed the intercom, a buzzer sounded, and the gates swung smoothly open. Dominic drove up the gravel drive parking outside the front door; his phone dinged with a text message "Don't park there!!" He drove the van past the BMW and a powder blue Bentley Turbo R, the ones he had seen on the Google Maps view.

His phone dinged again. "Come around the back to the kitchen door."

He walked through a gap in the nine-foot hedge onto the patio, a short, middle-aged woman with brown hair and bright green eyes came to meet him.

"Hello you must be Dominic, please follow me."

She took him through to a large high-ceilinged ornate hallway. The flooring was polished black and white marble tiles with expensive looking rugs. The walls carried tasteful art and beautiful occasional tables held sculptures of Greek Goddesses. The lady led Dominic into a large study that looked out over the well-kept gardens.

"Please take a seat, can I get you a drink or a cup of tea maybe?"

Dominic sat down on the leather chesterfield sofa and replied: "No thank you."

She left Dominic alone giving him the opportunity to look around the room. He couldn't see any obvious cameras or already installed sensors. The ornate desk had an Apple Mac Pro laptop and a Panasonic phone system.

After a few minutes, the middle-aged lady returned with a leather folder under her arm. Dominic took out his notebook and pen and said, "How did you hear about my services?

The lady just smiled and said, "Ms Fielding will be with you shortly" and placed the folder on the classic leather desktop and exited the room. Dominic realising his mistake got up and walked over to the bookshelves. Scanning the titles, he noticed several business books and autobiographies of famous racing drivers and well-known celebrities.

To Dominic's surprise, there was a selection of rare paperback books including "Venus in Furs" "120 days of Sodden" and a "Mistress Handbook". By Mistress Lorelei. He selected the book opened it to find it was signed by the author, to Mistress D.

Just as Dominic started to study the book, a well-spoken female voice behind him said, "Have you read my requirements, or are you too busy being nosey?"

Feeling embarrassed Dominic flushed and quickly replaced the book. He felt like a naughty schoolboy being caught trying to reach the top shelf girly magazines in the local newsagents. Standing before him with long flowing dark hair, and a perfectly proportioned curvy womanly figure was Debra Fielding.

Debra was dressed in a tight fitting white blouse, a black knee length pencil skirt, high red stilettos and perfect makeup. Dominic couldn't stop staring; she looked Italian or Spanish with her dark hair and eyes and evenly tanned skin. Her look was somewhat fierce with dark eye shadow, false eyelashes, and full red lips, which carried half a smile at his obvious discomfort at being caught out.

Dominic was in awe, he could not believe eyes, was this really Debra, the Mistress, in front of him. Dominic hurried to the desk and picked up the folder. Fumbling to hold it, in his haste all papers inside dropped out onto the floor.

As he bent down to collect the fallen papers, a high stiletto heel stood on them preventing him from picking them up. Looking up Dominic gazed directly into the face of a goddess. Debra Fielding was The MISTRESS, right here, right now, in person. He could not take his eyes off her or utter a single word.

"Clumsy boy," she said and stepping away she turned to face the windows.

Taking a long slim cigarette from a silver box on the bookshelf she put it to her perfect lips. Dominic hurried to pick up all the papers and put the folder back on the desk. With her back to him, she pointed with a red-manicured finger towards a gold lighter on the coffee table. Dominic picked it up and handed it to her. Debra flicked it, lit the cigarette drawing deeply on the smoke.

She looked directly at him and said, "Do you always wear your dirty boots inside?"

"I'm so sorry Ms Fielding" his head was still screaming it's Mistress Debra!

Dropping to one knee, he struggled to remove his boots. Then standing there in his socks he looked at Debra who exhaled smoke, opened the patio doors in a swift motion she said, "Walk with me."

As she left a steady breeze, blew the voile curtains into his face. Pushing the light material aside and still in his socks Dominic hurried to catch up with her. He almost walked into the back of Debra as she suddenly stopped, turned, and looked at him. In her heels she stood nearly three inches taller than Dominic; still smoking she looked him up and down.

Dominic suddenly remembered he had left the folder on the desk and didn't have it with him. He mumbled, "I'm sorry Ms Fielding, let me just go and get the folder."

Dominic rushed back to the study. Debra flicked her now half smoked cigarette butt into the flowerbeds and walked back towards the study. Nearly colliding with Dominic as he came rushing out of the door again.

Debra paused before re-entering the room and said,

"Not a great start?"

As she sat in the chair, she watched Dominic read through the notes. Lighting another cigarette Debra waited for him to look up. When he did, she extended a long fingered hand as if to shake hands and greet Dominic. But as Dominic put his hand out to shake hers she turned his palm over flicking the cigarette ash into his palm. He withdrew his hand quickly, not because it burned him but more through surprise.

She laughed and sat back drawing again on the cigarette, draping an elegant arm over the back of her chair. Dominic cleared his throat and thinking this wasn't going anything like he had imagined!

Dominic said, "I have a lot of experience in this line of work, but I was curious as to what the grey coloured box near your chimney was for."

Before answering Debra smiled and then said, "You are very observant Dominic but can you see an ashtray in here?"

He looked around and saw a cut glass ashtray on the sideboard. Rising he brushed the ash from his palm into it, returning to his seat he placed it on the desk next to Debra.

Dominic studied the contents of the folder. The list of the materials was impressive. Some of the items weren't domestic specification and Dominic was surprised that these were available outside of the military or specialist agencies. Dominic had to think hard to recall how some of this equipment functioned.

He felt a tingle of excitement as obtaining these items would be a real challenge. He would need to call in a favour or two from his underworld contacts to get this type of gear.

Debra put out her second cigarette. Blowing smoke over Dominic's head she said, "Can you handle a job like this?"

He had installed similar equipment on a large project for a business premises with his ex-boss, but had never handled something of this level alone.

He said to Debra, "This is a big job and may take some time to install once I have the gear together."

"That's not the question I asked you, Dominic."

Not smiling she repeated, "I said could you handle a job like this?"

He looked at her again taken aback by her beautiful velvet brown eyes and perfect skin.

"Yes," he said.

"Are you sure"

"Yes," he said again, "but it will cost a lot and will take me some time to get necessary hardware and do the programming."

"The cost is not an issue you need to worry about!"

"How long will you need to do the complete project?" Debra asked.

Dominic thought for a moment, he estimated it would take a day to do the site recon, two days to put in the equipment, a day to test it and a further day to be on call if there were any problems.

"Five days total, as soon as I have the equipment."

Debra looked at Dominic and said, "I want it done urgently and certainly not taking five days. Can you do that?"

She looked at him in his socks and with the folder perched on his lap. Dominic looked at Debra who was looking straight back at him.

"I think so."

"You think so?"

"Yes" he replied

"Good," she said, "Can you start the recon now?"

Dominic stuttered "Right now? But we will need to order the gear and have it delivered before I can start."

Debra stared at Dominic with her intense brown eyes and said, "Look can you do it or not, it's very simple Dominic?"

"I suppose so…. But wait."

"Problem?" she said again raising her eyebrow.

"Er, no…it's just the gear will need special ordering, may take weeks,"

"We have all the equipment already," Debra said not breaking eye contact with Dominic.

He was surprised and said "You have all of this already?" holding up the sheet.

Debra smiled and just nodded.

Dominic scanned the list again shaking his head in amazement.

Rising from her chair Debra stood before Dominic in her high heels, looking down at him. As she moved closer, his face was just above her plunging cleavage.

Debra's perfume was strong and heady, and she smelt amazing.

As she passed him, she said "The gear' as you call it, is in the pool house, Marcus will show you where to start."

"Marcus?" asked Dominic

"Marcus is my PA, and he will show you where I want things to be set up."

With that, she left the room.

The door opened again it was Carol. She smiled and said, "You need to come with me to find Marcus, he will show you around and where everything is."

"Ok thank you," said Dominic.

He followed Carol out of the open patio doors, stopping to put his boots on again. They walked across the courtyard towards the outbuildings. As they neared the pool house, Dominic looked back and up at the top floor windows. He thought he caught a glimpse of Debra smoking and watching him. Dominic nearly tripped over a low flowerbed; stumbling forward he almost knocked into Carol. Regaining his balance, Dominic looked up again at the windows, but Debra had gone.

Carol took no notice and carried on towards the pool house. As they approached the buildings, the pool house door opened, and a young athletic looking man stepped out to meet them.

Carol said "Marcus will show you where everything is" and left. Marcus didn't speak he just held the door open for Dominic and followed him into the outbuilding.

The pool pump house was warm and smelt slightly of chlorine. In the corner of the building was a wrought iron staircase, which Marcus ascended with effortless grace, indicating Dominic follow him.

Once on the level Marcus turned to Dominic and said in a well-spoken but slightly camp manner, "It's all here, everything that's on the spec sheets. Check it, and then we can go across to the house."

Dominic opened the folder and surveyed the pile of boxes. He could see they varied in size ranging from a matchbox to a washing machine. There was no indication as to the contents of the boxes other than a bar code label on each side and top. Marcus went back down the staircase skipping off the last step and headed for the door.

He called over his shoulder, "Carol will serve tea in the

kitchen later."

Dominic nodded and set about the task of opening each box to check its contents, ticking it off the spec sheet.

After an hour Dominic had ticked off all of the equipment and went out of the pool house into the grounds. The sun was now shining, and the pool cover had been removed, the water looked clear and inviting.

As Dominic went out of the side entrance, he noticed the powder blue Bentley was gone, and Marcus was washing the BMW. A wet patch still showed on the gravel where the Bentley had been washed before it left.

Marcus ignored Dominic and carried on washing the car.

Returning to the pool house Dominic started to move the external equipment boxes down and load them onto a trolley. As he was doing so, Carol appeared and asked him if he would like tea.

Dominic said, "Yes please" and followed her into the spacious kitchen. He sat at the breakfast bar as Carol served him tea in a Royal Crown Derby china cup and saucer. He remembered how his mother used to drink her tea from a similar bone china cup. His father would fuss over her with a tea tray laying out chocolate biscuits on a matching Crown Derby plate.

Carol asked how it was going, and Dominic said it was all fine. Then he asked if Debra was still here. Carol said, "No she has business in Winchester, but will be back later."

Carol offered him a plate of sandwiches which he ate without asking any more of the many questions he had in his mind. Finishing his tea he returned to the pool house.

Dominic spent the rest of the afternoon planning and placing the cameras in the right locations. He worked hard putting cameras on the entrance gates, the front and back doors, and spent some time up on the roof positioning the roof cameras to get maximum coverage for each one.

It was almost 6pm when the gates swept open, and the powder blue Bentley drove in, coming to a halt in the now dry spot behind the newly washed and polished BMW. From his vantage point on the roof, Dominic could see the car and the driveway clearly. Dominic expected Debra to get out of the car. However, when the car door opened, a young woman with shoulder length straight dark hair got out. She was speaking on her phone and went straight to the house without pausing. Dominic was still standing on the high roof when Carol called his name from below. Once on the ground Marcus was waiting with a few smaller boxes and told Dominic to follow him. They went through the kitchen to a laundry room where a red velvet curtain was draped across the back wall.

Behind the curtain was an ornate lift door panel. Marcus swiped a card across a flat LED control panel, and the elevator door slid open.

"The control room is below here," Marcus said.

Stepping into the lift compartment, which was lined with purple velvet and had gold buttons, Marcus pressed "B", and the doors smoothly slide silently shut.

Dominic was conscious that there was not a lot of room in the lift and Marcus's aftershave was pungent; he had probably showered after cleaning the cars and changed into clean clothes. The elevator stopped without a jolt after its short decent and the doors slide silently open to reveal a well-lit space. The walls held exotic artwork, and the carpet was red and thick. Marcus stepped out, and Dominic followed him down the passage past Baroque style furniture and ornate golden light fittings. On both sides of the passage were black deep-buttoned leather covered doors. They both had gold lion head door knockers.

The doors were numbered "Room 1" and "Room 2". Marcus paid no attention to these doors, passing them without a word. He led Dominic to a plain black door on the left-hand side of the passageway. He ran his card over another panel and keyed in a code, the door slide open to reveal another room. Inside were banks of monitors and a console desk full of switches. Dominic was surprised to see that it appeared the house already had CCTV installed, as he could see the set of square screened monitors were all blank and the modems were not powered up.

Marcus pointed to the left of these monitors to an empty wall mounted rack. "The new screens will go here", he said.

"What about these? Dominic asked.

"They are nothing you need to worry about," Marcus said with a dismissive wave of his hand.

"Ok," said Dominic wondering what they did and where they were connected to.

Marcus said, "We will go back upstairs and I'll help you bring the rest of the kit down. The cameras will need to be networked and connected to the laptop Wi-Fi in the study too."

As they passed the black leather-clad doors, Dominic asked, "What's in those?" Marcus just said "Private" and scanned his card for the lift.

Returning, Dominic unboxed the items and worked through the kit setting up the new flat screen monitors on the wall brackets and connecting the equipment wirelessly to the remote cameras and began testing the feeds.

Once they were all live he activated the state of the art cameras. One by one they came online and began to work through their set up demo's, scanning left and right and zooming in and out. Dominic was impressed by the external cameras' lens range and the clarity of the image. As they continued to run through the default demos, Dominic turned and studied the other monitors.

Although the equipment was of an older design, it was undoubtedly expensive and of a high technical specification. Dominic studied the control console and pressed a few buttons. At his touch, the screens came to life and the consoles light up.

The older screens showed a red and black coloured room that resembled an S&M dungeon. Dominic couldn't believe his eyes, He thumbed the joystick, and the camera panned left and came to focus on a large gold cage, covered with a large black silk cloth. Studying the control panel again he found the camera microphone pushing up the slider he increased the playback volume. There were speakers mounted on the control room wall, and he could hear some sounds, which appeared to be coming from the gold cage. Dominic zoomed the camera to the base of the cage and could clearly see a human foot showing just below the hem of the silk cover. He increased the volume to maximum and the sound improved. To his surprise he could make out what seemed like a man crying and sobbing.

As he listened, a deafening voice came over the speakers "Turn that off!"

It was Marcus's voice. Dominic quickly hit the "kill" button on the console, and the monitors went dark again.

Marcus's camp and still angry voice came over the speakers again "If you are done down there come back up and meet me in the study."

Dominic stacked the empty boxes back onto the trolley and left the room. As he passed the black doors, he paused putting his ear to the leather covering and listened carefully. Unable to hear anything he pushed the trolley to the open lift door and got inside.

The elevator ascended and as the doors opened he was met by Marcus's angry face and folded arms.

"Follow me," he instructed and walked into the study, past the pile of kit boxes and perched his bottom on the edge of Debra's desk. He glared at Dominic and said, "You are not permitted to work that equipment under any circumstances. If I catch you doing anything other than what Debra requires I will remove you immediately and you will not be paid, is that clear?"

Dominic felt like an 11-year-old again being dressed down by his mother. He didn't speak at first then asked, "What's in those rooms then?"

Marcus jumped up and shouted in Dominic's face "I told you that is none of your bloody business! It's private, and I will not tell you again!!"

"Now get on with it and hurry up, I want you finished for today within the hour" and at that, he strutted past Dominic and left the room.

Chapter 34

Dominic sat at the ornate desk and set about configuring the Mac Air-Book Pro. The outside gate cameras came online, and he saw an identical blue Bentley pull up to the gates. He flicked to another camera and watched the twin car drive up to the house and stop. As the car pulled in behind the other Bentley, a silver-haired gentleman in a long grey coat and peaked cap got out of the car and opened the back door. The camera picked up the detail as Debra wearing her high-heeled shoes got out of the car and walked towards the house.

She had her hair down, and her fringe held back with a bejewelled clasp, and she wore a long fur coat. She was carrying a tan coloured attaché case; Carol met her at the door and took the case from her. Dominic heard her heels clicking on the hall tiles then silence as she passed onto the carpeted areas. Dominic wished he had hooked up the internal cameras so he could track her movements. As he turned around, Debra was standing in the study doorway.

She looked at Dominic and said, "I hear you have been a noisy Parker again."

He blushed and said, "I'm sorry Ms Fielding"

She walked towards him.

"I should think you are" she scolded him.

"I'm sorry," he repeated again.

Lighting a cigarette she said, "You are here to do a simple job, nothing more, do you understand me, Dominic?"

"Yes Madam," he said.

She blew smoke into the air.

"Very well, how much have you achieved today?"

He gave a brief summary of the work he had done that day. He said he still needed to install the alarm systems and hook up the internal cameras.

"Well you had better get busy then hadn't you?" she stated.

He rose to leave the study, as he did she said, "One more thing, what did you see downstairs?"

"Nothing!"

"Good and make sure it stays that way," she snapped.

As he went over the various room plans, Dominic made sure he had everything he needed. The hallway was the next installation, then the lounge, dining room, the study and lastly the back door to the kitchen. Taking an arm full of smaller camera boxes he went into the kitchen and put them in the hallway. It was clear that the upstairs was not to be included and there were only enough internal cameras for the downstairs areas.

After positioning all the cameras in the right places, Dominic went into the study to mount the ceiling units. He would still need to configure the laptop and activate the feeds. On entering the study, he was surprised to see that Debra had gone, but sitting at the desk was the young lady with the shorter dark hair.

She bore a striking resemblance to Debra, just about thirty years younger. Her makeup was subtle, and she wore a tight fitting navy blue skirt and a pale blue cashmere jumper. Like Debra, she wore high-heeled shoes. A quick glance at her thighs Dominic could see the suspender clasps under her skirt and knew instantly, like Debra, she was wearing stockings rather than tights. She was speaking on her mobile phone as Dominic entered.

"Look I don't care about that, I'm going, and that's final!"

Dominic put the camera boxes on the desk and said, "Excuse me I need to put up this camera and use the laptop."

The young woman looked him up and down, swiped her phone, and without saying another word stood up and walked past him out of the patio doors into the garden. Dominic fixed the camera in the ceiling corner and checked its position.

Sitting down at the desk, Dominic imagined he could still feel the warmth left from the young ladie's shapely bottom. He clicked a few screens logging into the cameras online programs then quickly activated the Wi-Fi again, and the cameras began to run through their test mode as before. While these were running, he took out his iPhone, tapped a few other screens and accessed his own online network. There was still no data on his previous searches.

Suddenly a screen popped up on his phone asking if he would like remote access to the new network he was installing. Dominic paused for a second wondering if he could hide the fact he had access if he set it up. If he did have remote access he could patch into the local Wi-Fi and monitor the systems for his house and van.

With this he could spy on the house and possibly on Debra. He would need to add some code to the install program in the control room downstairs to get full remote access. Dominic would need to bury the code deep within the operating system, where only a professional programmer would be able to trace and find it. He seriously doubted if Carol or the flamboyant Marcus would have that sort of IT expertise.

Once the systems were all functioning and the cameras working on the desktop Mac, Dominic went to find Marcus to get the access codes to the server room to complete the setup, and if possible to set up his spy feed.

He found Marcus in the kitchen talking to Carol.

"Charles won't be happy if she goes..." but he stopped speaking as soon as Dominic walked in and crossed his arms.

Marcus said to Dominic, "Took your time didn't you?"

Dominic didn't reply.

Marcus set off towards the lift saying, "Follow me."

Marcus called the lift, and after swiping his card, punched in the code, and this time Dominic memorised it. 2468 in a perfect cross. Not the most original code but one people could remember by sight. Dominic knew that a vast amount of passwords and key codes could be guessed in less than 2 seconds.

Once on the lower floor, Marcus waited by the lift, so Dominic went straight to the server room, not glancing at the leather covered doors. He configured the new cameras and put in a memory stick that in twenty seconds uploaded an access key into the operating systems command code. Dominic didn't access the full server module for fear of Marcus catching him. With the .exe program from the stick, he would try to get in via the Internet as he had the IP addresses of the servers.

On returning to the kitchen, Marcus informed Dominic that the next job was to install the alarm system. This involved a complex set of pressure sensors with sensitive door and window movement detectors. Like the rest of the equipment, the alarm system was state of the art and used temperature and air density monitors.

Dominic had installed similar systems in celebrity houses. He used Marcus's iPhone to set him up as the first responder. The alarm system was entirely web based, so Dominic sent a quick email from Marcus's phone to his own as "Back Up."

The time was now 9.45 pm and Dominic was exhausted and hungry. He would normally string a private job out over days, sometimes weeks, blaming technical reasons why the situation was more complicated or needed more time and consequently more money in fees. But with this job he was surprised that he had worked so hard without a break and that Debra had such an effect on him.

On returning to the kitchen, he found Carol making fresh coffee and setting out a plate of sandwiches and biscuits.

"All done?" she inquired pleasantly.

Dominic realised he had estimated five working days but had almost completed the job in just under 11 hours.

"Please tell me, Dominic, what is your day rate?" she asked

Dominic replied, "£350 plus expenses."

"Here is £500" and she passed him a small pile of £50 notes.

Dominic was momentarily stuck for words.

Then managed to say, "Thank you, but a few more things need to be tested."

At that point, Marcus walked back in.

"Is it all working correctly both inside and out?"

Dominic nodded as his mouth was full of chicken

sandwich.

"If that's the case I can take care of those last tests."

"Oh, ok then" replied Dominic

"Good in that case when you have finished your sandwich I will show you out."

Dominic said goodbye to Carol and thanked her for the sandwich. As they went into the hallway Dominic looked around to see if there was any sign of Debra, but there was none. He thought this woman Debra Fielding could be the answer to all his prayers, and he must find a way to see her again.

As Marcus opened the front door, Dominic asked, "Is Debra here?"

Sensing his interest, Marcus opened the large door but didn't reply.

Dominic paused on the threshold and asked, "Is Debra going to want anything else doing?"

Marcus said sternly, "No, she isn't!" and closed the front door on him.

Dominic was left on the doorstep and suddenly felt alone. Glancing up he was hoping to see Debra watching from an upstairs window, but there was no one there.

Unbeknown to Dominic, the new front of house camera panned silently left, watching him walk despondently to his cold van and climb in. As he drove the van out of the gates heading home his phone chirped with a text message. Opening his phone, he saw it was from the same number as earlier.

It read: "You did well today I'm pleased …Good Boy"

He found his way to the motorway and headed towards London, replaying the day's events in his head as he drove. He couldn't believe it, but he had met Debra Fielding, a real Mistress. Dominic knew then he had to see Debra again, to somehow tell her about his need to have her as his new Mistress.

That night he lay on his bed looking at downloads of the photos of Debra that he had retrieved from Lucian's phone. His mind was racing as he planned to destroy Lucian and find a way to take his place with Debra.

Chapter 35

Lucian woke early on Friday morning and his head filled immediately with thoughts of Debra. His heart began to beat faster as he remembered her rules and the fact he hadn't said "No." Lucian did find Debra very attractive. The wealth and the power she commanded made his head spin. He had been both excited and nervous when he was with her, and he missed that intensity when she had left.

Lucian had been in mental turmoil thinking about what being her "Submissive" would entail.

He had spent several more hours reading up on BDSM, learning what a Dom Mistress was and what was involved in being a "Sub" or "Slave". Lucian had downloaded a book called "The Mistresses Handbook by Mistress Lorelei. In the book, he had read about the different types of Mistresses: The Amazon Mistresses, School Madam Mistresses, and The Goddess Mistress.

He was sure Debra must be a Goddess Mistress.

She didn't seem to want to feminise him and make him

dress like a girl. Debra did not appear to want to whip or beat the shit out of him, as the Amazon Mistresses seem to do.

She was very controlling, and the rules were very precise regarding his sexuality. But then no more than a lover being faithful to his or her partner, it just was rather one sided in that she calls the shots, and he does everything she wants.

He had thought about this for a long time, and he actually liked the idea. He never had been an Alpha Male type, who needed to be the Top Dog. These types of men believed women were there to please them. Lucian, in fact, felt he was probably the opposite, he found the thought pleasing a lady turned him on.

Debra was clearly a wealthy and sophisticated woman, but she could be blunt, crude, and used harsh language to shock Lucian. He suspected she enjoyed offending his sensitivities; it was evident she had a very intense sexual side and wasn't shy about asking for her wants and desires to be satisfied.

He was worried about the weird messages and the freaky blood thing. Thankfully the emails from Furious Boy had not been repeated. Although from time to time he felt he was being watched.

He was due to meet Debra that evening at her house in

Winchester, so he had taken the afternoon off to get his haircut and to get ready to see her again.

Debra had sent a set of rules for Lucian to follow, which made him both excited and nervous after reading them. Lucian was in the shower, and as he washed his body, he recalled the instructions Debra had sent. Taking a razor, he took a deep breath as he began to shave his face and as per her instructions, his balls.

He shook his head in disbelief and smiled to himself, and in his best Sean Connery accent, said , "Just what have you got yourself into Mr Bond."

Dressing in one of the new outfits from the cruise, Lucian left for Winchester, but after fifteen minutes he pulled the car over and re-read Debra's instructions.

'Lucian I am granting you an audience with your Mistress. 5 minutes before your arrival you will text "5 minutes Mistress" to my mobile. You will arrive at 5.30pm precisely. Do not be late. If you are late for any reason, don't bother, just text the words "I'm not worthy Mistress".

Once you are at the house, Marcus will show you where to go. Do not speak to Marcus or do anything other than following his lead. Once in the room undress, pour me a glass of red wine, place it on the side table. Then kneel naked in front of my chair.

Put your head on the ground, ~~and~~ hands palm down in front of you. The cock strap will be tightly attached to your balls, which will be shaved as instructed. ....'

Lucian froze "Fuck, Fuck, Shit, and Bollocks!!" he cried out.

He had put the gold cock strap out in the bathroom to put in his pocket so he wouldn't forget it. What had happened... he had done just that. He had fucking forgotten it!

Screeching the car around in a fast 180 degrees, he floored it, racing back to his apartment. Driving too fast and not concentrating Lucian nearly mowed down a cyclist, who yelled "Fucking wanker!!" at him as he accelerated away. He sped through the streets like a maniac, taking corners like a stunt man in the movies; Lucian had never been so reckless in his entire life.

He screeched to a halt outside the apartment block and leaving the car running on the kerb, Lucian took the stairs two at a time. He dashed into the bathroom grabbed the gold leather cock strap and sprinted down the stairs again.

As he pulled the front door closed behind him, a traffic warden was looking into the open door; he stumbled back as Lucian pushed him out of the way saying, "Sorry, very late, sorry I'm so sorry."

The angry warden shouted at Lucian "Oi, you can't treat me like that, I'm a Special don't you know!"

He picked up his hat, straightened his jacket as Lucian sped away again. Lucian cursed himself for being so apologetic about everything. He even said he was sorry to a bloody traffic warden for God's sake.

"I'm not bloody sorry, I'm desperate" Lucian called back to him, although he was far out of sight.

He had been reading about extremely successful men who sought to find humiliation or abuse to impress and be accepted by a Mistress or Madam. They seemed to enjoy being abused and it made them stronger and even more successful. He had found it fascinating to read about these grown men who were a success in every aspect of their lives but lacked happiness.

Lucian was determined to show Debra he was strong and tough he was and could take as much as she wanted to give. He would be accepted by Debra, and like Samson, in the film, she would be impressed by his strength. Well, that was the plan whether he could actually do it remained to be seen.

As he raced at eighty-five miles an hour in the outside lane, he checked the time. According to the Sat Nav, he should get there with five minutes to spare.

As he turned off the motorway and joined the A road, he was just fifteen minutes away.

Waiting at the traffic lights, Lucian took out his phone and typed "5 Minutes Mistress" but didn't press send, just yet.

As he passed slowly through the traffic lights, he noticed a large workman in high visibility clothing staring at him. Checking his reflection in the driving mirror he was surprised to see how wild his eyes were and how flushed he was. His cheeks and neck were red, Lucian was sweating, and his hair was damp around his collar. Turning up the air-con on the dashboard and taking a sip of water from his glove box he tried to calm himself down.

As Lucian pulled into Debra's road, he sent the text "5 minutes Mistress" and got an immediate response.

"Good Boy."

He smiled as he approached the gates. Smoothly and silently they opened, Lucian drove up to the house and parked the car to the right of the main doors. The Bentley he had seen at the Westonbirt auction was there and another BMW. Getting out the car, Lucian felt in his pocket for the cock strap. He left his bag in the boot, as Debra's instructions were to pack for a couple of days, but not to bring anything into the house.

As he approached the door, it opened. Marcus stood there with a knowing smile and said simply "Follow me".

He took Lucian through the spacious kitchen and through a laundry room. A red curtain concealed a lift door at the rear. Lucian would never have known it was there. As the elevator descended, Marcus turned to Lucian.

"Debra is expecting you, do you have your instructions?"

Lucian dared not to speak but gave a quick series of nods, indicating he understood. He was clenching his fists to stop his hands shaking. Marcus opened the lift door to a red-carpeted hallway with black leather covered doors. Taking the lead, he walked to the end of the corridor to a door that faced straight towards them.

The other doors had number 1 and 2, but the one at the end didn't have a number. The door was slightly larger and had a gold lions head on the panel and a doorbell. Lucian felt his heart beat faster, and as Marcus pressed the doorbell, a buzzer sounded. The door catches released signalling it was open, and they could enter.

Marcus stepped aside and said grandly, "This is where I leave you, Mr Palmer Jones."

He bowed his head and Lucian nodded again. Marcus got back in the lift and the door slid silently closed. Lucian took a deep breath and pushed the door open to reveal a room that resembled a Hollywood film set. The theme was ancient Greece with red and black marble columns, giant urns of gold and long veils hanging from raised balconies. Real torches burned and water flowed from black marble ducts in the floor and walls. A large sunken bath with rose petals overflowed into the carved canals that ran the length of the room. The lighting was controlled and hidden behind decorative architraves. The room had a slight perfumed scent and subtle classical opera music played from hidden speakers.

Lucian looked around in amazement at the chamber's creation, a clever blend of modern technology and traditional styling. He walked across the room touching the first column thinking it might be cardboard or fake. The column was real, cold to the touch and solid marble. Across to one side through a veiled curtain was the bedchamber, with a huge Egyptian-style bed. It was a representation of a huge chariot and was covered with heavy cotton sheets and pillows. There were what looked like solid gold tables and a seven-foot dressing table with a triple mirror. On the dressing table was an array of makeup, perfumes, creams and potions. Lucian was lost in wonder when his phone pinged with a text.

Fumbling in his pocket for his phone he read a single message. "Ready?"

He realised he had been distracted by the room and wasn't doing as instructed. Turning to his left, there was an ornate candlelit recess. Lucian could see a large golden throne with a purple velvet seat. The striking high back of the throne was bejewelled with sparkling coloured gems. Just in front was a matching ornate footstool. Both were situated on a raised marble platform. The floor had a thick, luxurious red carpet. It covered the whole area apart from a ten-foot square of cream marble tiles in front of the throne.

Lucian remembered Debra's instructions and looked around for somewhere to change.

He saw a curtain on a circular rail, similar to a clothes shop changing room. Lucian undressed, hanging his clothes on the coat hangers supplied. Once naked he put on the cock strap and walked to the marble-floored area in front of the bejewelled throne. Lucian placed his foot on the slabs. To his surprise the floor was hot to the touch.

He knew he must do as he was instructed and maybe this was the first test. Walking onto the heated floor, Lucian had visions of burning coals. He had to concentrate to ignore the hotness as his feet absorbed the heat. Immediately in front of the thrones platform, the floor looked different. While the heated floor under his feet was highly polished marble, there was a smaller square approximately four feet square that was dull and matt.

He stepped onto it then instantly jumped back. It was freezing cold! Bending down Lucian touched the icy surface with his palm. Slowly he descended onto all fours and crawled onto the cold stone. Once fully onto the icy cold square, he realised both areas, the heat and the cold, were just about bearable. Maybe this was the first test, to take simple things that were uncomfortable. Lucian could manage them with a bit of willpower and effort.

Lucian had read this was a requirement in the "Lifestyle" to go beyond your comfort zone and endure unpleasantness. He had read about men and woman who trained to be in the SAS and slept on the moors and pushed themselves to extremes. Many athletes trained to the point of exhaustion for the Olympics. They went far beyond their limits to set personal bests, achieve gold medals and qualify. This group of people did it to be regarded as heroes by other athletes and fellow officers.

The old Meat Loaf song "I would do anything for love…." came to mind.

Lucian could feel the cold under his palms and knees,

but he remembered that Debra had instructed him to push his hands forward and place his forehead and chest on the floor. He hadn't thought anything about it assuming it would be carpet or at worst a wooden floor. This was different, it was icy, and Lucian had to press his naked chest against the floor.

He had always thought the best way to get into a cold swimming pool, or the sea was to just dive in. This avoided the prolonged torture of the cold water inching up his body. He would take this approach now and gritted his teeth as he pressed his chest down hard onto the cold stone. With his head on the ground and trying to deal with the cold he didn't notice Debra enter the chamber.

He jumped as he heard her high heels step onto the hard flooring and ascend the step to the throne. Lucian didn't look up, but his heart raced, and he was aware of how shrunken and small his cock had become.

The cock strap was still on, and he was thankful he had put it on the second clasp, or it would have slipped off.

Debra spoke, "Welcome Lucian, I see you are following my instructions."

Lucian didn't look up.

"Yes, Mistress."

"Are you cold Lucian?"

Lucian didn't reply, simply nodded.

Debra laughed and said, "Look at me, Lucian."

Lucian raised his head and was stunned by Debra's beauty, and like Cleopatra, she looked like a queen or goddess sitting on her gold throne. Lucian looked up at her, and despite the cold, his cock began to stiffen. He looked at her black underwear; lace topped stockings and very high pointed black shiny shoes. As before her makeup was heavy and theatrical but perfectly applied. Debra's hair was down and fell in thick waves over her shoulders and back. It was held from her face with a jewelled clasp in the shape of a red peacock.

Debra pointed to a gold box with her shoe.

Lucian reached out for it and carefully opened the small gold casket. It contained slim white cigarettes and a solid gold Dunhill lighter. Taking out a cigarette and picking up the lighter, Lucian reached up to pass it to Debra. But she didn't reach forward or move to accept it from him. She just made a gesture with her hand to indicate he light it for her. He did so, rising onto one knee to pass her the cigarette. Debra took it from him with red painted nails, and took a deep inhale, blowing the smoke into the air.

"Still cold Lucian?" she asked.

Lucian gave a slight nod.

She smiled and said, "Good then lay on your back for me Lucian."

Lucian placed his bare buttocks on the freezing tiles and braced himself as he put his whole back and shoulders onto the floor. His cock was still slightly swollen but quickly receded as the cold passed through his body. Debra was amused by Lucian's discomfort. As Lucian looked through his raised knees watching Debra smoke, he got the sensation that the floor was warming up. After a few minutes, he could feel the heat under his buttocks and soles of his feet.

Debra looked down at Lucian and smiled and said "Better?"

Lucian said, "Yes Mistress, thank you, Mistress."

Debra didn't say anything else just sat back and smoked.

After a few minutes, Lucian found he was now getting rather hot. The floor was increasing in heat, and his back began to sweat, Lucian had to lift one foot then the other to stop them from burning. Sweat was running down his face and neck, and he was really feeling the heat. Debra had been flicking her cigarette ash into a gold ashtray, she suddenly stood up, stubbing out the cigarette butt and stepping down from the throne.

She took a couple of steps down straddling Lucian's body. She placed a stiletto heel in the centre of his chest and applied pressure, pushing his burning back onto the heated floor. He gritted his teeth but didn't call out. To his horror, Debra pulled her black panties to one side and pissed on his hot body. The yellow liquid cooled him, but he couldn't help but twist under her foot as she directed the warm urine onto his chest and face, stinging his eyes and soaking his hair.

Stepping off Lucian, Debra laughed and walking towards the bedchamber she said, "Wash in the bathing pool and join me in the bedchamber."

Lying there on the hot floor covered in Debra's piss, Lucian felt revulsion and disgust. He looked at the door and was tempted to make a run for the exit.

But when Lucian looked at the changing area his clothes were gone. They had been replaced with a white bathrobe. Rising he hurried to the sunken bath and stepped in. Thankfully it was cool but not cold, and he sank down under the water. After washing himself down, he took a large towel from the side and dried himself off. The cock strap was now wet, and he could feel the wet leather around his balls.

Putting on the bathrobe, he went to find Debra.

She was lying on the large Egyptian style bed. As Lucian got a closer, he could see the headboard and footboard were covered with ornate decorations. There were scenes carved into the wood and hieroglyphics with serpent heads and slaves finished in jewels and gold leaf. The four posts were draped with fabrics that were partially see-through. Small crystals sewn into the weave glistened like tiny stars caught the flaming torchlight.

Debra had taken her shoes off and relaxed back, laying on the beautiful silk pillows. As Lucian came closer, Debra extended a hand. Lucian couldn't help himself and kissed her hand.

Smiling she said, "Still here then?"

Lucian flushed and murmured, "Yes, Mistress."

She laughed.

"Go and fetch me some wine then come and sit with me."

Lucian collected an unopened bottle of wine and a single glass from a red and gold cabinet. Taking it into Debra, who had removed her stockings and draped them over the end of the bed. Lucian poured the wine, and passed it to her.

She said, "Are you thirsty Lucian?"

He said he was.

Laughing again she said, "Do you know what Mistress Champaign is Lucian?"

He thought for a moment and said, "I think I was just bathing in it?"

Debra smiled.

"Yes Lucian you were, and yet you are still here… why it that?"

Lucian mumbled, "I don't Know Mistress."

Debra leant forward showing Lucian a full view of her ample chest.

"Do you want to stay with me for a few days Lucian?"

He looked down and said, "Yes, Mistress if I can handle it, Mistress."

Debra slapped his face hard.

"I will decide if you can handle it or not, now get on your knees!"

Stunned, Lucian fell to his knees and placed his head on the floor. His mind was spinning and his cheek burning from the slap. Debra pushed the cushions to one side and then opened her legs wide and began to rub her fingers between her thighs. Slowly she began to breathe more heavily. Lucian was aware she was touching herself.

Debra reached out for Lucian and grabbed his hair. Pulling him onto the bed, she directed his head between her legs.

"Lick me Lucian. Please, your Mistress."

He buried his face between her legs and began to lick and kiss her pussy.

Lucian thought it was wonderful and from the sounds that Debra was making, he knew he was pleasing her.

Later that evening, upstairs, Lucian sat in suede and leather armchair sipping red wine and watching Debra as she stood at the patio doors smoking. They had enjoyed a light dinner that Carol had prepared. Now dressed in casual clothes from the cruise, Lucian felt calm and relaxed. It was strange, all the nervousness and tension was gone, and he felt amazing.

Debra turned back into the room and sat on the matching two seater sofa.

"My husband never liked this house, he preferred to live in London or Hong Kong. I love this house and the

English countryside. London was always too busy, and Hong Kong is so hot and humid. Tell me, Lucian, why have you never been to Venice?"

Lucian replied, "I have travelled to other parts of Europe but I just never got to Venice."

"I'm going in three weeks you must come with me."

"I would like that Mistress, but why me?" replied Lucian

Debra smiled and said, "I wasn't looking for a lover or partner, but I miss my husband and the lifestyle. I have no shortage of "Players" who would have a session if I wanted one."

Lucian nodded and said, "The room downstairs is fantastic."

Debra replied, "A submissive Swiss architect built the rooms downstairs. They were a gift to my husband and me for hosting parties."

"The bed and the furniture were custom made by a Dutch craftsman. We regularly had people stay and use the rooms".

"But not the Red Room that is mine and nobody touches my things in there."

Lucian asked, "What happens in the other rooms?"

Debra said, "Recently a high court judge was imprisoned for two days in a golden cage, fed dog food and cold porridge from a silver bowl."

"He had a photo of me to keep him company, but I was away in Dubai."

"I don't like group sessions, I only had one on one sessions with my husband."

"We had a heavy session the evening before he left for Aruba, I haven't indulged again in any kind of session until I met you, Lucian."

Debra paused.

"So, to answer your question, I didn't choose you, in a funny way you chose me. By being so innocently shy and gentle, I felt moved to be with you."

Lucian couldn't answer he just looked at the floor.

Debra said, "It's late, and you have done well for your first session. Carol has prepared a room for you in the apartment by the pool. I don't rise early when I'm at home, so breakfast will be at ten."

Lucian got up, and as he did he asked, "Did I please you, Mistress?"

Debra smiled and said, "Good night Lucian."

Lucian went around the pool looking at the lights in the water.

It was a perfect English night, although just after 10.30pm, there was still some light in the sky and the evening stars twinkled silently.

As he lay in bed, he replayed the session in his mind his and hand gently massaged his hard cock.

Lucian felt guilty rubbing his cock without Debra's permission. He took his hand away, not allowing himself to jerk off.

Debra had told him she had filmed the session, and he could take the discs when he left. He had promised he would keep them safe. Debra had insisted the films were for his personal viewing pleasure. He was not under any circumstances allowed to show them to anyone else.

It was very unlikely Lucian would show videos of himself being pissed on, slapped and God knows what else.

He had told Christina he was on holiday for a long weekend in Bournemouth, visiting a cousin and wouldn't be back until the following Tuesday.

He slowly drifted off to sleep, he imagined Debra as a younger woman, having a succession of adoring men kneeling at her feet and worshipping her every move.

Chapter 36

The next morning Lucian awoke with the sun shining through the curtains and a low hum of a pool vacuum cleaner. He opened the curtains and saw Marcus in tight green shorts and a white vest cleaning the pool.

Lucian got dressed and went outside, Marcus looked up and smiled and said: "Still here then?"

Lucian replied, "Looks like it!"

Marcus didn't say anything just smiled and carried on vacuuming the pool steps.

As Lucian went into the kitchen, Carol was there and had prepared tea and toast with a selection of fruit, cereal, yoghurt, and preserves.

Seeing Lucian come in she said, "Good Morning Lucian I see you are still here then?"

Lucian reacted sharply.

"Look, I told Marcus, and I'm telling you, I'm here for the weekend, and that's it OK? "

Carol smiled and said, "Debra told me you would be, and I think you will stay until Monday. It's just we have seen men twice your size come out of the red rooms in tears and run for the gates."

Lucian was sat at the breakfast table staring at her

"Well they are not me are they?"

Carol poured tea and said, "I'm sure your right dear."

Lucian ate his breakfast in silence, watching Marcus finishing off cleaning the pool and then trimming the low-level hedges.

He asked Carol if Debra was up yet.

Carol looked surprised and said, "Debra left early this morning and told me she wouldn't be back until this evening, didn't you know?"

Lucian didn't sound convincing at all when he said, "Oh yes, of course."

He spent the day in his room, surfing the Internet on his laptop, dozing and enjoying the peace and quiet. At four 'o' clock, Marcus tapped on the door opened it and popped his head around.

"There is a note from Debra, you need to check your email."

Lucian picked up his laptop to check. Sure enough, there was a message from Debra, but also one without a subject.

He opened that one first and immediately regretted it as the screen went bright red. A finger started to draw in the fake blood tracing out the words.

"Hate and Fury will lay claim to your soul!"

He deleted it and opened Debra's, which read in two simple lines.

Lucian

You have passed the first day; tonight you will feel my pain. Prepare and be ready in body and mind, see you at 7.30 pm.

Mistress D xx

Later that day, as Lucian lay on the bed, an envelope was pushed under his door. Inside was a DVD. Opening his laptop, he put the silver disc into the disc holder. After it had loaded, the picture showed the red room with Lucian on his knees in front of Debra on the gold throne. The camera panned left and right showing the room then zoomed in on Debra as she smoked.

Even seeing her on DVD made Lucian's heart beat faster. He watched in shock as the events of last night replayed in front of his eyes. Closing the lid of the laptop, he stared at the ceiling wondering what was in store for him tonight.

It was now 6.30 pm, and in less than an hour he would be kneeling before Debra once again.

Carol had brought over some hot food earlier. Lucian wished he hadn't eaten anything, as he was feeling sick with butterflies in his stomach.

At seven twenty-five he went into the house to find Marcus waiting in the lift with the door open. Descending to the basement, Lucian was sweating in the small elevator space. Marcus didn't speak; his aftershave was sickly and choking. Leaving the lift, Lucian headed towards the end room, but Marcus paused by room 1.

Lucian came back, and Marcus said.

"Change in Room 1 and then go to Room 2, wait until you are told what to do. Do you understand?"

Lucian nodded and entered room 1.

The room was a lot smaller than the red room at the end; it consisted of a pommel horse and a large black cross, fixed to the wall. The floor was a rubberized tile, and there was a black silk robe draped over the pommel horse.

Stripping naked Lucian put on the gown, the silk felt lovely and cool against his hot body.

He noticed a black leather bag by the legs of the pommel horse. Lucian put his hands in the gown pockets and felt something cold and metal. Taking it out he held a silver key in the palm of his hand. The bag at his feet had a silver lock and Lucian bent down and tried the key. It worked, and the leather doctor's bag opened at the top.

Inside were several things that made Lucian's heart beat faster. The first was a black rubber cock and a tube of lubricant; the second item he pulled out was a pair of nipple clamps on a metal chain.

The third was a studded collar and a black leather lead with a diamante handle.

He put the collar on and picked up the bag.

Opening the door, he glanced left and right expecting to see Marcus.

There was no sign of him, carrying the bag and in bare feet, Lucian headed towards room 2, he pushed it, but it was locked. He looked for a doorbell, but there was nothing on the frame or on the button studded leather door panel.

Lucian saw a camera on the ceiling slowly panning

towards him. He tried the door again pushing harder this time, but it was solid. Lucian waited and listened. He tried the once more, putting both hands on the panel and pushing as hard as he could.

Lucian walked to the lift and was about to press the button when he had a thought. Lucian walked back to the door and instead of pushing the door again he took hold of the gold doorknob and pulled it towards him. There was a slight click as if a magnet had been released and the door came slightly towards Lucian.

Lucian pulled the door open and nervously entered room 2. To his amazement, the room was pitch black.

The light from the doorway caused a small shaft of light but as the door closed that vanished, leaving Lucian in the complete darkness. Lucian stood still waiting for his eyes to get accustomed to the dark.

It made no difference, he couldn't even see his hand in front of his face. Lucian sensed movement close by so he stood completely still. He felt a light breeze blow across his naked legs and up his back.

Lucian called out.

"Is that you Mistress?"

No reply, then suddenly a cigarette lighter flicked.

Lucian could just make out Debra sitting on an ornate high-backed chair to his right. Debra took a long draw on her cigarette, and it illuminated her face and red lips.

She exhaled the smoke, but it was too dark to see her face.

Lucian felt a sharp prick in his right calf muscle, he immediately felt faint. Dropping to his knees his head swam, and he passed out.

When Lucian came round, he was naked lying spread-eagled on what felt like an operating table.

His wrists and ankles were tightly strapped down. Lucian had several things attached to his body. His nipples were clamped with sharp pinching pegs that were taped down.

His balls were strapped up with the cock strap, and he could feel something big up his anal passage. His mouth was filled with a rubber bridal gag. The wide strap across his forehead and neck meant that he could not move.

Lucian strained against the ties, but despite his best efforts, he was completely immobilised.

Suddenly a shooting pain went through his nipples, and his arse was suddenly hurting with a deep vibration.

He began to sweat and gritted his teeth against the pain.

A voice spoke close to his ear, it said:

"Pain is all in the mind Lucian you can deal with the pain if you concentrate on something else."

He recognised Debra's voice.

He couldn't see her as the room was still in total darkness.

After forty-five seconds of the agony, Debra moved into his line of sight. As she looked down on Lucian, she smiled, and the pain receded slightly.

Lucian stared at her beautiful features and red lips.

She reached out stroking his face and tracing the sweat as it ran from his hairline.

"There's a good boy," Debra cooed, and the pain died away.

Then as she moved out of sight, the pain came back twice as strong. This made Lucian twist and buck in the restraints.

Debra spoke again.

"Will you suffer for me, Lucian? Take the pain for me?"

Lucian couldn't talk but forced his head to give the slightest of nods.

Clenching his fists, Lucian tried to resist the burning sharp pain in his nipples. And the deep grinding hurt in his anal passage and bowls.

Debra's face came back into view, Lucian focused on her face the pain receded and then was gone.

Panting with relief, Lucian stared at Debra, who stroked his face and said, "You took it well, you are a good boy."

Lucian closed his eyes and breathed a deep sigh; Debra moved away again and whispered into his ear.

"I feel you may be able to take more for me than you think, Lucian?"

Lucian's heart started to race again in anticipation of the pain returning when he felt a sharp scratch on his forearm and again the same heady rush as he passed out.

He awoke in the apartment in the bed with the birds singing and the sun shining through the drapes.

Checking his phone it was eight thirty on Sunday morning, he must have been out for over twelve hours.

He lay in the bed thinking about what had happened, was it a dream or a nightmare about being drugged and tortured he wasn't sure.

Checking his forearm he did indeed have a small red mark where the injection had gone in and the same on his calf muscle. His body ached all over, and his nipples were sore, and his arse ached like he needed to go to the toilet.

He dressed and went into the house. Carol and Marcus were nowhere to be seen, and breakfast was laid out on the table.

He made some tea and ate some toast, feeling alone in the house.

After breakfast, he went into Debra's office and was surprised to see her sitting at her desk typing on her 17" Mac book Pro.

As he entered, she smiled and said, "Good Morning Lucian I trust you slept well?"

Lucian couldn't help himself. He put his hands on his hips and delivered his reply.

"Well yes but I have to say I've been here less than forty-eight hours. I've been boiled, frozen, drugged, tortured, and I'm not sure, if I'm honest, I can take any more Debra!"

Debra smiled.

"We are alone in the house today, I have given Carol and Marcus the day off. So you will be my servant today. So fetch me some coffee, I take it strong, black, no sugar."

She went back to her typing leaving Lucian speechless in the middle of the room, his hands still firmly placed on his hips.

Feeling somewhat embarrassed, that his protest was totally ignored. Lucian turned and went back into the kitchen. He put on the kettle to make Debra's coffee and got out some fancy china coffee cups and a shiny silver coffee pot.

Lucian put some coffee into the pot and poured in the boiling water. Next to the coffee was a matching silver tray, so Lucian placed everything on to the tray and carried it into Debra.

He re-entered the room and set the tray on the small table. Debra didn't look up, so he poured her a cup of coffee and went to place it on the desk.

She turned sharply to Lucian and said, "Kneel down and hold the coffee for me."

He did so, and she took the cup from the saucer and sipped the strong hot coffee.

Placing it back on the saucer she said, "There are some things I wish you to do today. I want you to "Worship" me by kissing my feet while I eat, and kissing my ass while I smoke."

Lucian looked at Debra in disbelief but the words "Yes, Mistress" came out anyway.

Debra rose and said, "Good you can begin by lighting me a cigarette."

Lucian saw a silver cigarette box on the side and the gold Dunhill Lighter.

He got to his feet, and Debra took the coffee cup from him and walked to the patio doors.

As Debra walked past Lucian, he saw she had on very high red stilettos and seamed stockings, with a white blouse and a tight black pencil skirt. Her hair was combed back in a tight ponytail, and she had on fresh lipstick.

Debra stood by the open patio doors, and as Lucian approached her, she said, "Kneel behind me light my cigarette and then raise my skirt and kiss my ass while I smoke. Or do you want to whinge and moan about things some more?"

Lucian was taken aback by her harsh tone of voice and dropped to his knees feeling ashamed. Lighting her cigarette, he mumbled.

"Sorry Mistress."

She took the cigarette from him and said, "If you don't want to do it you can leave right now."

Lucian didn't reply just looked at the floor.

Debra lifted his chin with a red painted fingernail and said,

"I'm not forcing you Lucian, and if you can't take it you can get out right now!"

Lucian didn't get up and knelt with his head bowed but his cheeks burning with shame. He felt so drawn to this beautiful woman and even when she scolded him he still wanted to stay.

Seeing he hadn't moved Debra's voice softened, and she gently said, "Worship me, Lucian, show me you are a good boy and deserve to be my sub."

She then turned and looked out of the doors, blowing smoke out of the open windows.

Lucian looked down at her red Lou Boutin stiletto shoes. Debra didn't speak again but raised her ankle and rubbed the back of her calf with the top of her red shoe.

He was beginning to learn that a simple gesture or sign would indicate her desires. Lucian remembered on the ship that she didn't have to always command him to do things verbally.

Lucian knelt on the wooden parquet flooring behind her, she gazed out over the pool and well-kept gardens and continued to aimlessly rub her calf.

After a couple of minutes kneeling at her back, he placed his hands on her hips and waited.

Sensing his movement Debra snapped, "Go on then!"

He raised her black pencil skirt over her thighs exposing lace topped stockings and black panties. The metal suspender clamps caught the light and distracted him momentarily.

"I'm waiting," she said.

He took a deep breath and adhered to his task of removing her black panties and carefully drawing them down her long legs and over her seamed stockings to her ankles.

He then again paused and waited.

Debra raised one heel at a time so he could slip the flimsy fabric out from under each heel. She shifted her weight and leant forward arching her back and spreading her legs.

He shuffled forward, his knees sliding on the wooden floor, so his face was close to her now naked buttocks.

He waited, his heart pounding in anticipation as of his next task. He almost felt compelled to turn away at the thought of what she wanted him to do.

Lucian's head flipped at the idea of such a degrading and humiliating task.

He could see Debra had a very attractive bottom but the idea of putting his tongue up her arse, made his guts churn. It was a phase people banded around often but to actually do it for real he wasn't sure he could do it. He kissed her cheeks and placed his face against her warm buttocks.

Debra spoke again.

"Wait! Before you worship me, I want another cigarette."

He rose and fetched the silver box, fumbling to remove a cigarette and light it. Lucian passed it up to her with shaking hands.

As he didn't smoke, he was careful to make sure it was burning properly. Lucian took care not inhale the smoke and cough, which would displease her. Debra took the cigarette from him without looking down.

"Ok do it deep Lucian, I want you to worship me, and I want to feel your tongue right up my shit hole."

His heart pounded hard in his chest as he gently held Debra's cheeks apart with his hands. Pushing his face deep into her bottom crease Lucian thrust his tongue into her tight arse hole.

Debra pushed back onto his face and tongue, smoothing his face with her arse cheeks.

After several minutes of this, Debra pulled way flicking the finished cigarette into the garden and turned to face him.

Debra looked down at Lucian, who was red-faced and kneeling before her. She looked at him and swiftly slapped his face and spat into his eyes.

"What do you say!!" she demanded.

Shocked, Lucian gasped, "Thank you, Mistress."

"Good now run me a bath," she snapped and stepped past him as he sat red-faced and shaking.

Chapter 37

Lucian didn't sleep well. He spent most of the night staring at the ceiling, trying to pluck up enough courage to get in his car and to go home. He replayed the day's events and what he had done with Debra. The night-time memories came flooding back. The evening sessions were indescribable. Lucian couldn't believe the things he had experienced in that red room.

Lucian was conscious this time, as the feelings and sights were racing around in his head. His body ached, and his cock and balls were sore for being tortured and finally being allowed to cum in the most unbelievable way.

He could still taste the bitter tang of his own semen as she had made him lick it out of her hand. Debra had been a total bitch and utterly wonderful at the same time.

Finally around 4.30am sleep came to him.

Lucian woke after what only seemed a few minutes. He checked his watch, and it was 9.30am on Monday morning.

He dressed and went into the house. There was no sign of Marcus or Carol, and there was no breakfast set or coffee made.

Lucian made a coffee and went to see if Debra was in her office.

She wasn't so he sat on the sofa, drank his coffee and waited.

At 10.00 he took out his phone to call Christina when he saw he had received a text message.

It read:

My Dear Lucian

I have enjoyed our weekend together. I feel that you need time to digest what has happened. To explore how you feel about me, your Mistress. Do you think the lifestyle is for you, Lucian?

Please message me tonight from your home. If you look on my desk, you will see the recordings of the sessions that we had this weekend. As before, these DVD's are for your personal viewing and not to be shared.

You are truly a special person, and I enjoyed your company very much.

With fondest regards

Debra (Mistress D) X

Later that day Lucian sat at his desk having opened his emails and caught up with work events. Christina had gone home early as she had a dentist appointment and hadn't expected him back until Tuesday. Lucian sat alone thinking about the weekend.

He had been very scared but also hadn't felt so excited in his entire life.

His head was fizzing and was filled with images of torches, marble and hazy pictures of Debra in flowing gowns. He could envisage himself kneeling with his tongue up her ass. Lucian also remembered how calm he had felt after the sessions ended.

Lucian had never felt this way before, and his emotions were in turmoil.

He really liked Debra, and he was sexually excited by her and the things they had done. But he found it a battle to give into his submissive side.

The forums had spoken about the growing from the ground up as in the military boot camps. They break you down to nothing, those who can take it, grow to be strong and powerful.

Lucian had read about the same theory in BDSM.

Several Mistresses had stated that they would be devastated if they really "hurt or harmed" their partners.

Outsiders found it difficult to understand the trust and respect. Even though both parties were involved in some very extreme sessions, afterwards, they cuddled up and returned to everyday life as loving partners.

Lucian reached into his bag and retrieved the DVD that he had brought back from Debra's house. With sweating palms, he put the disc into the tray and pressed play.

The scene opened with Debra smoking and Lucian on all fours at her feet.

He was soaked in sweat, and he looked spaced out and dazed.

He watched the next twenty-five minutes in disbelief. Lucian was shocked to see how amazing Debra was, she did things to him that he didn't remember.

"What a mind fuck!"

It was evident he was drugged and out of his head, but

Debra was in complete control.

That evening he messaged Debra, she was warm and friendly, and they chatted about films, music, places to visit and restaurants they had eaten in. Debra was interested in Lucian's tastes, and when they signed off, Lucian saw they had been online for over two and half hours.

They didn't actually discuss the sessions until near the end of the chat. She typed:

"Did you watch the DVD's Lucian?"

Lucian typed he had, and she asked if he was turned on by watching it. Lucian admitted that he was but was shocked and couldn't believe it was him in the footage.

Debra said he had done very well. She said he was a natural sub and was a very easy to train and willing to please her. He had taken all she desired like a man.

Lucian said he didn't remember much about it and kept having flashbacks.

The next few days passed rapidly.

Lucian attended meetings in London and Reading and had to work hard to make up the lost time. He was looking forward to seeing Debra again; she had invited him to her cottage in Berkshire for another long weekend.

Carole had sent him the address and he was awaiting for a time and date from Debra.

Although he was extremely nervous, Lucian was looking forward to it, and to experiencing more of the Lifestyle.

Chapter 38

Dominic opened his work email and smiled when he saw an email from Debra. Opening it, he was disappointed when he saw it was actually from Marcus.

It read:

'The testing of the systems has shown there are several errors in the positioning and operation of the equipment you installed on Ms Fielding's property. It is evident the range, and focus of the cameras are below par. We expect you to return at 10 am tomorrow to correct these errors. Please note as payment has been made in full we will expect this work to be carried out at your expense.

Regards Marcus'

Feeling the anger rising in his chest Dominic read through the email again. He had checked the system twice and found no operating errors. He pushed back his chair stomped across the room and shouted at himself "No!!" "I did a great job, a fucking great, fucking job!"

Dominic's rage grew and grew. He shook his head violently trying to stop Marcus's camp effeminate voice screaming inside his head.

"No, No, No, I am not useless you cunt, I am fucking great!!"

He looked in the mirror, then red with rage he shouted at his reflection.

"How dare they tell me it's fucking wrong, No, No, Fucking No! You fuckers no!"

He could picture his mother's sour face her bony finger pointing at him saying, "You bloody useless stupid boy!!!"

He turned from the mirror and hollered once more "No!" at the top of his voice.

After sitting with his knees drawn up and rocking back and forth, he managed to calm down. Then climbing into his van set off for Hampshire.

The traffic was light, and the weather was bright as he headed south. Dominic listened to the radio as he drove his mind filled with images of Debra. Her raven coloured hair, her beauty, her perfect makeup and her curvaceous figure.

He tried to think about the house system and what

could possibly have gone wrong. As he approached Winchester, his phone chirped advising him he had a text message. He pulled over and reached for his phone, the message was from Marcus. "System working 100% no call out needed."

Dominic called Marcus straight back. Pressing the phone to his ear, Dominic waited to be answered. After three rings Marcus picked up.

"Hello, can I help you?"

Dominic identified himself and resisted yelling at Marcus.

Marcus sighed and said, "It's all ok now, probably just a glitch in the power supply. Ms Fielding won't need you again."

"But I am nearly at the house!" complained Dominic

Marcus didn't seem to hear him and hung up.

Dominic threw the phone onto the passenger seat and slammed his fists onto the steering wheel.

"How dare they fucking treat me like this!"

He went to the back of the van and sat at the van's mobile console in front of his screens. He had purposely planted a backdoor access code in the CCTV system. By using the 4G mobile connection, Dominic was able to log into his own servers at home. From there he tried to locate the tiny hole he had created in the program systems at Debra's house. If he could access it from the van, he could send a small pilot virus that would temporarily disable the system causing it to fail.

This could generate an error message to come up on Marcus's screens. They would then have to call Dominic, as he was the only one who could fix the problem.

After a few minutes, the screen flashed with a message stating the system was restricted and the tiny pilot file could not be accessed. Dominic tried every back door access program he knew of to get into Debra's system but again the same response. He reconfigured the files and re-sent the command again but after a few minutes of spooling it timed out and came back again with no joy.

Dominic felt angry and frustrated, he had always been able to easily crack domestic systems.

Images of Debra smoking kept flashing in his mind as he fumbled with his boots. Her looking down at him as he scrambled to pick up the plans. Since they first met, he just couldn't stop fantasising about this beautiful, wealthy woman with a BDSM playroom.

He was determined to see this amazing woman again, and Dominic vowed he had to be part of her life somehow.

The Winchester property wasn't far away, and he decided he would park nearby and see if he could do a local access system invasion.

Eleven minutes later Dominic drove past the gates. Dominic tried to access the system from a local perspective but got no better results than remotely. He extended a telescopic spy camera from the roof of the van and began to watch the property. After a few minutes, Marcus came out, opened the boot of the BMW and removed a black leather attaché case.

Shortly after, a car drew up to the gates. An Aston Martin DB9 swept into the drive and stopped directly outside the front door. The car door opened an older man dressed in a well-tailored navy blue suit, and a bright green tie got out. Debra came to the door to greet the man in the blue suit and tie. She looked incredible in her pencil-thin high heeled stilettos and a figure-hugging red dress. With her hair tied back, Debra looked like a Spanish or Italian movie star on the steps of her mansion. She hugged the man and kissed both cheeks as she greeted him on the doorstep.

Dominic felt a pang of jealousy at this obvious show of affection to the man, who was good looking with distinguished grey hair. Debra pointed at the cameras on the outside, and the gate and the man nodded in approval. They went inside, leaving Dominic powerless to do anything except watch the front of the house again. If he could access the system, he could see and even hear the conversations inside. To pass the time he zoomed in on the Aston's number plate. Then accessing the DVLA's database, found the car belonged to a certain Charles McCreedy.

A quick Google search found that he was sixty-three years old and was the senior partner in several property development firms. He searched the HMRC and Companies House databases, feeling another pang of jealousy when he discovered the end of year accounts. Dominic saw the previous tax year for one of the companies made pre-tax profits of £13 million.

The front door opened, and the man and Debra came out, they exchanged cheek kisses again. Dominic had set up and pointed a directional microphone at the front door. His camera zoomed into Debra's face, and he could see the affection in her eyes.

This incensed Dominic even more.

Debra hugged the man, and the powerful directional microphone could clearly pick up Debra's words.

"We will do everything we can to find her Charles,

please don't worry she will turn up."

The man looked emotional as he got back into the Aston and drove away. Dominic wondered what type of relationship they shared and who they were referring to.

Dominic wished he could have Debra as his Mistress and have her stroke his face with her perfect soft hands and kiss his cheek with her perfect red lips.

Dominic watched as Debra came out of the house again. She had changed and was dressed in an immaculate black straight skirt and tight fitting tailored jacket. She wore a white blouse with high collar and black and white high heel shoes.

Marcus followed on with two large suitcases, which he put in the boot of the Bentley. The driver opened the door, and Debra sat in the back closing the car door behind her.

As he did so, the front door opened Carol came rushing out holding the slim black briefcase and got into the other side of the car from Debra.

Once both were inside the driver got back in, and the Bentley drove out of the gates.

Dominic started the van, turned it around and gave chase as the car sped away.

He was determined to follow the car and find a way to get closer to this extraordinary woman. He couldn't see Debra or Carol due to the tinted back windows.

After only a few miles, Dominic lost sight of her Bentley as he waited at some temporary traffic lights. He was stuck at the lights angry and frustrated as Debra's car accelerated up onto the M27. He followed seconds later but the car was gone. Pulling into the motorway services he tried to calm down before heading home.

Chapter 39

Dominic's finger stabbed the enter key for the final time and slumped back in his high-backed leather chair. Running his hands over his bald head as the sweat ran down his forehead. The room was stuffy and smelt of sour food and stale perspiration. For the last two days and nights, he had been very busy.

Dominic had not slept, keeping alert by drinking cans of energy drinks and running on hate driven adrenaline. He had created a large folder of photos and data relating to Debra and Lucian's affair and had posted it everywhere.

Dominic chose the most damming and intimate photos from the weekend sessions. Using Photoshop, Dominic added loads of false information and explicit captions. He inserted faked pictures of Lucian and edited voice clips.

He created fake Facebook, Twitter and Linked In accounts. Dominic uploaded all of the "session" videos onto the YouTube channel. He copied extracts from the conversations Debra and Lucian had on Yahoo messenger. He posted these on many blogs.

It was all designed to show Lucian as a kinky womaniser, liar, and in the poorest of light.

It had taken all of Dominic's skill to prepare the data, and now last part of the task was done. Dominic, using one of his many hacking talents, created what looked like a news article. In the "Trending" section of Facebook, he had attached this to Marcus's homepage feed. Dominic knew that soon the ultimate betrayal would be exposed to Debra.

Dominic's skills had been tested to the full to create the backlog of information on Debra and Lucian.

He would post more when he had the time. After he had disposed of Lucian Palmer Jones, he would present the additional evidence to Debra. She would praise him for ridding her of that cowardly liar Lucian and select him, Dominic, to be her faithful sub.

Dominic watched a moth circling the light on his desk.

He casually took a long handled BBQ lighter from the office draw and turned up the flame. Then pointing the lighter at the unsuspecting moth, clicked the button. A three-inch flame leapt out and incinerated the moth burning it to nothing. Smiling, Dominic swivelled in his chair and said to himself.

"Burn you fucker burn."

Chapter 40

Back at the Winchester house, Marcus was sat at his desk reading random online profiles on Gaydar and Mancrunch,

"No newbies today," Marcus said to himself as he flicked over to his Facebook posts.

He was surprised to see Lucian's face staring back at him from the trending list. He followed the link and was immediately very concerned about what he read.

He followed the other links. Marcus was shocked and appalled, as they revealed some extremely disturbing things. Marcus felt sick to his stomach, as he knew Debra would go absolutely crazy.

Lucian was photographed in places that Marcus knew he shouldn't have been. There were entries about Lucian that were quite frankly unbelievable and very alarming.

There were links to other sites that exposed Lucian as a paedophile, having sexual harassment charges against him and a criminal record for violence.

There was also a newspaper article dating back to the mid-eighties showing Lucian as a teacher and a scandal with under aged girls.

Other links reported that he was involved in money laundering and a property scam that robbed thousands of people of their life savings.

It highlighted the scam was to do with properties in Portugal, that were never built. The money was taken from genuine investors, against a set of plans. The properties never materialised, and the land was then sold off to and turned into a car park next to a theme park.

Marcus was disturbed to learn that Lucian Palmer Jones may not be the man Marcus thought he was. He found it almost impossible to believe, but the articles and the photographs seemed genuine. The most concerning was the information on Debra's involvement in the BDSM lifestyle. It was all over the Internet and on social media channels for everyone to see.

If all of this or even part of this was true, then Debra was in a very dangerous situation.

Marcus's gut feeling was that something was not quite

right and despite his reservations, Marcus copied the data, zipped it up in a file marked it "TOP URGENT" and sent it to Debra.

Chapter 41

Debra sat smoking looking out over the London skyline sipping red wine. She had been in Chelsea Harbour having dinner then taken a car back to her hotel in Kensington. She was enjoying a quiet drink in the roof top bar in with a young city broker when Marcus texted her.

"Top urgent found something you need to see!"

Debra finished her cigarette stubbing the red lipstick coated filter into the sand filled champagne bucket. She turned to the young broker, telling him he was very sweet but she was tired and was going to bed. He thanked Debra for her company and reluctantly bade her goodnight.

Returning to her suite, she mixed a large gin martini and made herself comfortable on the bed. Powering up her IPad, she opened Marcus's email, which contained an extensive list of links. As Debra clicked on the first link her heart sank; the article was about a property fraud and named Lucian as one of the conspirators.

The next was a link to Lucian's Facebook, which showed photos of Lucian in recent weeks attending parties.

Debra's hands were shaking as she scrolled down to yet another photo showing Lucian in bed with a young red haired woman. Debra walked over to bar poured another large gin martini and lit a cigarette. She needed to calm her nerves and pause to digest the information.

The phone ringing, jolting her back to reality, it was Marcus

"Are you ok Debra?" he asked.

"I'm okay Marcus, but I think Lucian has a lot explaining to do!" With that she hung up.

Marcus was surprised at her relatively calm voice and concluded she hadn't seen all of the links he had sent.

Debra returned to the IPad and continued with the list of links, she forced herself to read every one. She spent the next forty-five minutes following the leads in utter disbelief. Although she found it difficult to believe, she could not ignore what she was seeing.

The older information was agonising to read. Debra knew some of the recent dates and times were when Lucian wasn't with her. It appeared he had lied about where he had been on various occasions. Debra forced herself to continue reading, desperately trying to block out the feeling of utter betrayal.

Debra was getting more and more emotional as she watched video clips of the man she thought she knew as Lucian Palmer Jones.

She refilled her glass, lit another cigarette and continued to watch through tears that were now rolling down her cheeks.

The final clips were too much; it was their weekend session and clearly showed Lucian in various situations. The scenes were from the DVD Debra had given to Lucian and was now publically available for everyone to see!

Debra snapped, violent anger and rage filled her veins.

She hurled the crystal tumbler at the wall shattering it into a thousand pieces.

With one clean sweep cleared the dressing table scattering the contents and sending them in all directions across the floor.

On the wall facing Debra was a piece of art depicting a lady sat on a chair staring into the room, Debra jumped up screaming.

"Don't you dare fucking look at me?"

She ripped the picture off the wall and with all her might brought it crashing down on a coffee table.

Her agonising screams could be heard echoing down the corridors.

The phone rang, Debra picked it up, and a young woman asked,

"Are you ok Ms Fielding?"

Debra screamed "Fuck off you stupid bitch" at the top of her voice, slammed down the receiver, ripped it out from the socket and threw it across the room.

The tears flowed uncontrollably now she curled up in a ball on the chaise long, trying desperately to ease the pain.

As she sobbed into her hands, Debra smelt something burning. Looking across at the stripped bed she saw that the cigarette she had been smoking had fallen onto the bed and was smouldering and burning a hole in the mattress

Debra snatched a pot of fresh flowers from the dresser. She poured the water and contents on the smouldering bed and then threw the glass vase across the lounge area.

Still fuming she made her way over to the window

drinking neat gin straight from the bottle.

Debra was feeling very light headed and sick to her stomach, which was in knots and saliva filled her mouth.

Stumbling her way towards the bathroom, Debra didn't make it, and projectile vomited up the hallway.

Debra lay in ruins on the floor, too tired to cry anymore, her world and the room in a thousand pieces.

There was a light tap on the door and Marcus's voice called out her name. Still slumped on the floor, Debra reached up, turned the knob, and Marcus entered. He helped Debra to her feet and carried her to the chaise long.

Debra managed to say "Thank you Marcus" and gave him a weak smile.

Marcus looked around the room at the devastation.

"How long did this take?"

Debra looked at the damage she had done to the room and whispered, "Not long", and they both smiled.

Marcus quickly collected up her things and put them into her bag. Debra felt much calmer now her trusted

Marcus had come to rescue her.

Marcus held his hand out to Debra.

"Your car is waiting to take you home, are you ready to go Mistress?"

"One minute Marcus, in for a penny, in for a pound."

Debra replied and with that she picked up the broken coffee table leg and swung it like a baseball player at the bronze bust placed on a column, knocking the heavy head onto the floor.

"That's going to be Lucian's head" Debra announced.

With that last symbolic gesture, they left the hotel.

Sitting in the back of the car Debra lit a cigarette and texted Lucian a simple message.

"Lucian met me on Thursday at 3.30 pm at my country cottage.   D XX"

Chapter 42

The cottage was located near to Windsor on the outskirts of London. Debra used it as a weekend retreat as it was private and peaceful.

Lucian's car pulled into the gravel drive with a Wisteria tree forming an arch over the entrance. The cottage was small and beautifully kept, with a stone porch and original wooden sash windows.

Lucian went down the narrow pathway that led to the small courtyard at the back.

With his heart pounding, Lucian entered through a low doorway into a pretty country style kitchen.

He passed the dark wood dining room and entered the sun-dappled living room, with two French windows looking out over a bright, colourful garden.

As Lucian entered the room, Debra was by the window smoking a long slim cigarette held between her two raised fingers. Her red painted fingernails pointed straight upward.

He stopped and froze as he remembered the previous times when those perfectly manicured nails and long fingers had been raised like that.

He had seen on the DVD how she had pushed those manicured fingers deep up his arse hole. Debra then removed them swiftly and placed them in his mouth. They tickled the back of his throat making him gag; it had taken all his concentration not to throw up. That was not allowed, he was forbidden to lose control in her presence.

She had laughed at his panting and watched as he struggled to maintain his hard on and "Wank" as she had instructed.

Debra seemed to take delight in knowing that it was all he could do not to be sick. The foul taste of lubricant and the salty saliva from his churning stomach tormented his tongue.

Since returning from the cruise, they had indulged in many different activities.

Debra now knew it was the cruel attention that Lucian craved. The acts themselves were secondary.

During the weekend sessions, his nipples had been clamped with metal pegs. Debra had leant forward as if to whisper something, but then raised his chin and spat into his open mouth.

On other occasions, Debra hadn't been satisfied enough with his discomfort. She had removed the metal pegs and replaced them with plastic ones, which she called her piranhas. Named after the serrated edges and very sharp bite they gave. He remembered her placing these on the very end of his burning nipples and saying,

"Now wank and cum for me."

He hadn't been able to resist the intense pain of these pegs and had begged her to allow him to cum.

Pausing for a second or two Debra had looked around the beautifully decorated room, with it flaming lanterns then said, "Yes, but in your hand."

He came hard into his own upturned palm, and she laughed as he twisted and jerked at the intensity.

She had looked at him and waited until his eyes focused on her face and said, "Now eat it."

He forced his head up and quickly licked his palm and consumed the white slimy liquid.

"Good Boy,"

She said and removed the pegs allowing Lucian to fall back exhausted after his efforts to please her.

Afterwards, he recalled how she had smiled and put her warm hands on him and rubbed his chest. She had felt his racing heart begin to slow its pounding rhythm.

He had asked her if he had pleased her and she had stroked his hair saying, "Yes, Lucian you are such a good boy."

Debra and Lucian spent several hours discussing the Lifestyle and chatting between the intense sessions. Lucian had asked many questions, he wanted to know why he felt this way and how the pain was necessary.

Debra explained that she expected Lucian to take as much pain as possible and it was a matter of enduring until she was satisfied.

She enjoyed seeing him suffer Debra told him, the next time they were having a session, he would be expected to take more challenging and uncomfortable tasks. She wanted to push him to his limits in his devotion to her, seeing his love and affection increase with each session.

The cottage had an entirely different feel from the red room. That afternoon the sun was over the garden and the honeysuckle flowers gave off a heady scent that blew in on the gentle breeze.

Debra didn't turn around when Lucian entered the

room for this time things would be very different.

She ignored him as he stood there behind her. She checked her diamond watch and picked up her glass of red wine, and slowly sipped it while she waited.

Lucian didn't speak. He just gazed at her in silence, then thinking maybe she hadn't heard him come in, he whispered so as not to startle her.

"I'm here Mistress what would you like me to do?"

In an instant, she spun around her hair flying and slapped him full force across the face with her open palm. Lucian reeled back, nearly being knocked off his feet from the sheer force. His hand went to his cheek, and he couldn't speak from the shock.

His cheek was burning, and he was sure he could feel it swelling.

Lucian looked at Debra sensing something was very wrong, he could see the hurt and anger in her blazing eyes.

Lucian was filled with fear and panic.

She screamed at him.

"You lied and betrayed me you bastard!"

Lucian was rooted to the spot. Debra circled him making him feel dizzy.

"You deceived me! You fucked dirty whores behind my back! You're a criminal and filthy child molester."

Lucian couldn't speak just stood looking at Debra.

Her accusations spinning round in his head, Lucian was dumbfounded.

She stepped forward and grabbed Lucian's hair yanking his head back.

"If that wasn't bad enough, you revolting prick, you shared our sessions online!"

Lucian couldn't believe what he was hearing, the blood drained from his face.

He stammered, "What do you mean? I haven't done anything Mistress, I swear I haven't!"

"You fucking liar."

She screamed swinging at him again clawing his neck with her long red nails.

Lucian panicked and jumped back away from her. She was wild. He had never seen her so upset. Normally she was cool refined and totally in control. This time, her eyes blazed with tears, her perfectly made up face was contorted with anger.

"It's not true Mistress, please Mistress listen to me."

He tried to plead with her.

Debra shrieked, "You lying filthy bastard Lucian, I have seen it all over the social media and the Internet."

"How dare you fucking betray me you disgusting shit?"

She yelled and raising her hand slapped him again hard across the face.

She walked across the room picked up a pair of wrist restraints, turned and threw them at him

"Get your fucking clothes off and put these on."

Lucian hesitated, his head reeling and his face burning, she screamed at him.

"Hurry up you vile little pig!!"

He picked them up and started to get undressed. He was sweating, and his heart was beating so fast he thought it would explode. He put one restraint onto his wrist.

Debra screamed, "NO! Put them on your fucking ankles."

Lucian looked up with fear in his eyes.

Debra had never needed to tie him down. She never used any ropes or restraints. She liked Lucian to submit and consent willingly. This time, Debra was stone cold and acting like a crazed woman.

Lucian put the restraints around his ankles and stood before her, still trembling and petrified. Maybe if he pleased her, doing what she wanted, she might calm down and explain what was going on. The next action convinced Lucian that Debra wasn't kidding or acting out a role-play.

She slapped his face a third time and said, "Kneel before your Mistress you fucking filthy piece of shit."

He knelt down, and she put her sharp stiletto heel on his chest pushing him onto his back.

She towered over him as he lay naked cold and shivering on the hard floor. She turned and went to a cupboard and collected a length of chain. Clipping the end of the chain to the rings on the restraints, she attached it to rope pulley mounted on the wall.

Lucian pleaded again.

"Please Mistress, I have done nothing, I swear".

She ordered him to put his legs out straight. Lucian did,

his heart racing, he dreaded what she was going to do next.

This time all he could feel was Debra's detachment and the connection wasn't there for him. He then realised that it wasn't pain he craved or the act of hurting that excited him. Somewhere in both their heads a trigger would go off, and the sexual chemistry would work. It was the connection between them that made it work.

With one swift movement, she connected the rope to an electric hoist and the pressed a button on the wall.

Lucian was raised slowly into the air. As his ankles rose above waist height, she stopped the hoist. He was suspended with his shoulders still touching the floor and his head bent forward with his chin on his chest.

She came over to Lucian and stood astride his shoulders. Looking down at him, she spat in his face. Then, taking his cock and balls in her hand she gripped them tightly and said, "You are going to tell me everything about the articles on-line, or I shall hurt you so badly that you will wish you were dead."

"Mistress please, I don't understand what you are talking about. I haven't shared anything we have done. I wouldn't do something like that."

"I swear it's not true Mistress, hurt me all you want it

won't change anything it must be a mistake.... Please believe me."

Stepping off him she said, "We will soon see?"

Lucian's mind raced as he tried to see what she was doing behind him.

She was certainly capable of inflicting very intense pain, and he feared that she would cause him some serious damage this time.

Coming back into view Debra squatted down, so she was nearer to Lucian's face.

To his horror, she had a large kitchen knife in her hand.

Debra placed the knife in between Lucian's balls and he felt the cold sharpness of the blade's point.

She gritted her teeth and hissed, "Tell me why you did it, you bastard!!"

Lucian pleaded with her again.

"I didn't do anything I swear Mistress!"

Debra grabbed his cock and balls, pulling them up and placing the knives sharp edge across his stretched scrotum.

"Tell me!" she screamed.

"I didn't know, I wouldn't, and I love you, Debra!"
Lucian cried.

Pressing the blade point into his balls, Debra said, "Last
chance before I cut your balls off and stuff them down
your lying throat!"

Lucian sobbed, as the sharp edged knife pressed into
his skin.

Getting no reply, Debra stared at Lucian.

Debra was torn. In her rage she wanted to slaughter
Lucian, repeatedly stabbing him in a frenzied
bloodbath. But in her heart, she was yearning for it not
to be true. Debra hoped this kind man, who she had
fallen for, was innocent of these unforgivable crimes of
disclosure.

"Right. You have forty-eight hours to prove this is a
setup and that you Lucian Palmer Jones had nothing to
do with it."

Lucian nodded feverously.

She continued, "If you can provide me with proof. I will
continue to see you, however, if you do not convince
me it's over, and you will never see me again."

As Debra delivered this statement, she pressed the knife deeper into his scrotum piercing the skin and drawing blood.

Watching a small trickle of blood run down his stomach, Debra continued by saying, "In forty-eight hours, you will meet me at The Park Lane Hilton International hotel at 10.30 pm."

"If you are late or don't have the evidence, I will not wait, and will be gone forever".

Placing the blood-stained blade of the knife between Lucian's trembling buttocks she stepped back.

Debra didn't speak again or wait for an answer. She walked across the room and left, slamming the door behind her.

Lucian hung there stunned, with his feet in the air and warm blood trickling down his chest. It ran in a steady flow down his neck into his left ear. He replayed Debra's words in his head and wondered what the hell she had found online.

He had no idea how he was going to locate the proof and show he was innocent.

But first things first ... Getting down from this position before he bled to death would be a good start.

The chain was tied to the rope, which was attached to the pulley a few feet away. Lucian couldn't reach to unhook himself. He couldn't call out for help, as there didn't seem to be any other houses nearby.

If someone did come to his aid, what would he say? Upside down, naked and bleeding heavily at three in the afternoon!

"What a fucking predicament!" he said out loud.

Lucian summoned all his strength, twisting in the ankle restraints and managed to turn over onto his front. By doing an awkward press up kind of handstand, he was able to unhook the pulley from its hook. As he did so, he fell forward hitting his face on the floor. Cursing Lucian got to his feet took off the restraints. He went to the bathroom and looked at his blood-splattered torso, feeling relieved that he still had his balls.

As he stood looking in the mirror, he was aware that the blood was still flowing and was running steadily down his leg. He was surprised that such a small cut could bleed so heavily

Turning on the shower, Lucian quickly washed off the blood from his chest and neck. He let the hot water run between his legs.

Drying himself, Lucian took several pieces of toilet

tissue and wrapped it around his stinging nuts. He applied pressure hoping he wouldn't need stitches at the hospital, with awkward questions to answer.

He could imagine the doctor saying, "So Mr Palmer Jones just how did you get such a deep cut on your scrotum?"

After a few minutes, he checked the toilet tissue and thankfully the bleeding seemed to have stopped.

He got dressed; there was no sign of Debra as he left the cottage.

After driving home in a daze, Lucian poured himself a drink and sat at his laptop.

Lucian was absolutely horrified by what he found online about himself and Debra. Lucian spent some time reading things he hadn't done with people he hadn't meet in places he had never been to.

Some of the images of the man, in the video clips closely resembled Lucian's body shape and build. It didn't show his identity as the man wore a full-face leather hood. Other scenes showed the man tied to a cross having his nipples tortured and undergoing extreme punishments.

Lucian knew he hadn't done these things but how could he deny the photographic evidence?

He had never met with a Mistress in Scotland, even though he had been in Scotland on that date. The Mistress was blonde and skinny, a complete opposite to Debra.

He read in amazement, a conversation going back six months, with this woman leading up to the date of a session in Scotland at the time of Lucian's business trip.

He had never had this online chat, and there were others too.

One thread showed him talking online with a Mistress in London and to seeing her not once but twice. Checking back in his dairy he could see that the dates were exactly the days he was in London. He had been in London all that day, and he could well have found an hour or two to see this woman, but he definitely hadn't!

He didn't even know what a Mistress was until I met Debra!

The worst stuff was the video clips of him and Debra during their sessions. He could hardly bear to look at the photos and watch the clips. He could now see why Debra was so utterly furious with him.

There were photos showing Debra in bed on the cruise and Lucian dressed to please her serving her wine on a silver tray. These were photos he had taken on his iPhone! And now these were on his fake Facebook page.

 A video they had made of Debra doing her makeup the night they went to dinner was also on there too. Lucian knew he would never have aired this to the outside world.

Some of the photos were real; there was no denying it. But some were not, and the dates were hard to dispute.

Lucian felt desperate for Debra; he loved her and would never have done this.

This was out there for her family and friends to see, her business contacts around the world and the others in the "Lifestyle" would not be happy with Debra going so public.

Lucian was now in a state of panic. Anyone could see these posts, his ex-wife and children, his work colleagues and family. It was evident to Lucian that his identity had been stolen and an attempt had been made to ruin his relationship with Debra.

He didn't have any enemies that he was aware of?

Lucian thought "Who would do this to me?"

Maybe it was Debra that had enemies that would benefit from her being disgraced or embarrassed.

Lucian needed to find out who this person was as soon as possible. He was desperate to find a way to prove his innocence and restore her faith in him. He needed to clear his name, but the task was enormous, if not impossible.

Lucian was feeling at a total loss, the clock was ticking, and he didn't know where to start.

Panicking Lucian thought, who could he contact, who should he trust? Lucian paced the room shouting to himself "Think Lucian, fucking think."

In desperation, Lucian called his business IT guy Martin.

Martin was a techie who Lucian had used for the office IT and the company website for some years. Although it was embarrassing to involve someone else, he was sure Martin would be discreet.

Chapter 43

After a short conversation with Martin, Lucian explained the problem he faced.

"Can you close it all down and delete the pages?" Lucian asked.

After some thought Martin said, "I don't think so, it's beyond me, but I think I know someone who could."

"Ok who?" Said Lucian

"It's a guy I met from my Home Office days a few years ago. He knew about this sort of thing, I might be able to track him down."

Lucian felt a glimmer of hope and asked, "How long do you need?"

"Give me a day or so and can I pass on your number on."

"Please call him today Martin, I am in a desperate situation! My whole damned life depends on it." Lucian blurted out, choking back the tears as he thought about

Debra. He just wanted to hold her and tell her everything was going to be okay.

Martin replied, "I will try. Leave it with me."

Lucian thanked Martin and hung up. Martin sensing the urgency in Lucian's voice, made some calls.

Lucian lay on his bed, his heart aching more than the stinging wound on his balls. Debra had only given him forty-eight hours and he just prayed that Martin's contact would come back to help him in time.

Lucian called Marcus and asked if Debra was there.

Marcus was very unfriendly and informed him she wasn't there, and he was not to call again.

Lucian pleaded with Marcus and asked him if there had been any threatening letters, emails or strange things happening at the house.

He begged Marcus almost in tears "Please Marcus, please help me, this was not my doing!!"

Marcus seemed to soften a little and said there hadn't been anything unusual going on.

Lucian asked, "Did Debra have any problems or hassles with anyone in business in the last few months?"

Marcus listened and then said, "It's more likely she would tell you than me, darling."

Marcus was quick to point out that Debra was a very private person and even if she had been in a difficult situation she probably wouldn't have discussed it with him.

Lucian explained it was all a frame-up, and he was innocent. He told Marcus what had happened when he saw Debra that afternoon and that he wouldn't and couldn't have done it.

"I love Debra and would never hurt her Marcus, you have to believe me."

Marcus thought for a minute then said, "The only thing that is different is that she had a new security system fitted recently."

"Really," said Lucian grasping at anything that might help.

"Yes, a techie guy came to the house installed and fitted it, I didn't like him he was a creepy bugger."

"Not your type then Marcus" teased Lucian trying to lighten the mood and get Marcus to stay on the line.

"Not like you sweetie" camped up Marcus.

They both laughed then Marcus said, "He was here at the house for a few hours installing the cameras and alarms."

"Were they connected to the Net?" asked Lucian.

"Yes, but we are on a secure private network so it's very unlikely that someone like that could access us remotely."

"Is it possible?" asked Lucian

"I don't know, but give me a minute, I'll run some tests and see what I can find out for you. If you are innocent Lucian, the truth will eventually come out, if you are not then God help you!"

Lucian told Marcus that if he couldn't prove his innocence, then he would never see her again.

Marcus said, "It might be worse than that Lucian, you were lucky she didn't cut your balls off!"

Lucian hung up feeling utterly helpless. He sat on his bed looking at Debra's photo on his phone feeling crushed. Lucian loved this woman and would take anything for her, but this rejection was too much for him to bear.

Since Lucian had left Debra's cottage, he had tried to call her mobile dozens of times. He sent her endless text messages begging for her to see him or answer his calls.

Lucian sent a long email to try to explain how he would never worship another Mistress or betray her in this way.

Deep in thought, Lucian jumped when his mobile phone rang. He grasped the phone hoping it was Debra, but it was Marcus.

"Hello Lucian, I think I have found something."

"Go on" Lucian replied

"It's rather strange, but the alarm and the camera system are on a closed loop. But the server logs show the system has been tried multiple times to gain remote access, and that is most unusual."

"The firewall has prevented access, but the remote access port has been tried over 300 times."

"Oh my God by whom?" said Lucian.

"We can't tell for sure, but it could be the guy that fitted the cameras. I caught him snooping around Debra's private system when he was here."

"Has he been back since?" Asked Lucian

"Well, yes and no," Said Marcus

"The system shut down overnight because of a load of remote attacks," explained Marcus

"I called him to come back and fix it, but it reset its self. Everything was fine, so we cancelled his call back."

"Although" Marcus continued, "I think he did come back that day. Charles was at the house and we saw his van on the cameras outside the gates. I believe he followed Debra to the airport when she went to stay in London."

"Who is he?" asked Lucian

"His name is Dominic. He's someone Carol found, he works for CCTV Installations Limited."

"Do you have his details?" asked Lucian

"I think I have a card somewhere, he left one in the pool room. I will text the details to you."

Lucian thanked Marcus, hung up and started to review the posts and profiles that had been created by this mystery person.

As he was reading through his mobile rang with a withheld number. He picked up hardly daring to breathe, and a loud, camp voice said, "Lucian darling, it's Marcus. I called you on Debra's private line because it's more secure. I have the CCTV man's details."

"Ok," said Lucian, slightly disappointed.

"His name is Dominic Clayton, and his company is based in Hounslow."

Lucian jotted down the address, his website and email details.

Lucian thanked Marcus for the second time and hung up.

Lucian didn't trust the police, and they move far too slowly, and the clock was ticking. In desperation, he called Martin's number again, but it went to answer machine. He left a brief, tense message and hung up.

After another forty-five minutes, the phone rang and thankfully it was Martin.

Lucian asked if he had found someone who could help. Martin paused, and Lucian couldn't help pressing him.

"Well?"

Martin said he hadn't found his original contact, but he had found someone else.

Martin explained.

"Look this really isn't my thing, I will give you a name but would prefer you don't mention me as I don't want to be involved."

"Ok, please Martin, just give me the name," Lucian pleaded.

Martin told him that the contact was an ex -police detective, who had been involved in several high-profile cases. He had left the force under a cloud in the late 1990's who was now based in Elstree and worked as a private investigator.

"Ok, but is he any good and can he help me," asked Lucian.

"The word is that he is a rough diamond and tough as they come. I hear he doesn't play by the rules Lucian, so be careful and best not to mess with him."

"Thank you, Martin, I owe you," said Lucian as he hung up.

Chapter 44

Lucian dialed the number Martin had given him. The phone rang several times then a gruff voice said, "What?"

Lucian was taken aback and said, "Is that, Harry Wilson? I'm looking er calling for a Harry Wilson," stammered Lucian.

"Who wants to know?" said the voice.

"My name is Lucian Palmer Jones I'm an estate agent," said Lucian, immediately regretting saying that.

"I don't need a house son," said the Voice

"No. Er I have problem..." stammered Lucian

"I ain't a fucking shrink either mate I think you have the wrong number."

"No, no wait," said Lucian, "I need your help, Mr Wilson. I've have had my identity stolen and need to find who took it."

There was a long pause then silence, followed by a cough and sniff.

The Voice said, "Ok I'm Harry, so tell me about it."

Lucian gave a brief overview of the fake profile, the posts and the photos but didn't go into any details about Debra.

"Who else is involved?" asked Harry sensing Lucian's reluctance to go into detail.

"There is a wealthy woman. It's a very difficult situation."

Harry snorted again and said, "There is always a difficult situation when women are involved, who is she?"

"I'd rather not say over the phone," said Lucian.

"Well, it isn't Princess Diana mate. She's dead! "

"No, it's someone who is very much alive and in trouble!" said Lucian

"So what do you need me for Mr Palmer Jones? I'm a busy man, and the football is on soon" Harry grunted.

Lucian was getting very frustrated with the arrogance of this man, but Harry was his only chance and time was definitely not on his side.

 "I really need your help, Mr Wilson. Can I meet you tonight somewhere, please Harry I am desperate," pleaded Lucian.

Harry was quiet for a second then said "Tell me her name?"

"Ok but can I trust you to be discreet?" asked Lucian.

Harry snorted.

"Look mate if fucking Princess Diana could trust me I think you are safe to assume that you can son!"

Lucian gave Harry Debra's name and didn't say anything more.

Harry made a note of Debra's name and agreed to meet Lucian at 7.30 pm at The Three Rats in Hammersmith.

Before he signed off, he said, "Look, son, if this lady has the sort of money I suspect she has, I can be as discreet as you like. Just send me everything you have by email, and be sure you don't do it from your own email address."

He gave Lucian a Gmail address and hung up.

Lucian used Christina's personal Gmail and sent

everything he had got from Marcus and a brief summary of what they knew of Dominic's details so far.

After hitting the send button, he Googled The Three Rats in Hammersmith made a note of the address on his phone.

Lucian hurriedly left his apartment and made his way to Richmond tube station. He rode the Tube across town, walking the short distance up a semi dark side street to the pub called The Three Rats. It was one of those traditional old drinking houses that were fast going out of business.

Lucian got himself a drink and sat surveying the dreary inside surroundings while he waited for Harry to arrive.

The décor was tired and dated, and the carpet looked like it hadn't been changed for fifty years. The ceiling was stained dark yellow from years of tobacco smoke. It hadn't been repainted since the smoking ban came in. Umpteen signs and trinkets decorated the high shelves that ran the length of the walls.

It clearly didn't benefit from a trendy lunchtime or after work crowd and was in need of a fresh lick of paint.

There were only three people in the pub, a man reading

a paper and two young men who looked sheepish as they held hands under the table. They naturally favoured a quiet place where they could chat and be close without the prejudiced stares of others.

The landlady was a typical London barmaid type with a bottle-bleached beehive hairdo, a smudge of peach lipstick and poorly applied blobby blue mascara.

Debra made up like a movie star, while this landlady looked like she had applied her makeup with a palette knife and no mirror.

After twenty minutes Harry still hadn't turned up.

Lucian was feeling very desperate and anxious, he called the number, but it just rang and rang.

Angry, Lucian stood up and left the pub. Crossing the road he saw a car parked alongside the kerb. It was away from the streetlights, deep in shadow with the engine running.

As Lucian looked closer, the car lights flashed once. Lucian turned and walked towards the car, as he did so the car pulled away from the kerb and speed at Lucian. Thinking he would be knocked down, he threw himself back to the kerb landing on his arse.

The car skidded sideways on to a halt, the driver wound down the window and shouted: "Get in!"

Stunned for a moment, Lucian said, "What? Hold on, who are you?"

The driver yelled again.

"I'm Harry, get in the fucking car."

Lucian picked himself up, ran around the front of the car and jumped in the passenger seat. He was pushed back in his seat as the car accelerated away. Nobody spoke. After a mile the car turned sharply into an abandoned warehouse and skidded to a stop.

Turning to the driver, Lucian said, "If you are Harry, your bloody forty-five minutes late!"

Harry grunted a reply "Yes I am Harry, and I wasn't late. I was here before you arrived to watch the pub making sure you weren't followed."

Harry turned to Lucian and looked him square in the face "You should be more careful."

Lucian looked at the scruffy, unshaven man with longish grey hair. He wore a leather coat with a black V-neck jumper underneath.

Harry sat at the wheel of a Jaguar S type smoking and blowing the smoke out of the window.

He really didn't know what he was getting into with

this scruffy man. Lucian was taken aback as he had never considered the possibility of being followed. All that Lucian knew was he had to find the person who was creating these profiles and stop him.

As he turned to Harry, someone sniffed in the back seat. Lucian jumped startled by the fact they weren't alone in the car. Lucian spun around and could see a young lad sitting back on the back seat in the shadows.

"That's Mikey," said Harry as a way of introduction to the young black youth in the back seat.

Lucian couldn't see his face clearly due to the dark hoodie top that he was wearing.

"Mikey is my step son." explained Harry. "Mikey has particular talents when it comes to cybercrime."

Lucian was silent for a moment and then said, "What do we do now?"

Harry laughed a smoky laugh and said, "Well Lucian my son. First, we talk money. My day rate is £1,200 plus expenses and Mikey's is £340.00."

Lucian was slightly taken aback by the frankness of the man but knew he had little choice. If he was going to get the information within the forty-eight hours he would have to trust and pay Harry.

"Ok let me tell you about what I know so far." Lucian started to explain when Harry laughed again.

"Look I don't need to know about your kinky sessions with an older woman," he said. "It isn't the first time and certainly won't be the last."

"So let take it as read, that this lady doesn't want her personal life out there and has a lot to lose."

Lucian took a breath and said, "Ok but we don't have a lot of time, I need to find this person and fast. I have to get back to Debra and show her it's all a setup."

Harry paused and then said, "Tell him, Mikey."

Lucian turned around. The figure in the shadows sat forward, showing that he was a youth of about seventeen to nineteen years old. He was mixed race and had a thin wispy moustache over his lip and short-cropped hair.

Mikey looked at Lucian and said, "The guy you want is called Dominic Clayton, and he is like well smart."

"What do you mean?" said Lucian.

Harry spoke up, "After we had spoken earlier, Mikey went on the grid and did some quiet digging."

"We also talked to Marcus and Carol and got a line into

this guy's life. He is a smart boy and has been active in some dodgy online stuff for some time."

Lucian nodded and continued to listen.

Harry continued, "If this guy is anything like as good as we suspect he is, he will be all over your communications. He may be watching your movements and has possibly bugged your office and flat."

"It's good that you used Christina's Gmail, but you have to assume all your computers and phones are compromised."

"I suggest you get a new Gmail address one that is not related to you or your business. Also, get a new pay as you go mobile phone."

Lucian couldn't believe what he was hearing.

Right, Harry continued, "Don't go home tonight, stay in a hotel you have never stayed in before."

"Oh my God, really," said Lucian feeling stupid and quite sick.

"No shit Sherlock," said Harry.

"It's not often that Mikey comes off a recce looking worried, eh Mikey?"

"Yeah man" was Mikey's soft reply.

"This guy has some crafty tricks set up to stop people like Mikey doing what we did."

"He is a major league player, and you need to know this is serious shit."

"Yeah like, serious man!" Mikey echoed again from the back seat.

Lucian sat in silence and tried to take in all the information that Harry had just told him.

Harry continued, "Ok, we know who he is, we also know where he lives. But we have to be very careful, do you have a gun?"

"A gun! Jesus No I don't have a gun. I'm an estate agent, not a fucking gangster." exclaimed Lucian, who was now feeling very scared and sick to his stomach.

Harry opened the glove box and passed Lucian a parcel wrapped in a black towel.

"Here take this."

Lucian reeled back and said, "No, I have never fired a gun in my life. I have never even held one, what good would it do if I can't even point it!"

Harry put the gun back in the glove box and said:, "Ok, but don't say I didn't offer you it."

He started the car and drove down a few streets, turning left and then right, until he passed West Kensington Tube station.

Lucian was sure he went a complete circle. Harry pulled over and said, "Take the Tube, get a new phone and check into a hotel. Here's my number call me when you are in the room."

He gave Lucian a card, and when Lucian was out of the car, he sped away.

Lucian stood at the tube entrance, dazed by the last few minutes and wondering what the hell he had got involved in. Before getting out of the car, Lucian had given his credit card details to a complete stranger that had a gun in his vehicle glove box!

"This is just crazy, fucking crazy," Lucian said out loud making a lady on the pavement give him a strange look.

Shaking his head, he crossed over the road to a small phone shop with a flashing neon sign saying "Phones unlocked."

He walked out twenty minutes later, with a simple pay as you go mobile phone. But it had been so complicated, Lucian felt like he had just taken out a lease on the whole phone shop.

Lucian took the District Line entrance. Now alone on the crowded Tube station he kept looking around thinking he was being watched. Even though he had only just met Harry and Mikey, he took some comfort from being in their company. Lucian had watched a lot of movies and always enjoyed the spy thriller plots. But now he was in his own real life one. His stomach was tense, and he was sweating.

Taking the next train, Lucian emerged from the Tube station at Bayswater.

It had started to rain and he nervously checked behind him. But all he saw was a sea of faces as they hurried along. Crossing the street, and pulling up his collar against the drizzle, Lucian turned right towards a row of inexpensive hotels. With its white facade and green over door awning, the Lord John Hotel looked welcoming.

Lucian was glad to get out of the drizzle as he stood in the small cramped reception behind an American couple.

They were asking about West End shows and restaurants. They were speaking to an Eastern European girl, who clearly knew nothing about the city.

Lucian was just about to turn around and leave when a man's voice asked, "Can I help you, Sir."

Lucian turned, and a well-dressed middle-aged man was now standing behind the counter.

"Yes, I would like a room," said Lucian.

"How many nights," asked the man

"Just tonight please," said Lucian

"Oh Ok Let me see what we have left," man said.

The man clicked the mouse and pressed a few keys "I don't have any standard rooms I'm afraid. It's a busy time, with London Fashion Week and The Ideal Home Show."

Lucian cursed and said, "What do you have then?"

The man tapped a few more keys and said, "We do have one vacancy left at our sister hotel in Kensington. It's a deluxe room, but it's £250 a night."

"Oh that's a lot!" said Lucian.

The man again tapped a few keys and then said, "I can give you a 20% discount sir if you would like to book it now?"

Lucian looked at the rain as it fell heavily outside and

said reluctantly, "Ok, thank you I'll take it."

The man tapped some keys and said, "That's booked shall I call a taxi for you sir?

"Thank you and yes please for the cab," said Lucian.

He stood for few moments on the steps of the hotel sheltering from the downpour. The taxi arrived after a few minutes, and he got in the back. The cab pulled away after Lucian gave the taxi driver the hotel address. Lucian had been in too much of hurry to notice a bald headed man standing against the railings opposite the hotel.

He didn't see as he got into a silver van on the other side of the road. The rain fell harder as the van did a U-turn and followed Lucian's cab as it picked its way through the traffic.

Chapter 45

Sitting behind the wheel of his van, Dominic watched the silhouette of Lucian's head in the rear window of the cab.

Dominic imaged the Kennedy assassination in slow motion. He pictured Lucian's head snapping forward, as a large calibre bullet entered the back of his skull, his face exploding all over the Perspex dividing screen.

Dominic smiled a wry smile and muttered to himself.

"Oh no, my handsome friend, that would be far too quick and easy for you. I would want you to suffer a while before I allow you to escape into death."

As the cab passed through the traffic lights, Dominic could see on his phone that they were heading towards Kensington High Street.

He had followed Lucian since he left his apartment nearly losing him when he got into the Jaguar at The Three Rats.

He had made a mental note of the number plate and would find out later who it belonged to.

As the cab pulled over, Dominic drove past and parked at the next corner. He got out of the van with a leather bag. Dominic caught a glimpse of Lucian ascending the steps of the Kensington Grand Hotel.

Opposite the hotel was a coffee bar advertising "Free Wi-Fi."

Dominic went inside bought a takeout cappuccino, and took a seat facing the hotel entrance.

Dominic waited ten minutes for Lucian to check in and made sure he wasn't changing hotel again. Dominic pulled his IPad Mini from his jacket and tapped a few onscreen keys. It had been easy to plant the GPS tracker, as he brushed past Lucian in the West Kensington tube station.

The tiny tracker in Lucian's jacket showed that he was on the sixth floor and was stationary.

Dominic drank his coffee and watched and waited. After twenty minutes he went over to the hotel and asked the receptionist if his friend Lucian Palmer Jones had checked in and what his room number was.

The girl didn't have any hesitation in giving Dominic Lucian's room number and confirming he had signed in under his real name. She offered to call his suite to let him know his friend was here.

"Oh No, that's Ok I will see him in the bar later." said Dominic.

"Is there, anything else I can help you with?" asked the girl.

"No," said Dominic "You have been more help than you know."

And with that he headed towards the lifts.

In the room, Lucian laid on the bed his head spinning, his thoughts on Debra. It had been such a whirlwind, he only had hours to find this man and get to Debra before the deadline. Harry seemed to think this man was very dangerous but who was he and what could Lucian do to fight a cyber-criminal?

Lucian went to the bathroom. Looking at himself in the mirror he was shocked as to how wild he looked. His eyes were bloodshot from lack of sleep, his skin pale and blotchy. A real contrast to how he and Debra looked on the cruise ship. He recalled how happy and contented he had appeared, his skin slightly tanned and his posture relaxed.

Now Lucian looked tense and stressed, and his whole body felt taught and burned with emotion. Taking some Aspirin in his jacket pocket, he crushed two with the glass tumbler on the hard marble sink surface. With his credit card, Lucian scraped the white powder into a glass. Mixing it with Scotch from the mini bar, he drank down the contents in one go, gasping at the rawness of the whisky and the sharpness of the Aspirin.

Falling back onto the bed he tried Debra's private number again, but it went unanswered.

He had seen her ignore calls before when she was driving or doing something that required her attention. She would look at the screen, see who it was, smile a knowing smile and turn the ringer off.

He called Harry's number, and Mikey answered in a panic.

"My Dad is on his way to pick you up, but you must get out of the hotel right away!"

"Why, what is going on?" said Lucian.

"We have been looking into Dominic's profile and found a lot of crazy scary stuff."

"What stuff?" Lucian butted in.

"It's bad man, just get out, he knows where you are, and

he is coming!! Hurry man run!"

"Ok, ok but I just got here!"

The waiter over the road picked up Dominic's half-drunk coffee and placed it on the tray. He was surprised to see there were deep bite marks all around the rim of the cardboard cup.

The lift doors opened, Dominic got in and pressed floor Six, Lucian's floor.

As the elevator started its ascent, he drew a large carving knife out of the leather bag he was carrying. Dominic ran the point down the mirror leaving a scratch across his reflected face, from one side of his face from ear to ear, and then drew a Z-shape across his eyes.

When the lift reached level Three, it stopped, and the doors opened, a well-dressed couple got in the man asked

"Going down?"

Dominic didn't speak just indicated with his head that he was going up. Undeterred the couple entered the lift and stood with their backs to Dominic.

The woman was middle-aged, her hair was put up in an elegant twist. Dominic could smell her expensive perfume. Her low cut cocktail dress showed her shoulders and slender neck and her earrings were sparkling in the lifts lights.

Dominic imagined punching her in the mouth; her perfect white teeth shattering under his gold coin signet ring. Refocusing his eyes, he was staring at her expensive designer shoes and slim ankles. Dominic looked her up and down and was tempted to run the point of his knife down her exposed spine. He imagined watching her face turning into a scream of sheer terror as he pushed the knife in deeper.

Her partner, in contrast, was a plump, balding man with an ill-fitting suit. His white shirt collar was open and held together with a thin blue tie.

Dominic put his head back against the mirror closing his eyes, an image flashed through his mind of the man with his throat cut and his face slashed in several places. The woman on her knees blood running from her nose and mouth, her hair now free and falling across her tear and blood stained face.

At that point, the lift stopped Dominic was jolted from his daydream. As the doors opened the couple parted so Dominic could step out. As they did, he had an overwhelming desire to bite the woman's neck sinking his teeth deep into her flesh.

Dominic didn't and the lift door closed, and the couple made their descent unscathed.

Looking down Dominic saw that he had been stabbing his leg with the point of the knife. Dominic had been unaware of his actions, his mind on the murder of the couple.

Room 629 was to the right, Dominic set out to find it and complete his task. He was determined to kill the man who stood between him and his rightful Mistress, Debra Fielding.

Lucian's phone rang. It was Harry.

"Where the fuck are you, Lucian? Did you speak to Mikey?"

Lucian was still lying on the bed having tried Debra's phone again.

He sat up and said, "Yes, I did... but how could he know where I am, and what room I'm in?"

Lucian continued, "Mikey told me you had found some stuff about Dominic. Harry you've got to tell me what is going on!"

Harry just yelled at the top of his voice, "There isn't

fucking time to explain! If you want to live to see Debra again, get the fuck out of the hotel. Now!"

"Ok ok I'm leaving," said Lucian jumping up from the bed.

"Get out and meet me in the alley beside the hotel entrance, and for fuck's sake hurry up!"

Hanging up Lucian was thrown into a panic. Grabbing his coat and wallet he headed towards to door.

As he opened it standing outside was a young girl about six years old. She was dressed in pink and yellow pyjamas, a red fluffy dressing gown and holding a teddy bear.

Looking at Lucian, the girl said, "Is this room 529?"

Lucian looked at the door and said: "No, it's 629 I think you are on the wrong floor."

The little girl hugged the bear looking at Lucian and said, "Mummy will be worried can you help me find her?"

Lucian smiled and said, "Come with me I'll take you down one floor."

The little girl grabbed Lucian's hand, as he turned left towards the lifts.

The girl pulled away saying, "Barney doesn't like the lift it scares him."

"Oh," said Lucian.

"He got stuck in one once," the little girl said as a way of explanation.

"Ok," said Lucian "If Barney is scared of the lift, we will take the stairs."

Taking the little girl's hand again, they turned to the right and walked away.

Dominic turned the corner, the knife at his side. He saw what he took for a father and daughter walking down the hall. Dominic ducked back against the wall so he would not be noticed. Once they were out of sight, he approached Lucian's room.

Pausing outside room 629, he took a pass card key reader out of his leather bag and slipped it into the door lock. The device went through over 10,000 key card combinations in less than two seconds. Then the lock clicked, disengaged and showed a green light

Opening the door quietly he entered the room only to find it empty. He checked the room and the en-suite, running his finger over the white powder residue on the bathroom sink. Dominic put the traces to his tongue. Reacting to the bitter taste disappointingly, it was only Aspirin; he hoped it might have been cocaine.

Dominic had tried several mood-altering drugs such as Cocaine and Speed. He had also experimented with a host of pills from E's to Quaaludes. None of these drugs had done anything for his mental state or enhanced his sexual performance. He found poppers gave him a headache, and Viagra made his cock itch.

Returning to the bedroom, he realised he was too late, and Lucian had escaped.

Throwing a chair across the room, breaking the mirrors and kicking the glass coffee table over, Dominic yelled "Fucking Shit!"

An uncontrollable rage came over him as he slashed the bedding with his knife, turned over the mini bar and ripped the telephone cable from the wall.

Violently shaking his head, he fell to his knees digging his fingers into his temples. Dominic pushed his head down into the carpet. The small glass fragments from the smashed coffee table made small cuts on his now sweating forehead.

Dominic pressed down harder and felt the needle bite of the glass particles. Still harder he pushed until the pounding in his mind started to ease.

When Dominic was calm, he lifted his head and several glass shards stayed stuck in his skull.

He went into the bathroom and looked at his face. Blood was starting to trickle down his forehead. He picked out each shard of glass, dropping them into the sink.

Suddenly Dominic punched the mirror with tremendous force, shattering it, his bloodied face reflected a dozen times in the spiral-shattered dent.

Lucian descended one flight of the hotel stairs and opened the door to the fifth floor.

He walked with the young girl towards room 529. Lucian found the room and knocked the door. An anxious looking woman answered it, about thirty years old. She looked at Lucian then the little girl. It took a couple of seconds before she swept the little girl up in her arms and hugged her saying, "Where have you been Katy?"

"I was lost Mummy," said the little girl, "This man helped me to find you."

The woman then focused on Lucian and said "Thank

you so much! I was so worried."

"It's Ok," said Lucian, smiling at the little girl.

Lucian turned to leave and said, "Take care of Barney."

The woman smiled hugging the child as Lucian headed towards the lift.

Pressing the elevator button, his thoughts came back to the man who was after him and meeting Harry in the alley by the side of the hotel.

The elevator pinged the doors opened. A tall man in a dinner jacket and a cowboy hat stepped back to allow Lucian to get into the lift carriage.

In a Texan drawl, the man in the hat said, "Going down?"

Lucian replied in his clipped English, "If you would be so kind."

"Surely," said the Texan.

Dominic splashed water on his face and wiped the blood from his forehead with a bath towel. Looking around he gritted his teeth as a voice in his head whispered: "Such a messy boy."

Ignoring the voice, he left the room, pausing for a second to check the passage was clear.

Dominic then headed for the stairs figuring that must have been the way Lucian had gone. Dominic would have seen him if he had used the lift. Going down one floor he came out into the hall just in time to see a lady with the same little girl heading for the lifts.

No sign of the man. Could that have been Lucian? He headed back to the stairs and ran down them two at a time.

Lucian had got out of the lift and crossed to the street exit. The receptionist looked like she was going to say something to him but he continued without pausing.

He turned towards the side alley. As he did a car with its lights on full beam speed towards him.

Sliding to a stop, Lucian could see Harry behind the wheel smoking a cigarette. Glancing over his shoulder Lucian got into the car and Harry sped off.

They turned sharp left before accelerating away.

Once the hotel was out of sight Harry turned to Lucian and said, "You took your Fucking time didn't you?"

Lucian ignored Harry's apparent anger and said, "Tell me what you found and who the fuck is this bloke?"

Dominic reached the bottom of the stairwell. He followed the sign that said Lobby and went out into the reception area.

He was greeted by the receptionist, who said, "Oh, your friend was just here, did you speak to him?

Dominic glared at her and said, "Where, when?"

The receptionist was taken aback at his anger and stammered, "He went outside just a second ago."

Dominic flew past the receptionist and caught a glimpse of a Jaguar car speeding away having come from the side alley.

Kicking a planter outside the hotel entrance, Dominic yelled "BOLLOCKS!"

As the car passed Wembley Park, Harry looked up at the famous football stadium.

"I grew up on Fulham Road, and my dad was a big Chelsea supporter."

"He took me to my first FA Cup final here in 1967. It was between Tottenham Hotspur and Chelsea. It was always known as the Cockney Cup Final."

"Oh" Lucian replied, not in the least bit interested.

"As it happens Tottenham won 2–1. Good match and I've hated Tottenham Hotspur ever since."

Lucian couldn't believe his ears.

"What the hell are you talking about?" he said.

Harry lit another cigarette, inhaled deeply and said, "I'm afraid our boy is a Tottenham supporter and an ingenious one at that."

"What's that got to do with anything?" Lucian asked.

"Nothing really" Harry replied.

Lucian sat in silence.

Finally, Harry spoke again.

"We did some searching and found a whole load of stuff."

"Dominic has posted quite a collection of photographs and data on you and the lovely Debra."

Sensing Lucian didn't smoke Harry lowered the window four inches and continued.

"It's very worrying that every photo of you on Instagram had been defaced in some way, this man clearly doesn't like you much at all."

"We found home movies on his Facebook page where he is slicing up a raw steak with a very sharp knife while staring a picture of your face."

Lucian said, "You are kidding me aren't you?"

Harry drew a long drag on his cigarette making the tip flare in the dark car.

"Lucian I couldn't be more serious, I have worked on serial killers cases in the past, and this is one very sick bunny."

"Where are we going now?" asked Lucian,

"To somewhere safe, but first we have to stop, and you have to get naked."

"What?" exclaimed Lucian.

"Look, he knew where you were so he must be tracking you somehow. Mikey reckons he has bugged your office, flat, car, and most probably planted a tracker in your clothes or shoes."

Harry pulled in a petrol station and got out of the car. He indicated for Lucian get out too. As he joined Harry at the back of the car, Harry handed Lucian, a pair of dark blue cotton mechanics overalls. They were well worn and smelled of grease and stale cigarettes.

"Go into the toilets and put these on, leave everything else in the bin."

Lucian pushed the overalls back at Harry.

"I am not wearing these disgusting, stinking things. And anyway Debra bought me these clothes!"

Harry shouted, "For fuck's sake, you've got bin them, Lucian!"

"I'm sure she will buy you some more, once this is all over."

Still muttering, Lucian walked over to the filling station building and went inside. To emerge five minutes later dressed in a bright patterned hoody, white T-shirt, blue nylon waterproof trousers, and dark green garden wellies.

Getting back in the car he sat with his arms folded and looked at Harry.

"Don't say a fucking word Ok, just drive."

Harry lit another cigarette, trying not to laugh. He pulled the car out of the service station, put his foot down and headed north.

Chapter 46

The Jaguar pulled out on to the North Circular Road and gathered speed. After about ten minutes Lucian asked where they were we going.

Harry kept his eyes on the wet road and his foot firmly on the pedal and replied, "My place."

After a few minutes of silence, Lucian asked, "So this Dominic bloke, what's his story? I'm completely in the dark here, I'm tired, stressed and had to escape from a hotel because I was going to get murdered!"

Harry sniffed and turned to Lucian.

"We are nearly at mine, and if you hadn't have fled when you did, you would be tired, stressed and fucking dead my son."

The Jag exited the North Circular after a short dual carriageway. Harry slowed the car and headed towards the M1 motorway. Taking the Watford exit, he branched off onto the A41 towards Elstree.

Lucian watched the leafy avenues slip past. His thoughts turned to Debra and how they had stood together on the cruise ship's balcony. She looked so beautiful in her dark sunglasses and red lipstick. Debra had said that she would like Lucian to take her driving in the English countryside.

She said that she would sit in the passenger seat smoking, while Lucian drove. He would wear a grey peaked chauffeur's hat, black leather driving gloves and grey coat to match.

Lucian was brought back from his thoughts as Harry turned the car into a driveway. They approached a set of high iron gates. Harry reached into the centre consul and picked up a small black remote control. He pointed the remote at the gates and they slowly began to swing open. Harry drove the car into the driveway and approached a small single storey house set back from the road.

Parking outside, Harry turned off the car and indicated for Lucian get out.

The front door opened, and Mikey who was wearing a different hoody, stood in the doorway. They all went inside.

Lucian looked around the hallway and was then shown into the dining room.

The house looked modest from the outside, similar to many bungalows owned by retired pensioners and older generation people. The house had apparently been updated with a modern kitchen extension.

Harry, sensing Lucian's curiosity, explained that the house had belonged to his mother and he had inherited it when she died. Harry went on to say it had a few special facilities as they had used it as a safe house in his MI5 days.

Sitting down at the kitchen table, Mikey asked Lucian if he wanted tea or coffee.

Ignoring Mikey, Lucian addressed Harry and said, "Look, I need to know what's going on, I don't have much time."

Harry sniffed, filled the kettle with fresh water and sat down at the kitchen table.

Lucian stood up and said "Please Harry! What can we do?"

Harry got up from the table and said, "Ok ok, come with me, and Mikey, tea for two mate."

Harry opened the kitchen door and walked outside lighting a cigarette. Lucian followed him out of the kitchen and onto a stone flagged patio. He followed Harry as he walked across the courtyard to a brick out building.

Harry opened the door; Lucian followed and stood staring at a spiral staircase leading underground.

After descending the stairs, they came to a large metal vault door. Harry placed his palm on a high-tech full-screen scanner. The door beeped, and the vault door opened inwards.

"Come on in," said Harry.

They entered a bright, white corridor. Lucian was surprised to see several rooms equipped with servers and high-tech equipment. Harry walked past the server rooms and entered a room with a desk and a several large Apple Mac monitors. Sitting at a desk, Harry fired up the Macs, and the screens came to life. They showed pictures of Debra and Lucian, plus several photos of a bald-headed man, sometimes wearing a 'Lakers' baseball cap.

There were more pictures of the man entering a property and getting in and out of a silver Mercedes van.

"That is our boy," said Harry.

Harry sat back in his chair and clicked through a few more screens.

Taking a deep breath, he began to explain.

"As we know his real name is Dominic Clayton, he installs CCTV and security systems and that is his connection to Debra Fielding. However, he uses several names and aliases and is a very dangerous man."

"It appears he installed Debra's systems in her Winchester house. He went to her house, met her briefly and then seemed to develop an unhealthy obsession with her. He has some deep mental problems and is a very unstable character with severe anger issues. He obviously has a talent for hacking and forging identities."

"Jesus Christ," said Lucian "where do I fit into all of this?"

Harry ignored Lucian's question and continued.

"He has been very active on blogs and forums calling Debra some very unpleasant things."

"Like what?" asked Lucian.

Harry clicked, and a screen came up with a blog called Spunky Monkey. There was a photo of Debra with a fur coat, dark glasses, wearing red lipstick, and smoking.

Underneath the picture was a long paragraph of typewritten capitals.

It read:

You are mine YOU FUCKING BITCH, YOU FUCKING BITCH, YOU FUCKING BITCH.....

Harry said, "He doesn't name her, but you can see that Dominic clearly has a serious problem with Debra. Marcus told me he was there for only one day, but he felt he was a little weird and caught him snooping around the private systems at the house."

Lucian looked worried, and Harry asked, "Can you explain what he meant by that?"

Lucian hesitated and didn't answer.

"Look this is important Lucian what has she got to hide?"

Lucian didn't want to elaborate on the special his relationship with Debra. He doubted if Harry would understand what a Mistress was and the role of Dominatrix and her submissive.

He could see that Harry and Mikey had been onto some BDSM portals trying to trace Dominic. They had to have some idea that Dominic was involved in some aspect of this world, and so was Debra.

Lucian didn't want to divulge the sexual nature of their relationship, so he said, "Debra has a separate set of cameras, and these are on a private network. She sometimes lets people use her house for, shall we say, elite parties."

Harry seized on this statement.

"Look I don't care if you and Debra are into kinky sex and enjoy swinging from the chandeliers."

Harry stared straight at Lucian.

"This man is a bloody psychopath, if he finds you or Debra, I think it will be very dangerous."

Lucian said, "Holy fuck! I didn't know it was this bad."

Harry replied, "It doesn't matter what the truth is he has done a job on you son, But what is interesting, is that he hasn't posted so much about Debra."

"We did some searching too, and even with my clearance and ex-police contacts I couldn't find much about your beloved Ms Fielding."

Lucian stood listening intently.

"How well do you know her and why can't we find her in any recent records?"

Lucian looked puzzled.

"There must be something, she never told me much.

Other than she was married and her husband was extremely wealthy. I think he died quite recently, and she was involved in some property businesses."

Harry listened and stroked his stubbly chin.

Lucian continued.

"But to be honest, we didn't talk about those sorts of things, we just enjoyed being together and spent our time planning things for the future and not discussing the past."

"How convenient," said Harry.

Harry then said, "We know who Debra was married to and yes she probably does want to keep that quiet as he was practically a billionaire. He was killed in plane crash in Venezuela and efficiently all history just disappeared."

"I know, Debra did tell me that," replied Lucian

"Well," said Harry, "She has almost no online profile and does not appear in any company records under Debra Fielding."

"Debra may have another business identity and have interests in several countries. She possibly has friends in very high places."

"She keeps everything very private, and all of our enquiries stopped at some lawyers in New York."

"We tried to speak to them, but they won't discuss their clients, but among their well-known clienele is an ex-presidents wife was is running for President!"

Lucian thought for a minute and realised just how little he knew about this woman. He was just swept away and started on the journey of discovery into the world of S&M.

Harry continued.

"Marcus did let it slip, that when Debra does have a 'Party' both he and Carol are asked to take the evening off. They are not to return until noon the next day."

Lucian remembered Debra telling him that and could feel himself blushing.

"He also confirmed that there are special cameras in the basement, and there are custom made rooms that are used for private functions. Would you care to elaborate on these "Rooms" Lucian?"

Lucian flushed and had to lie.

"I don't know what goes on in them. But I understand that Debra lets "People" use the rooms."

Lucian hoped that he sounded convincing.

Mikey came in with two cups of tea. Lucian thanked him for bringing in the sugar bowl in too.

Harry sat back, put his hands behind his head, sensing Lucian's reluctance to give details.

"So Lucian, are you in a relationship with Ms Fielding?"

"If so, what I would have to assume is that Debra is some sort of high-class Madam. Her house in Winchester is a private S&M knocking shop for the great and the good. It's probably used by politicians and celebrities to have kinky sex."

Lucian looked at the floor and said nothing.

"I would guess therefore, that if this Dominic character has got access to those cameras and possibly video footage, then there are going to be some very pissed off people."

Lucian then said, "So what can we do?"

Harry stood up pointing at the screen.

"We need to get into that van, that's what we need to do."

"We were able to access some of his files from what

was left in traces on the Internet, but even Mikey couldn't get past his security firewalls remotely. We need local access, and the van is the only way in. If we can get Mikey into that van, we can access his network and see what he has been looking at."

Lucian replied, "Do you know where the van is?"

"I have a mate at DVLA records and have an address. I'm not sure it will be there, but it's a start, and I suggest we go now."

Lucian was pleased to leave Harry's house. Back in the car they headed south again to the address listed in Hounslow. No one spoke for the first part of the forty-five-minute drive. Mikey sat in the back with DR Dray headphones under his hoody.

Lucian could hear the slight thump of the bass line of the tracks he was listening to, his face illuminated by the IPad he had propped against his knees.

 Lucian looked at Harry and asked, "Why did you quit the force?"

Harry didn't answer straight away then said, "Because of Mikey."

Lucian remained silent, and Harry continued, "I had been working on a complicated case with an informant. Her name was Beverley; she was the most beautiful black woman you have ever seen. She was talented and with a heart of gold. She was a singer and worked at a West End club. I had helped her Russian flatmate out with a rape case some years ago."

"One night she was in the private VIP suite after her set, when one of the businessmen asked her to join him for a drink. Beverley had learned Russian from her friend and while they were talking she overheard a conversation with the man's business partner and some Russians, about a large drugs and arms deal happening in the next couple of days. I was working Russian counter-intelligence then, so she called me to offer to get more details if I would look after her son if anything happened to her."

Lucian watched the road as Harry continued.

"I agreed and over the next few nights we meet up and she fed me information. As the day of the deal got nearer she was frightened for her teenage son Mikey, as he had low-level Asberger's disease."

Lucian looked at Mikey in the rear view mirror, but he wasn't listening just looking at his iPad grooving slightly to his tunes.

The car left the North Circular Road and joined the A4, still heading south. Drawing deeply on another new cigarette Harry resumed in his deep, gruff voice.

"I had found out who the Russians were and told Beverly to quit her job and to get out, as it wasn't worth getting hurt over."

Harry sounded a little choked up at this point and searched the side pocket for a bottle of water.

After guzzling almost half of the bottle, he continued.

"That night she told the club owner she was leaving. The manager threatened her with not paying her week's wages, so Beverley had to stay until the Saturday night."

Lucian watched as he fumbled and lit yet another cigarette, tossing the empty packet out of the window.

Harry coughed and continued with his story.

"We found out later from the club manager what had happened. It was Beverley's last night, and as she prepared to go back onto the VIP lounge stage, she heard the men say the deal was going down tomorrow and she overheard the location and time."

Lucian sat silent and watched the road as Harry spoke.

As Harry retold the story, the emotion in his voice was evident.

"She did her set and managed to text me the details of

the deal. That was the last time I heard from her."

Harry glanced in the rear view mirror, but Mikey was still staring at his iPhone with his earphones in and his hood up. Satisfied Mikey couldn't hear him he carried on with his story.

"She was found dead two days later, her throat had been cut. The autopsy showed terrible torture and abuse, all her fingers were broken, her face was wrecked, and her beautiful hair ripped out. She had been horribly sexually abused.

We put an operation in place at the site, but unlike the movies, the deal never happened.

We can only assume that after she was tortured, she talked, and the Russians moved the location. It happens all the time. The news and media never get wind of even a fraction of the deals that go down."

Lucian sat in shocked silence listening to Harry's story and wondered if Debra was involved in this sort of thing, surely not? But he was starting to think nothing was impossible or was, as it seemed.

The story had passed the time; Harry pulled the car over to the kerb, turning off the engine and lights

They scanned the road ahead, but there was no sign of Dominic's van.

They sat back, and Harry said, "We need to get into that van, but we will just have to wait until he comes back."

Turning and getting Mikey's attention Harry said, "Go check out the house, but be careful."

"Yeah Ok," said Mikey getting out of the car still wearing his headphones, but leaving his IPad on the back seat.

Lucian watched him walk towards to house then turned to Harry and said, "Tell me more about Beverly and Mikey. What happened next?"

Harry sniffed.

"He's a good kid. Despite his condition he works hard at school and never been in trouble with drugs or fighting. His mum was a wonderful lady and one day I will find those bastards. I'll kill 'em all, and it isn't going to be quick either."

He fumbled in his jacket pulled out a new pack of Marlborough cigarettes and lit one, blowing the smoke out of the window. He smoked in silence unable to continue for a moment as the emotion became too much.

At that moment a silver Mercedes van passed them and pulled into the kerb 100 yards ahead. Lucian shrank down in his seat.

Harry laughed and said, "You watch too many movies mate he won't see us this far away."

Harry leant out of the window and gave a short, sharp whistle. Mikey just carried on walking and didn't look back.

As they watched the van door opened, and Dominic got out, he didn't look in their direction just shut the van door and headed towards the house.

Harry got out of the car, and as Lucian went to get out, he said, "Sit tight for a minute I'm going check it out."

Lucian watched as Harry walked down the street and noticed he had something in his hand.

He had a dog lead and was whistling as he walked.

As Harry approached the rear of the van, Mikey appeared from the other side, holding a small black box in his hand.

Dropping to his knees, he turned onto his back and slid under the back wheels. Harry stood smoking and swinging the dog lead. After a few seconds, Mikey reappeared, and they came back towards the car.

Harry came round to the passenger door and opened it and said to Lucian, "Let's go."

"What now?" said Lucian feeling scared all over again.

"Yes now, no time like the present," replied Harry.

He went to the boot of the car and emerged with a handheld remote control about the size of a mobile phone. He tapped few keys and then pointed the device at the van.

Harry smiled and said, "Our boy probably has some pretty impressive security on this vehicle, but Mickey is the best at developing apps that are cable of temporality jamming any alarm signals. If Dominic has got an alert on his phone or anything funky inside to stop intruders, then Mikey's box of tricks will have disabled it."

With that, the indicators flashed. ~~and~~ Mikey gave thumbs up, opened the back doors and disappeared inside.

Harry pushed Lucian forward saying, "Come on Rambo, Chop Fucking Chop."

As they approached the van, Mikey opened the back door for them to climb in. Harry explained that Mikey had put a sensor on Dominic's front door, so if he came out again, they would get a thirty-second warning.

The van was full of high tech equipment and was racked out with screens and touch screen keypads, obviously state of the art technology.

Mikey was already on the console and had the screens flicking to life with images.

Harry looked over his shoulder and said "Let's see what he been up to."

As Mikey opened up the screens, a large white house with elegant gates was shown on the flat screen.

"That's Debra's house in Winchester," said Lucian.

"Cool pad," said Mikey. "Has it got a pool and everything?"

"Yes," said Lucian.

Mikey keyed in another command, and the rear of the house came into view.

"Is this live?" asked Lucian.

"No," said Harry. "These are screen shots showing the camera positions, probably taken when he was testing the camera zooms."

Mikey continued to click the mouse, and another room came up. Lucian pointed at the screen and said, "Hey, that's my fucking living room!"

Mikey clicked again, and the scene changed to a

bedroom, a bathroom and a kitchen in rapid succession. As he stayed on the kitchen view, a cat walked over the worktop and drank from the tap.

Lucian explained, "That's my neighbour's cat, he gets in the kitchen window at night and so that must be live footage from my place."

"What time is it?" asked Harry and Lucian checked his watch.

"8.45pm."

"Then it is live because look at the kitchen clock it says 8.55."

"That's right," said Lucian, "I keep it ten minutes fast so I'm not late for work in the mornings."

Lucian watched and said, "Holy fucking shit, he has been watching me all along."

"It looks that way," said Harry.

Mikey kept clicking around the desktop. Opening another folder, he found a video clip showing Debra in thigh length boots, stockings and a Basque standing in front of an elaborate French mirror smoking.

"Interesting," said, Harry.

"You don't need to run that one," said Lucian quickly knowing full well what it contained.

"How did he get those, they are from my PC or filmed on my iPhone."

"Like I said Lucian, he is intelligent and very dangerous," said Harry.

Mikey scrolled down showing at least a dozen videos and said, "Yeah man, looks like he is into all your shit."

"But how?"asked Lucian. "I haven't been without my phone."

Mikey turned and said, "Give me your phone man."

He opened it up and looked at it for ten seconds.

"You are connected to iCloud. It backs up all your photos and videos created on your phone to the cloud. He just hacked your cloud account, every time you do something new, like take a photo or video, he gets a copy. It's really easy dude."

"The bastard," cursed Lucian.

Harry laughed and said, "You posh folks, you even swear nicely!"

"Oh shut the fuck up, this is serious," complained

Lucian.

Suddenly Mikey's little black box beeped and he jumped up and said, "He's coming get out quick."

Mikey hit the shutdown button, and the screens went blank, and they opened the rear doors and jumped out.

Mikey leapt from the van and closed the doors.

They ran down the street keeping to the shadows of the pavements verges.

Harry paused and timed the press of the remote button to the precise split second Dominic tried to unlock his van. Pulling the door handle, Dominic looked puzzled by the door still being locked and pressed it again and this time, the lights flashed the vehicle unlocked.

Dominic got into the van fired it up and drove away.

Lucian and Harry sat in the Jag and got their breath back.

"That's was bloody close," said Lucian.

Harry sat breathing heavily for another twenty seconds then lighting another cigarette said, "Ok let's go see what he has indoors."

Lucian looked horrified. "What, now?"

Harry shouted, "Yes now!"

Lucian exclaimed, "What break into his house, what if he comes back?"

"We have got a few minutes, Mikey placed a tracker under the van, and it's tracking him. We will get enough time to get in and look around a bit."

"How far away is he now Mikey?"

"About three miles, he is speeding down the motorway heading south." said Mikey, looking at his iPhone for confirmation.

"He won't be back for at least fifteen minutes even if he turned back now."

"Ok let's go, Mr Bond!" Harry said, smiling to himself as he recalled some of the images he had just seen.

Lucian shot Harry a puzzled look and hesitated getting out, until Harry came around to the passenger door and opened it.

"You told me you only had forty-eight hours right? So come on," said Harry.

Lucian nodded and followed Harry and Mikey up the path to Dominic's front door. They stood back as Harry used skeleton keys to open the Yale lock.

"No fancy remotes for the front door then?" said Lucian.

"Some things never change, but we need Mikey for the alarm," said Harry putting the keys back in his jacket pocket.

Harry stood back to let Mikey through; he placed a small black device on the alarm box and started pressing buttons.

The alarm box let out a beeping sound, which carried on for five seconds, beeped once more, and the display dislayed, 'Disarmed'.

They entered the house and went through to the living room where they discovered a large dining table filled with computers and equipment. There was a high-backed leather gaming chair, with lots of buttons and LED lights built into the arms. On the floor was a mat that also had a lot of LED lights.

"Wow, Coolio," said Mikey and sat himself down in the chair.

He picked up a gloved handset that was attached to a 3D visor and headphones.

Putting the handset over his wrist and forearm and sat back in the chair and put his feet on to the rubberized mat. His fingers slotted into plastic rings, and he wiggled his fingers, and two massive sixty-inch plasma screens lit up on the wall. He clenched his fist, and they went black again.

"Far out init "squealed Mikey.

Harry called from the upstairs landing.

"Lucian, come quick, you had better have a look at this."

Lucian ran up the stairs and entered the room where Harry was standing in front of a wall completely filled with images of Debra.

Some were life size with her dressed in different outfits. The other wall was plastered with still photos taken from videos showing the worst scenes of torture you could imagine.

There were sexual images of vaginas stitched up with catgut and men's penises sliced down the middle. Testicles nailed or screwed to wooden chopping boards or planks.

Lucian turned away only to be confronted with a poster size image of himself. It was taken at Debra's house by the pool. He knew that Debra had taken that one, and it was on her phone as his call sign. The face had been punctured with what must have been over thousand pins and needles like from the movie 'Hell Raiser'.

The whole image reminded Lucian of those pin sculptures where you push your hand or face into them to make an impression.

Underneath the poster on the carpet, was a tin tray with what looked like a half melted action man figure. The legs were twisted at funny angles, and the head had been burned off. Lucian suddenly felt sick and turned to Harry who was still looking at the torture wall. They stood side by side looking at the masses of images of mutilations, extreme serial killers and gruesome murders.

"Jesus Christ!" Harry muttered, looking at Lucian. "Fuck me there are some sick bastards around."

As Harry headed for the door Lucian said, "Let's get the fuck out of here, this place gives me the creeps."

They went back downstairs, and Mikey was out of the chair and hunched over the Mac furiously tapping away at the keyboard.

"Any joy?" said Harry.

"I'm in just copying the files to a flash drive should be done in another ninety seconds," replied Mikey.

"Have you found anything?" asked Lucian

"Yeah man, but this is serious stuff and we gotta get

going as the Dominic dude is heading back this way and will be here in eight minutes."

Lucian looked scared.

"How long? Only eight minutes let's get out of here and fast!"

Harry sniffed, "Hold on Mr Bond."

Harry clicked a few screens and brought up an airline page with a booking confirmation of a First Class ticket to Aruba.

Harry brought up the details and said, "Looks like our boy is going on a trip to Aruba."

"Do you know where that is Harry?" asked Lucian

"It's in the Caribbean man," answered Mikey. "Best kite surfing in the world and the beaches are just total paradise, with the bluest seas you have ever seen."

Harry was reading the details. ~~and said:~~

"Dominic booked a flight in Business Class two hours ago, and the plane leaves in just a few hours."

Mikey passed the flash drive stick to Harry and said, "It's all on there, the fake Facebook logins and all the other stuff he did in Photoshop,"

Harry said, "With the evidence on here, this should be enough to convince Debra that it was all faked. I also took a few pictures of the walls upstairs and will send them to you. Did you set up a new Gmail address like I told you to?"

Lucian looked sheepish for a second and said, "I have to admit I didn't and with all the rush I completely forgot about that part."

"Ok," said Harry. "It's probably best as Dominic has your PC at work and at home bugged. He no doubt would get the password quicker than Mikey if you had done it from there."

Harry headed for the door and said over his shoulder, "Right Mr Bond let's get out of here before he gets back."

"Mikey can you do a clean down, Lucian you go and get in the car. I'll get a couple more photos and be right behind you."

Chapter 47

Minutes later they were driving away from Dominic's street. As they waited at the traffic lights, they saw a silver van. Lucian looked directly at Dominic Clayton. Making eye contact Lucian felt a cold shudder pass right through him as if someone had walked over his grave.

Dominic was waiting for the lights to change and was staring through the window.

As he did so, he looked across to the other lane and saw a Jaguar. With the streetlight reflecting on car windscreen it was impossible to see the driver, but the passenger looked like Lucian Palmer Jones.

Dominic's heart skipped a beat. As the lights changed the Jaguar pulled away, and Dominic watched as Lucian sped away out of sight.

He couldn't be sure, with the rain and the darkness the view was obscured, but when he went out earlier, he thought he saw a similar Jaguar parked down the road from his house.

He had lost track of Lucian after missing him at the hotel. He had found his clothes hanging in a service station toilet cubicle near the North Circular.

Dominic drove on towards his house, having made a mental note to check the licence plate.

When he got back to his house, he parked up and went inside. Dominic stood at the base of the stairs drawing air deep into his lungs through his nose he could sense the air had been disturbed. By tilting his head back, opening his nostrils and sniffed the air like a beast. Dominic could pick up smells even though they are latent scents. He could register a sharp, fresh scent, and his mind flashed up the Lynx advert.

Someone had been in here and recently. Dominic went into his living room, and the scent got stronger. To his horror, his gaming chair had been moved, and the handset and headphones were out of place. The handset had been thrown down and carelessly cast aside.

Dominic had massive OCD and he would lay down his handset with great care. Stamping his feet and throwing himself into his chair he booted up his system and ran a quick diagnostic report of the usage.

The system had been accessed less than ten minutes ago.

All the files of Lucian Palmer Jones and Debra Fielding had been viewed and almost certainly copied.

Red with rage Dominic clicked some keys, and the DVLA website came up he entered the licence plate that he had remembered from the Jaguar. The results came up giving the name of the owner as Harry Matthew Wilson, but only gave an area not an actual address in Elstree. Dominic changed screens Googled Harry Matthew Wilson: it came up with several references to the police force.

It showed a decorated officer with several press clipping articles that featured Harry and his cases. The most prominent was the case of the Yorkshire Ripper, Peter Sutcliffe. Although the top brass took the glory for the arrest of Sutcliffe, Harry had been the chief leading officer and the point man on the investigation.

There were some later references to Harry being linked to the Princess Diana incident. The press focus was on Trevor Rees-Jones, but Harry was mentioned as being in Paris with Diana and Dodi Fayed as part of the security detail on an earlier shift.

Dominic saved the articles into new folder printing out a full-faced photo of a younger Harry. After sitting and looking at his picture for a few minutes, Dominic got up from his desk and went into the kitchen. Picking up two kitchen knives, he ran upstairs into the room with the photos on the wall.

Dominic took the picture of Harry and stabbed one of the knives straight through his left eyeball, pinning the print out to the wall next to one of Lucian Palmer Jones. Then he took the other knife and stabbed it repeatedly into the printout, finally leaving the knife sticking out of the right eyeball.

He went into his bedroom, and stood in front of the mirrors staring at his reflection. As he stood there, he could hear his mother's piercing shrieking voice drilling through his head.

"You silly boy, you let those people take the piss out of you. You're useless Dominic and always will be."

He shook his head violently until his screeching mother's voice stopped.

Dominic opened the wardrobe to reveal clothes and shoes all lined up and folded neatly on each shelf. Taking a leather case down from the top shelf he laid it on the bed and began to pack.

Chapter 48

Lucian sat back in his seat breathing hard.

"What's the matter?" said Harry.

"Fucking hell Harry! Didn't you see that?" said Lucian.

Harry replied, "I saw a silver van at the lights but couldn't see the driver."

Harry knew it was Dominic's van but was enjoying seeing Lucian panic.

"I did, I did Harry, and it was him!" Lucian gasped.

Some James Bond he is, Harry thought, smiling to himself as he pictured Lucian in his black dinner suit.

"Faster Harry please I have to get to the hotel to show Debra before it's too late" Lucian checked his watch, it was 10.05pm.

"We only have twenty-five minutes, Harry" Lucian exclaimed.

"You aren't gonna make it man, bad traffic ahead," Mikey said from the back seat while checking for an alternative route.

Lucian was jumping up and down in his seat. He was sweating, shaking and almost hysterical.

"I've got to make it!" Lucian said. "She will be waiting for me."

Harry felt sorry for Lucian and hoped that Debra would wait for him.

"The only other way through would be if you cross over the dual carriageway and take a cab. It would be the opposite direction, but there will be a back way through in about a mile or so," Mikey said.

The traffic had ground to a halt, the minutes were ticking by and they would take ages getting to next junction to turn around.

"Ok, I will take it from here," said Lucian frantically opening the door.

"Ok," said Harry "I will get some backup, and we will go back and take down that son of a bitch!"

Lucian leant into the car shaking Harry's hand.

"Thanks, Harry I can't thank you enough."

Harry sniffed and said, "Just pay my bill mate that's all I ask, call me later and let me know you got there ok."

Lucian slammed the Jaguar door and hopped over the barrier separating the carriageway and hailed a cab.

As the cab slowed, Lucian turned back to Harry and Mikey and said, "By the way what's with the Mr Bond stuff?"

Harry and Mikey collapsed in fits of laughter, and Harry coughing said, "You are kidding right?"

Lucian said, "No? Come on, what?"

Harry couldn't speak with laughter but Mikey said, "Just look in the mirror man, you IS James Bond right!!"

Lucian shook his head in confusion and got into the cab.

The cabbie, getting the joke said, "Where to James?"

Lucian said "Oh Shut up! The Park Lane Hilton hotel and hurry up, I only have seventeen minutes!"

The cabbie winked at Harry and drove off.

Seconds had felt like hours in the taxi as it had made its slow painful way through the busy back streets. Lucian kept looking at his watch as the minutes slipped by and finally in desperation abandoned the taxi.

Throwing a ten-pound note through the window, he knew he would be quicker on foot.

Lucian ran desperately through the crowded streets, racing up a narrow alley. At the end, he saw a car parked by the kerb. A man got out and crossed the street to help his wife with several large bags and packages.

Lucian saw the car had been left running, he sprinted across the pavement and jumped into the idling vehicle.

The man raced up to the car banging his hand on the window yelling, "Hey, that's my car hey stop hey!"

Lucian mouthed he was sorry, floored the gas and drove wildly into the oncoming traffic. Lucian drove like a maniac through the back streets narrowly missing several parked cars.

At the Park Lane intersection, Lucian looked down at his watch, seeing that his time was almost up. He floored the pedal just as the traffic light turned from amber to red.

As Lucian sped across the lights, there was a screech of air brakes, and a large truck slammed into the side of the car. Turning the car over onto its roof and spinning it through 360 degrees. The impact smashed the passenger window showering Lucian with glass.

Lucian was dazed and bleeding from a deep cut on his forehead. His left wrist was twisted and broken. He managed free himself from his seatbelt and dragged himself out of the driver side window.

Limping badly and with blood running down the side of his face Lucian stumbled through the bustling tourists into the Park Lane International Hotel lobby. Lucian was desperately searching for the sign to the hotel bar.

He checked his watch and in his head screamed "Debra!" as he staggered to the lounge bar. Lucian's head was spinning, he was seeing double and thought he was going to pass out.

This had been his one and only chance to tell her the truth. He needed to show her the memory stick from Dominic's computer, and keep her as his Mistress.

Several times he felt he had failed her, either by not being able to "Take enough" to please her or by misunderstanding her wishes.

Sometimes he would let his attention wander, and she would slap his face to make him focus on the most important thing at that moment ... HER.

Debra's words were very clear.

"You have a single chance to convince me that you are true."

She had ended with:

"Do not under any circumstances be late as I will not wait for one-second longer."

Tears openly flowed down Lucian's blood stained cheeks.

She had been here!... A partially smoked Vogue cigarette was still smouldering in the cut glass ashtray. The fresh lipstick stain, pillar-box red that still coated the filter, was evidence enough she was gone! He was too late.

"Fuck it, fuck it!" shouted Lucian as he kicked at a table causing casual drinkers to turn and stare at him.

Lucian caught his reflection in the bar mirror. He looked like a wild man covered in blood and glass with his trouser leg ripped and missing a shoe.

From the table, Lucian picked up the used wine glass, running his thumb over the rim smearing the same red lipstick across the smooth surface.

Seeing the slight stain on his thumb, he couldn't resist putting to his lips and tasting the lipstick.

Lucian thought he could smell a slight trace of her perfume, that intoxicated his senses and made his head swim.

Lucian looked about desperately hoping maybe she had just gone to the restroom and would be standing behind him with that cruel smile on her lips.

But No! She was gone.

Lucian could search the world, Rio, New York, Dubai, Hong Kong, but never find her.

There may be rumours that she was seen at Ascot or Neka Island or in Miami, but he would always fail to find her because this time, he was too late!

Debra was a ghost, and he was abandoned forever.

Lucian stood for a few minutes, his heart beating violently in his chest. His legs then turned to jelly, and he collapsed into a nearby chair, dropping his head into his hands. The tears started to fall uncontrollably. Deep sobs ached in his chest and momentarily he couldn't breathe.

A waiter approached him and asked, "Are you, alright Sir?"

He looked up his face smeared with blood from his cut eyebrow and his cheeks wet with his tears.

He tried to speak, but words deserted him so he just shook his head and put his face back in his blood stained hands, his was heart smashed into a million pieces.

Chapter 49

The smiling air hostess took Debra's boarding pass and indicated she turn left for her first class seat.

She removed her fur coat and placed her gold Gucci handbag on the seat. The air steward, who had been carrying Debra's hand luggage, opened the overhead locker and offered Debra a pillow and blanket.

After placing her bag in the overhead locker, Debra said, "I won't need those, thank you."

Debra preferred her own items she had a cashmere wrap and a neck pillow. She also had a beautiful fur blanket that travelled everywhere with her.

The steward nodded his understanding and placed her other bag in the locker.

As she settled in her seat, her thoughts turned to Lucian and how he hadn't made the deadline.

She had stayed an extra two minutes in the bar hoping with all her heart that he would make it.

Her chauffeur had waited by the hotel door and had opened the car door for her.

Even then she paused for a few more seconds before getting into the car and driving to the airport.

Lucian had had his chance to explain and to show that all the evidence that she had seen was faked and untrue.

She wanted desperately to believe him.

Debra knew some people wouldn't like the fact she was exposed as Mistress on the Internet. And she expected a call or message at any time.

Debra couldn't forgive Lucian for that as he had broken her golden rule of complete privacy and confidentiality.

This was unforgivable, and his failure to meet the deadline with the proof meant she would never see him again.

As she sat in her seat, she was feeling devastated and grief-stricken.

Debra closed her eyes tightly to keep the hot tears from flooding out.

The captain announced tonight's flight to Aruba would be eleven hours, the temperature on arrival would be twenty-eight degrees, sunny and dry.

Then he announced, "Cabin crew prepare for take-off."

Debra settled back in her seat, wanting a cigarette.

She signalled the steward and ordered a large gin and tonic. Relaxing back in her seat, her mind replayed the last session with Lucian.

Debra had never enjoyed drawing blood or inflicting serious pain, but she was so upset she could have easily cut Lucian's balls clean off and stuffed them in his mouth.

She visualised Lucian strung up and bleeding begging her to believe him.

She had given him every chance, and she must now focus on going to Aruba and investigating her husband's death.

 The steward passed her, giving a drink to a passenger sitting a row behind, who had been reading The Times newspaper.

Debra caught the steward's attention and ordered another large gin and tonic. As the steward moved away, the passenger behind leant over the aisle and said, "Hello, Debra."

On hearing her name she looked across at a man wearing a Lakers baseball cap, he had a small goatee beard and moustache and was wearing large framed spectacles.

Debra looked at the man opposite and said, "Do I know you?"

The plane gained speed, and started to climb into the night sky.

The man smiled at her and said, "Well, no Debra you don't know me, even though we did meet briefly once. But I'm hoping to get to know you a whole lot better."

THE END

About the Authors

The Red Room written by Patrick Mallison and Debbie Mitchell, who feel passionately about great story telling. They began to write the books while on a winter break in Malta in December 2013. Patrick and Debbie have written a trilogy of books under the pen name P. D. Mitchellson featuring Debra Fielding as Mistress D, the leading lady. They live in the south of England and split their time between England and their Caribbean home in Aruba.

The next exciting Mistress D novel

"The Invitation"

The Invitation is the second in the trilogy of erotic
thrillers featuring Debra Fielding as Mistress D.

The story follows Debra as she leaves Lucian and
England behind and travels to the Caribbean island of
Aruba in search of answers to her husband's death.
Dominic advances his obsession with being Debra's
chosen submissive. The story features many of the
must see places on Aruba and works to a nail biting
climax at the most extreme and glamorous fetish ball.
Dominic is hell bent on attending the secret party and
claiming Debra once and for all. Debra of course has
different plans and the story twists and turns involving
kidnapping, murderous criminals, drug cartels, and
torture.

For more information go to

www.mistressd.co.uk

or email

p.d.mitchellson@gmail.com

www.ingramcontent.com/pod-product-compliance
Lightning Source LLC
Chambersburg PA
CBHW031942260626
47157CB00017B/2064